Uncle Billy / Aunt Wanda,
Thank you for so much!
Martin

**UNCOVER: A Tale of Caution**
Copyright © 2014
E. O. Shiflett


Library of Congress — Cataloged in Publication Data

Printed in the United States

ISBN  978-1493584178


Published By Jabez Books
(A Division of Clark's Consultant Group)
www.clarksconsultantgroup.com

1. Mystery    2. Crime    3. Suspense

# Dedication

This book is dedicated to my family: Susie, Owen, Abbey, Bobbi, Will, Addie, Merrick, Gar Bear, and Baxter the dog.

Also, this book is dedicated to my Savior, Christ Jesus because without Him or my family, this book would still just be thoughts running around in my mind.

# Acknowledgements

Uncover has been in my thoughts for many years, but it was the consistent urging by my son, Owen and my Daughter-in-law, Bobbi, that pushed me to get this story on paper.

- A huge thanks to Owen and Bobbi for reviewing the initial manuscripts.

- Jake for reading the first finished book and saying it was definitely something worth printing.

- Also, to Bernie, Dick, and Geri for reading "Uncover" and giving me their thoughts for improvements.

- For Abbey, Jerry, and Sharon, for suggesting improvements also.

- For Laura for direction in getting "Uncover" published, Jan for her encouragement, and Dr. Clark for her wisdom and direction.

- Last, but certainly not least, my wife, Susie, for her help. Her patience and understanding to complete this task to fruition was paramount for me.

# Table of Contents

# PROLOGUE
# 1955

*There comes a time when the mind takes a higher plane of knowledge but can never prove how it got there*- Albert Einstein
*When the mind reaches its full potential, there will be no weapon as dangerous* - Alfred Johnson

In the summer of 1955, Dr. Alfred Johnson's starched white shirt stuck to his arms and back. That summer in New Jersey was very hot even for the month of July. The music in the background was soothing, but the thick pipe smoke made the room more stifling than normal.

"Dr. Johnson, you are one of the smartest men I know and you should concentrate on this endeavor of advanced human development." The world's most famous scientist said in a thick Austrian accent. "I also think that as you get closer to your goal, the obstacles from mankind will be the toughest to overcome. Maybe if I leave you my brain when I die, you can use it to advance your theory." He laughed and continued to puff on his pipe.

Johnson was overwhelmed with the support and praise he had gotten from the world's greatest living physicist. The heat and resultant discomfort didn't faze him at all. If he and Einstein were right, modern civilization could be changed forever, but there was a lot of work to be done to get to that point. Also as brilliant as he was, he realized that the change he wanted would make enemies of every government and giant corporations that needed to maintain the status quo. So every transaction, documentation, and discovery would need to be kept very secret.

# Chapter One

# 1991

THE SUMMER TRAVEL SEASON WAS IN FULL SWING AT NEW York's JFK Airport. Excited families with vacation plans standing next to somber business men and women were all waiting for their turn to obtain their boarding passes. The one thing they all had in common was that everybody was trying to get to their destination as soon as possible, and Mondays were always the most hectic day to travel during the summer, whether it was business or pleasure.

Tim Maybrey walked by the sharply dressed dark-haired woman wearing a black straight skirt, matching jacket, and stiletto heels  standing at a bank of payphones. He noticed her as she looked over to the FBI undercover agent sitting in the seat next to the ticket gate and gave him a smile and a wink. It was the signal to the undercover agent that the man they were seeking had just passed her and was going toward the gate. Maybrey kept on walking.

The person of interest was very average looking; white, medium height, average weight, nothing to suggest he was dangerous or one of the FBI's most wanted men. Nevertheless, she knew she had to stay at the phones in order to cut off any retreat path, in case the subject got spooked closer to the boarding gates.

This investigation was on its fifteenth year, and for the first time, they would actually have a suspect to question. The Bureau personnel working it felt as if they were chasing a ghost. That the case had dragged on for so long was considered a great embarrassment in the Bureau. Never had the FBI failed so badly at solving a case. Because of this failure, very few people at the Bureau or any other Government agency that used letters in their name knew the details. Outside the current agents packed into the airport terminal, and a few people at FBI headquarters below the title of Assistant Executive Director knew anything about the case.

When criminal acts have been ongoing for over a decade, but proven impossible to find evidence or even a link to possible suspects, the Executive Directors would take notice. Even though there were three different heads of the FBI during this time, they all felt it was best to keep it a secret.

The case began when major US banks noticed that funds were being siphoned from their accounts. The dollar amounts were fairly small -- about one hundredth of a cent from every account transaction. Oddly enough, as far as the banks were concerned, it had to be a rounding error in the programs. This had happened before and usually it was perpetrated by bank employees, skimming the fractions away into another account. The thieves were always caught -- until this case.

This time, the money left no trail of its existence. The anomaly was re-enforced once independent examiners found it consistent with most banks and determined it to be a software issue. The investigation was on hold until new software from another manufacturer was installed and the same errors were found. Then the FBI was brought in to investigate major fraud by the software providers. They thought it could have been a conspiracy between manufacturers. It wouldn't be the first time, so there was logic behind the suspicions.

After two years of testing and reviewing their files, they determined it wasn't the software. Then the FBI was faced with a larger question: who or what was taking the money out of the banks by breaking through the firewalls and where was it going. Computer hackers were notorious for breaking into banks and restrictive government programs. Most of the time, the hackers were caught and the damage proved minimal since law enforcement could determine what functions they had tried to perform. Usually, once a year, a person with an extremely fast computer and special software capability would hack into select programs and get away without being caught. This group escaped notice for a few months, until they would make a mistake and get caught.

In essence, the fastest computer performing the most computations would win and the banks and the government had the largest supercomputers available. It was only a matter of time before international efforts were underway, because all the major world banks were involved.

The first break came two years earlier, when Federal Reserve security consultants looking for vulnerable areas in their telecommunications system accidentally found a physical tap on a major fiber optic trunk line that carried banking information in downtown Manhattan. At first, they had no idea what they were looking at, since fiber taps hadn't been taken beyond the theoretical stage. Once AT&T lab engineers got a look at it, they determined it was the first active tap they had ever known to work on a cable. Fiber optics carries information in digital form, ones and zeros. The advantage was that a fiber optic system can carry billions of ones and zeros every second. The fiber itself is glass, with a primary and secondary coating. Several of these were bundled together into a tube filled with gel that was covered by multiple layers of Kevlar and thick jackets of polyethylene.

The tap had its own power source and a laser built into a square about the size of one cubic inch. It was able to bend the glass enough and inject a coded stream of data so that the signal processors never saw any signal drop or degradation. Once the tap had been taken off, a major effort was undertaken to find out who made it and how. None of those efforts bore fruit.

Then a breakthrough, FBI investigators were able to determine when the tap had been placed on the line by looking through records of when people had access to that particular manhole. They found a face because of a strategically placed camera that everyone thought was out of order was actually working and sending its data to an off-site storage area. The US Government cranked up their supercomputers and matched face scans until they found one that couldn't be accounted for, in either the construction companies or utilities. So they knew when and who, but no name. It was then that law enforcement started looking for that person on a broader scale. The FBI computer sent up a flag at a regional airport in Kansas and agents had been tracking the subject ever since. Fingerprints, if his, had no records attached to them. As well, the credit card leads were useless, since they were accepted cards, but the owners could not be traced. There were too many shell companies and dead ends.

The man they were looking for did not exist in any system and seemed totally off the grid. The FBI had several names that could be traced back to him: James Salmon, Henry Casteel and Andrew Cook, however, none of them could lead the Bureau to a real person until now. They never really understood why he was in Kansas, but, regardless, they were able to track his next stop. He was traveling to France via New York.

In cases which have proven particularly hard to solve, the FBI used teams to separate the evidence, then each team would be assigned to go in different directions and follow where the lead took them. One agent would run the operation and direct the different teams. This agent was called the Special Agent in Charge or SAC. Communication was vital, because this was usually, the tripping point of the operation.

For this case, it was handled by three people: the Director and two senior agents that only reported to the Director. To have an open case over a decade that involved so much money was an embarrassment that had to be controlled within this tight FBI circle. The senior agents weren't even sure that the President knew about the banking issue. Now that they were this close to capturing a real person, they brought help in only on a need to know basis. The Director had also placed a few calls to alert Interpol of a potential criminal suspect that might be landing in Paris, encouraging the agency to be ready to assist

FBI agents on the plane. It was decided that they would detain the subject once he landed in Europe.

Tim Maybrey had been with the Bureau for twelve years. Mark Goldberg, a ten-year veteran, had been brought in to assist. Maybrey was the SAC and knew the case inside and out. Goldberg had been added at the last minute. Tim went over the instructions with Goldberg, and how they wanted the "Ghost" apprehended.

Goldberg was chosen for two reasons. He followed orders, but was also a bit of a wild hair. He often made very questionable decisions that lead to successful arrest. Maybrey needed that creativity in a complicated case like this.

Goldberg looked at Tim and stuck his finger in his chest and said. "Maybrey, if anyone else in the Bureau had told me this, I would have laughed my but off. You make this sound like the Kennedy assassination conspiracy theory. Where in the world is the money going? Someone with this much money is spending it on something, somewhere. In essence our Director, along with some other Directors with fancy titles at Interpol, are the only guys in play?"

Maybrey replied. "This breach of the banks' firewalls has been going on for decades and maybe longer. What would happen if this information got back to the NSA or CIA? They would unofficially take the investigation over because it's international and all we would hear is the thump on the papers thrown on our desk, showing how they had nabbed some high tech bank robbers. Oh, and by the way, the FBI has been working on this case for almost twenty years and never caught the bastards."

Goldberg shook his head and was a little stunned by Maybrey's response.

Maybrey continued. "We need to make sure the rest of the team knows the importance of getting this guy alive, and when we walk to the gate area, look at our positions and tell me -- No. You go ahead and re-adjust positions as you see fit. I need another set of eyes on this and you certainly can give me that."

Goldberg looked straight into Maybrey's eyes and said. "You want this guy alive, but what if he gets spooked and ends up dead. What's your back up plan?"

"It shouldn't happen. He's probably not armed and if he had been alerted, he wouldn't be here. We have a pretty good impersonator ready to get on the jet, if we have to, but we have no voice recognition or mannerisms. We would just have to get lucky in Paris that someone will join him and start from there. And, if he's got a confederate in the airport here, the deal is blown if we have to 'bag him.'"

With a puzzled look on his face, Goldberg started scratching his head, and then he said, "I have been working major crime for three years and we never had anyone that has taken so much money from so many places and now you say we can't even arrest this person, because we have no evidence. That is usually a problem when the trials start, along with the fact you can't really charge the Ghost because one, he doesn't exist, and two, you can never go to court with what we have on him."

Maybrey was smoothing the carpet with his foot while listening to Goldberg. It was almost the same comment he gave the Director of the FBI. Maybrey said. "That's pretty much the case except one, he does exist and we will find his name, and two, who said this was going to court?"

"Did I hear you right?" Goldberg asked.

"Yes, you did," Maybrey nodded, lighting a Marlboro. "We have no intentions on letting this guy get a trial. We are sure he is insane, including everyone else that is associated with him, and if we catch all of them, they will never see the light of day again."

Goldberg had a crooked smile on his face and replied. "Alright then, one last question, why haven't you guys used the NSA computer and try to solve it that way?"

"We tried it and even used the latest Cray and IBM Supercomputers. It seems that, as fast as our computer goes to find the intrusion, the faster their computer goes ahead and puts up firewalls against the system. One day, they had the computer locked out from Citibank for over thirty hours. They had to suspend trading, and once the system was back on line, over one billion dollars was gone. It does sound strange, doesn't it? We've tried everything in our major computer tool kit, but have come up with nothing...nada, zilch. Today, though, we will contain the "Ghost" and find out where the trail leads."

They ended their conversation near the gate, and sat down well before the suspect (the walking enigma) was close enough to tell they were talking about him.

Agent Goldberg, as the suspect got closer, stood up, stretched and casually looked at the "Ghost" as the man approached the gate. Today, the Ghost was named Andrew Cook. The FBI had three agents on his flight, all with seats strategically placed to keep the Ghost in full view. Agent Goldberg turned and walked around the gate booth, as if he were going to make a call. He looked at the third agent, Maybrey, who had stationed himself within his line of sight. The suspect went to the counter, got his seat assignment and crossed over to a kiosk where he got a beer.  He ended up sitting in front of Maybrey.  The Ghost had a new electronic organizer and checked it while turning and asking Maybrey if the flight would be on time?

Maybrey looked at him not wanting to arouse any suspicions, and said, "According to my travel agent, everything's on time."  Then Maybrey paused and said, "I don't think I've seen that model of an organizer before."

"I'm in the electronics business and this is an experimental model," the Ghost explained. "It will eventually allow access to the Internet, when it's complete."

Maybrey was genuinely impressed and nodded his head as he asked, "When would it be available?"

"The Internet functional one will take a few years, but this model will be out in a couple of months. Here's my card. Let me know if you're interested in a beta test unit."

"Thanks. I appreciate that. I'll dig up a card for you." Maybrey took the card and was happy to get an additional set of prints, but was also a little concerned that, of all the people on this flight, the Ghost had chosen him to strike up a conversation with. Maybrey hoped he hadn't blown it.

The flight crew started the boarding process, and as everyone was settling in their seats, they put their large bags in the overhead bins and the smaller bags containing the items they might need during flight under the seat in front of them. Maybrey had already gotten situated for the long flight and resisted the temptation to look back and check out the Ghost.

They were all on board, and they weren't going to lose him on the aircraft.

Flight number 300 took off on time and the fully loaded 747 slowly made its way North and East, to get to its cruising altitude of thirty-five thousand feet. A slight vibration started, it ran from left to right on the aircraft. It wasn't turbulence, but like a wave in a pond that rolls under someone while in the water. Maybrey had been a fighter pilot during Vietnam and somehow instinct told him this motion wasn't normal. And he knew something was very wrong when they hit a pocket of turbulence. The left side of the aircraft dipped and the number one engine started smoking.

Passengers could see the smoke plume and many were almost out of their seats trying to get a glimpse. The Captain's voice came over the intercom. "We have some issue with our number one engine, as many of you can see. There is nothing to worry about, while we make our way back to Kennedy, our agents will check connections and determine the best way to get everyone to their final destination. We will have no issues in returning to the airport, since the other three engines are running fine. International Airlines regrets any inconvenience and we'll get you back into the air as quickly as possible."

Maybrey was already thinking how they could detain the Ghost at the airport, instead of taking the chance of losing him during a change of planes. He looked over to Goldberg and gave him a nod. The nod was a silent signal that they would stick to the plan. If they had to turn back, they had pre-determined they would apprehend the Ghost as soon as he was off the aircraft. After the announcement, the Ghost got out of his seat and went to the bathroom. The flight attendant suggested he take his seat, but he stated that he really needed to go. Since they were in the air, there was no need to follow him. It was a full flight, where could he go? The Ghost got back to his seat and there was a sudden jerk, similar to hitting a pocket of turbulence.

With that, Flight 300's number one engine exploded, parts flying in every direction. The Jet couldn't stay level in flight and it noticeably began to lose altitude. Then right after this, the alarms started sounding, the oxygen masks dropped down, and passengers starting grabbing for them, while screaming wildly in a hit pitch tone. Either a piece of engine or wing crashed into the aircraft, ripping open a huge hole behind the wing, sucking everything loose out of the jet. People, who weren't buckled in, were sucked out of the plane.

Maybrey, his instincts fine-tuned over years of coping with unexpected consequences, looked for his suspect, but couldn't believe what he saw. His suspect was struggling to get to the gap. The screams and noise from the hole were deafening and if the jet wasn't corrected, this would only last a few seconds. Maybrey knew the jet was corkscrewing itself into a death spiral. The Ghost braced himself and seemed to be timing when he was to leap out to his death. Maybrey wasn't about to have his target get away, even if it was to his death. Maybrey was out of his seat and moving toward him. None of the other agents seemed to be able to move. Maybrey was three rows from the gap, holding on to an armrest as his legs were being lifted behind him.

The Ghost crossed his arms, tucked into a ball and was out the gap, free falling from what had to be fifteen thousand feet. John Keller had made this jump multiple times with this advanced parasail type suit, but the free falling through the skies was still a rush to him. Maybrey thought about this as he saw the Ghost free himself from the tumbling aircraft. However, he realized, they had done their job. Then Maybrey also realized at the same instant that the aircraft was doomed. No one was going to make it. The few precious seconds that remained to Maybrey were spent saying a prayer, hoping for a miracle.

**\*\*\*\*\*\*\*\*\*\*\*\*\*\*\*\*\*\*\*\*\*\*\*\*\*\*\*\*\*\*\*\*\*\*\*\*\*\*\*\*\*\***

Keller could faintly make out the aircraft as it augured down into the Atlantic, fifty miles or so northeast of Long Island. There was a fireball for an instant, then it was gone. His face was numb with cold, his lungs aching. The slipstream around him tore at his exposed skin, his loose fitting sport coat and slacks. The roar of the wind enveloping him was maddening.

Judging himself to be at an altitude of a little more than two thousand feet, he deployed three-foot wide wing like chutes from each side of the sports coat, a harness built into the garment secure around his torso and at his shoulders. He had fitted it when he went to the bathroom on the jet. The sudden slowing jerked at him, knocked the breath from him for an instant. As he grasped at the canopy's control lines, he surveyed the ocean below him. He glided on a gentle wind, ever closer to the low white caps, drawing his feet up into almost a sitting position and turning just as he was about to touch the surface. He landed rear end first, releasing the chutes, keeping only a retaining line for their recovery.

John Keller had spotted the fishing boat seconds after deploying his parachutes and, within only a few minutes after his splash down, he was aboard, cocooned within a heavy woolen blanket.

Keller knew the man who had fished him out of the water and the captain of the boat as Dave Smithfield, which likely wasn't his real name, no more than the various aliases Keller had used earning him the sobriquet "Ghost" were real. "I called the crash in," Dave related, sitting down beside Keller near the prow. He offered Keller a players' cigarette. Smoking something that distinctive in the USA wasn't a good idea, Keller thought absently. But regardless, he took it anyway. Dave told out his cigarette lighter and lit Keller's cigarette. Then Dave said, "I bet that we have around thirty minutes before the Coast Guard shows up. How did the ultrasonic burst feel in the 747?"

"You could feel the vibration, but most people ignored it because of the immediate turbulence. You know that there were three FBI agents on that flight?"

"There were four hundred fifty-six people on that aircraft, and all but one died. If there had been another way, we wouldn't have gone to these extremes."

"Then, is it done?" Keller asked.

"The old man thinks so and he's seldom wrong."

"How close are they to catching up to us? I'm not talking just about capturing one of us, but also having our technology?"

"Today was abnormal," Smithfield responded, lighting a cigarette. "I doubt that we are more than five to ten years ahead on most of our weapons and computer systems, but probably ten to twenty years ahead in genetics. Let's get out of here, before people start the search."

Everyone on board flight 300 had died and Keller had "pulled the trigger." The authorities could study whatever scraps of wreckage they might recover for years and they'd never learn a thing about what caused the crash.

# Chapter Two

# 2010

PETER WINDOM COULDN'T HELP BUT LOOK AT THE WOMAN checking in at the hotel front desk. Her figure, accentuated under the close fitting red knit dress, was beyond shapely, and her skin was smooth and flawless, neither pale nor tanned. Her auburn hair was pulled back on the sides and caught up at the crown of her head, only to cascade to well pass her shoulders. Her nails gleamed, but didn't look at all artificial. Windom thought she looked as though she should have been in a beauty pageant rather than showing up for America's largest technology show in San Jose, California. She definitely looked like she was from New York, L.A. or Chicago. In contrast, the other female attendees were dressed in basic black and white business suits.

She apparently noticed him looking at her and smiled flirtatiously? Then she walked over to him and asked, "Are you Professor Windom, from Future Way Technologies?"

He returned her smile and turned red. It was one thing for people in the industry to recognize him, but for someone this classy to speak to him, he just wasn't used to that kind of attention. "Yes, I am Peter Windom." He made sure he added his first name. "But I can't say that I have the pleasure of knowing your name."

"My name is Pamela King. I'm from New York and I have heard so much about you. You are the Bio-technology God." She reached out her hand. He took her fingers in his and very gently shook them, lest he damage so beautiful and delicate features.

"Not really the 'Bio-tech God.' I just use biological material to self-organize through selective biochemical reactions."

"I know, Bioluminescent Bioreporter Integrated Circuits or BBIC."

Peter was impressed. "How is it that you know of my work on illuminating dangerous chemicals?"

"I'm with a unique venture capital firm that was involved with telecommunications and laser development. Since then, we've looked at many new technologies and decided that Bio-technology using virus protein was worth further investigation. So, I'm here to gather information and find specific directions, not necessarily specific companies at this point.

"Since you were one of the first pioneers at NASA to try it and then move on to more complex systems," she went on, "I wanted to see if I could talk to you while we're at the show."

"You're staying at this hotel, then?" He nodded toward the front desk.

"I am, because I know that the Four Seasons is your favorite chain. I tried to make arrangements with you before the show, but never got pass your assistant or voicemail."

"Do you do this much planning for every encounter you make?" He felt he had a twinkle in his eye and Pamela wasn't going to let up.

Pamela looked him straight in the eyes as she told him, "I only do it for the good looking men who think for a living."

"You know, you are the most striking woman that I have met in this business."

She seemed genuine as she murmured her thanks, but Windom figured, she had been told this every day of her life.

Pamela asked, "Could we meet in my suite this evening. I'm looking into a few start-ups that maybe you could give me some guidance on."

"I usually don't get into those issues with VCs, since I may have a conflict of interest, but, I'll make an exception in this case."

"Wonderful," she said, smiling. She told him what room number and they settled on seven.

Peter, widowed for two years, didn't know if he were being set-up or flattered. Either way, he was going to make that meeting.

Before the meeting, however, Windom had to see two old friends that were waiting for him. The three had a few drinks, although one of Peter's friends, Jake, only drank ginger ale.

Peter related whom he had just met. The kidding was brutal. But, finally, his closest friend in the entire world, Jake Bryant said, "Go ahead and drop us for that cheap skirt, but remember; we meet for breakfast at seven o'clock, so, don't be late."

As Peter got up to walk away, his other friend, Evan Cannon, cautioned, "I saw that woman in the lobby. She looked more like a model than any VC. I hope you know what you're doing." Peter hoped that, too.

As Pamela King ushered him into her suite, Peter was stunned. She looked even more beautiful than before, somehow, albeit she was dressed the same. And her suite was beyond anything he had imagined in the hotel. It, too, was magnificent. The ceilings were ten foot and the fixtures were plated in what looked like gold. "Is this the Presidential suite?"

"No, Peter. It's actually called the 'Emperor's Suite.' If the President of the United States comes here, he has to take a lesser suite, because of the security. This one has a second floor."

"Your employer must have very good taste."

"Only the best...our company President will be out here tomorrow, so he insisted on the best room. As I said, he has pretty deep pockets when he wants something"

"Okay," Peter nodded. "I'm dying to know your background and how you got into the jungle of VCs."

Pam offered him a drink from the full bar. He requested scotch. Of course, there were several brands all aged single malts. She poured his scotch into a glass and handed it to him, then she took two fingers of Jack Daniels for herself. As she started to review her background from childhood on, Peter couldn't help but think she seemed somehow even more remarkable. When it was his turn, Peter went over his life's high and lows and remarked that he usually didn't get personal during business meetings. He even recounted how his wife of twenty years had died of a heart attack while jogging.

The more alcohol they consumed, the more personal the conversation was becoming and the closer they were sitting. Maybe it was because she was speaking in a softer voice that required Peter to move closer to listen. Or, maybe, it was merely an excuse to move closer. He didn't mind, since it had been a long time since he'd been this socially intimate with a woman so beautiful and so intelligent.

Pamela told him how hard it was for a technologist like him to take her seriously and that it was frustrating, because she was sort of an outcast at these type of conventions. "I find myself being very alone in these situations." At that, her cheeks started to turn red and he could see the tears starting to well up in her eyes.

She looked downward deliberately, so he couldn't see. He reached over to her and placed a hand on her shoulder. She looked up and apologized and placed her hand on his. For a moment they locked eyes together, and she leaned into him and kissed him on his lips. Not a deep, passionate kiss, yet it was one that seemed to say that she sought a companion, and she wanted to determine how far they would go.

Peter was more than surprised, but found he cared for this woman. He placed his arms around her, bringing her close to him. He looked into her eyes, saw the hint of tears and kissed her, harder than he had kissed anyone since the sudden death of his wife, the kiss bringing back the longing he had repressed for so long a time.

Peter could smell her – the perfume mixed with her body – and the scent were very intoxicating. They moved together, finding each other's rhythm as they embraced one another even more tightly. Peter feeling a sense of pure joy, knowing she felt that, too. Peter arched his back, stiffened, and started seeing stars or just imagining them? As he laid on Pamela, he wanted to tell her his feelings, but something was very wrong. His head was starting to explode and he couldn't sound out any words.

Pam put her hands around Peter's head and looked into his face. Something was very wrong. The muscles in his face were contorted and emesis was coming out of his mouth. Pam screamed and in the next instant, Peter's eyes rolled back, staring blankly at nothing. Eliot Huggins, a lithe Englishman about six feet tall with black hair, walked down from the second story room after he heard the scream. He knocked on the door and Pam ran to the door in a somewhat frightened state slinging the door open frantically.

"What happened?" Eliot asked.

"I think he's dead!" Pam said in a high pitch voice.

"What in the world did you do to him?" Eliot asked. "I mean, I know you're hot stuff and all," he went on as he felt for a pulse. He picked up her purse, spilled its contents onto the coffee table, selected her eye shadow and opened the case, holding the mirror near to Peter's mouth and nose. "Yes, he is dead. He's showing facial nerve palsy and vomit around his mouth. He either just had a stroke or was poisoned."

"We had sex and then he just sort of collapsed," Pamela said while getting dress.

"Well, you were right. And with him dead, this puts a hole in our plan. Dr. Harris is not going to like this. We'll have to see if another candidate shows up and if you can work your magic again sweetheart."

"Don't get mad at me. We just moved faster than I expected. He was kind of nice."

"And now he's kind of dead. We have to call security and the police. At least this time, there's nothing that we did wrong. On the plus side, he appears to have died a happy man. Just finish getting dressed and I'll call Harris. Huh...he was perfect. I know we could have gotten the technology head start if he just hadn't died."

"I don't think he was favoring this conclusion either," Pamela noted.

The doctor did his exam and proclaimed to those that had crowded around the body to assist that Windom probably had an aneurism in his brain and it chose that time to let go. Once the body made it to the morgue, an attendant started feeling the back of Windom's head. He found the spot he needed and took a palm size tool kit and placed the forward edge to the back of the skull. There was a slurping sound and the bloody plug was placed into another canister. If anyone had been looking at the camera in the morgue, they would have never seen the attendant's face. Once the coroner did his exam, a note was made about a very strange hole in the back of Dr. Windom's head. It was perfectly round and had burn marks around the edges, made by something like a laser, the doctor concluded. Since Peter Windom died long before the hole was drilled and he was to be cremated, there wouldn't likely be much effort made to solve the whole issue. If the examiner paid more attention, he would have found that it wasn't just a small hole, but one that turned into a forty-five degree angle, removing a part of the brain called hippocampus, the part that carries its memory. A note on the paper work would likely be, however, that it was a puncture and the body would be released.

News of Peter's death reached the conference and his friends from the night before were crushed. They would leave San Jose knowing that they would never see their friend again and that a great ally was no longer able to help them.

# Chapter Three

# Central America

THE OFFICE WAS LIT WITH A SOFT WARMNESS, NATURAL LIGHTING that suggested the first blush of spring time; yet, there were no windows through which to watch what poets called "The merry month of May. The light that flooded the room came from no visible fixtures. The furniture was dark mahogany and expensive. Unlike most executive offices, this one had three screens displayed on the desk. Missing were the common office tools, including the telephone and computer. Yet, Dr. Alfred Johnson was communicating comfortably from behind the desk, while viewing a 3-D Hologram coming from his glasses.

Alfred stood. He was conscious of his appearance, tall, lean and exuding perfect health. He had a full head of gray hair with brushy eyebrows. He'd been told that, although he appeared to be a vigorous man in his sixties, but he moved and talked like someone much younger. At his age, he found that to be pleasant.

He spoke into the hologram. "There was no permanent damage to Peter Windom's tissue and the transplant went as scheduled?"

John Keller was the figure on the other end of the hologram. "We were close on losing this transplant, because of time, but the stroke that killed him actually helped us, by allowing the tissue to be engorged with blood before we placed it into our transport cylinder. And recovering the data was relative easy before we shipped it here."

"It's nice to have a little luck now and then, but I would have preferred Peter alive. Were we able to cover up the procedure, though?"

"The computer notes, of course, have been changed, but not the written notes. We don't expect that to come up again, since he was cremated." With that, Alfred leaned against his desk for a moment, and then began again to walk around the room.

"Who was the woman?"

"She's Pamela King an ex-CIA and FBI contract field agent that does work for corporations that require her unique talents. Her clients usually need information and they don't really care how she obtains it. Her client this time is Dynamic Industries."

That was another piece of unfinished business that would be dealt with at a more appropriate time. Dr. Harris, president of Dynamic Industries, wasn't well liked and a special plan was already being arranged. Another piece of the puzzle put into place, Alfred thought.

"Now tell me about what our Russian friends are doing," he asked the hologram of John Keller.

"We expect them to push the Iran task force into the Turkey region where they will run into light or no resistance. It's in the mountain region that the strike force can hit the columns."

"I understand that we are using a fiber optic guided missile to destroy the column?"

"That's right, sir, and the F-O-G-M completely destroys the armor as well as the support vehicles with ninety-five percent efficiency, according to the simulations," Keller confirmed. "Let me show you the scenario." Instantly, the hologram changed scenes, showing mountains and rocky trails with tanks, armored personnel carriers and trucks slowly moving through a pass that had the look of being used for centuries by invading countries and traveling caravans. The scene changed as missiles came from the sky and started landing on the lead elements -- tanks and communication vehicles. Adolph watched for about a minute, watching the destruction unfolding before him.

"I'm satisfied with your evaluation. Please proceed with the arrangements."

Dr. Johnson had been correct when he speculated about his research. When one advanced the human brain, adding two or three people's knowledge base into a person that had a high IQ to begin with, there was no limit to what the enhanced person could accomplish. Those hot days in Georgia had been the start of the most fantastic development in mankind's history and only his group knew about it. TOK was indeed a huge success. Here, they were intercepting information and planning an attack, based around an armament system that the military rejected. Of course, they would add their own features to it, but the whole project would be completed before any major country knew what had happened, leaving Iran and Russia wondering who had stopped them.

"There is one thing that you should know, sir," Keller added. "Jake Bryant is the CTO of Cannon Electronics, which is where we intend to purchase these fiber coils."

Surprise wasn't quite the emotion that Alfred felt. It was more like satisfaction, and for the first time, he smiled into the hologram. "Why haven't we crossed paths with him before now?"

"He has been very careful, keeping his paper and electronic trail at a minimum. Evan Cannon, Founder and President of Cannon Electronics, as you know, and Jake were classmates at VMI and it was Evan who picked Jake out of the rehab center and brought him into the company."

Alfred was thinking. He knew that Keller would let him have the time to think before responding again.

"Keep track of Jake and this Evan character. I'm afraid this could draw both men into harm's way. We don't want another disaster, like the International Airlines crash, to draw attention to us."

"Yes, sir. We'll start the surveillance background immediately."

With that, the room was quiet again. "Jake," Alfred whispered to himself. "I knew if you ever defeated the bottle and made it back to civilization that our paths would meet, and there's no time like the present." With that, a smile came over Dr. Johnson's face. He was impressed with Jake Bryant, but their work wasn't finished and he knew Jake could be a key to their success.

\*\*\*\*\*\*\*\*\*\*\*\*\*\*\*\*\*\*\*\*\*\*\*\*\*\*\*\*\*\*\*\*\*\*\*\*

"Jake, I don't know how you do it. Twenty plus hours of flight time, and not only did you not drink, but you look just as alert as when we started." Jake merely smiled, shrugging out of his coat. It was the last of May and already hot as summer in most states. Evan marveled at the man. Jake was born in West Texas to parents that were as poor as church mice. He wore jeans and boots everywhere he went. He was what many described as raw boned. He could have been the Marlboro man, if he had ever smoked. With sandy hair that was thick and slightly curly, he was thoroughly Texas -- if one could call someone that.

What separated Jake Bryant from all, but perhaps, three-tenths of a percent of the rest of humanity was his intelligence. It was off the charts, but Jake wasn't eccentric like many people with high IQ. He had his own quirks that most thought of as "different," but he worked around them most of the time and others accepted him because he was just plain smart.

Jake avoided a collision with a woman going the opposite way with computer bag and purse slung over her shoulder, causing her to run awkwardly as she rushed by. (Where are they?)

"I'm tired, but keeping my mind occupied with these new requirements and new cards that need to be developed have kept me alert."

Evan just smiled and shook his head. "If I know you, the layouts are done as well as the power draw."

Jake nodded his head in the affirmative and said, "It's really pretty easy, but the hard part will be to manufacture the fiber strand with a layer of LCP. At the speed that these Europeans want to fire the missile, it's got to have built-in reinforcement, and that means, Liquid Crystal Polymer."

Evan replied. "I know that Larry can make the process changes to get the cable made, but why do they want that speed and that much data, except to go after helicopters or slow planes?"

Jake looked Evan in the eye and said, "That's your department, to determine the application and close the sale." Jake made a big grin appear.

Even though Evan was the President and had established Cannon Electronics as a viable company, since Jake had come to the company, it had tripled in size, thanks to his product innovations. It was clear to everybody that Evan needed Jake, but few realized that Jake owed Evan his life and would never leave Cannon for another company. Evan intended to keep that confidence.

Evan reached into his pocket for his keys and tossed them to Jake. "Take my car. It's in short term parking by C16."

"Exactly how are you getting home?" Jake asked.

"I'll take a shuttle and see you tomorrow and we can switch cars then."

"Hey, I'm not arguing with you, since it's not every day that you get to drive your boss's Hummer." Evan gave him a smile and walked toward the shuttle counter to make his arrangements.

*****************************************

Evan was asleep before the limo left DFW airport parking lot. Amazingly, Evan woke up about three miles from home. It was strange how one could go from a dead sleep to waking up at a specific destination, Evan mused. He remembered how their family dachshund used to sleep in the car on the way to his in-law's house in Myrtle Beach, and wake up two turns away from the house -- every time. Evan pondered whether he might have "inherited" the knack from Emily, the dog.

Oscar, the shuttle driver, had taken him to his house many times before, so he didn't need directions. Oscar was a young Hispanic who loved to box and was partially sponsored by Cannon Electronics. He had a great personality, but really only wanted to box. Evan liked him, and as soon as he woke up, he started talking to him about his next bout.

"Mr. Cannon, I get a shot at last year's Golden Gloves champion. We will actually be boxing at Reunion Arena in downtown Dallas. Can you believe it?"

"Oscar, I would say that you have arrived, my man. Do you think you can take him?"

"He's a good match for me. Since I'm a lefty with quick feet, he'll have to move faster than normal."

"When's the match?"

"The match is next month on June 14."

"You know, that's the date of Flag Day?"

"Yes, sir! I'm wearing red, white and blue colors that night. Sid Chavez will be wearing his normal black colors. It will match his soul and the bruises I will give him during the fight."

Evan laughed and said, "Just don't get too cocky."

"I can't. My trainer and my mother keep telling me what I need to improve. Of course, my mom wants me to go back to school. But, she's given me two years to make it in boxing. If I'm not ranked in the top ten, she wants me to stop."

"Is two years enough?"

"I'm already in the top twenty, so with a little more than a year left, I can do it."

"Oscar, follow your dream. We only go around once on this world. Tell your mother I said 'hi.'"

"I will. She always says that I should listen to you. She says you have been blessed by God with a good heart."

"I wish your mom was right, but I don't think many people would agree with her." Evan thought back to the time when he got married on June 14 and how his ex-wife would definitely disagree with Oscar's mother. They turned into the driveway and Evan opened the garage door remotely. Oscar drove the car into the garage, jumped out and grabbed the bags over Evan's protest, then proceeded to the door, which Evan told him was automatically unlocked once the garage door was opened remotely.

It was a slight movement of a shadow that got Evan's attention. He looked at the opened space inside the house and saw a flash, but heard no sound. Everything was in slow motion. Oscar's head jerked and the back of his head exploded. The back and top of his head peeled away as if something invisible were ripping apart a grapefruit. It appeared that Oscar was falling backward in slow motion with the expression of surprise frozen on his face.

In fewer than two seconds, a wonderful person full of potential was lying on the ground, dead. To Evan, time had totally stopped. Fear, adrenalin, and instinct drove him to leap behind the car and out of the garage. Just as he was almost out of the garage, the wood frame exploded beside his head, sending splinters into his face. The stinging pain of the splinters did little to slow his run to safety. If he could just make it pass the edge of the house and into the neighbor's backyard, there was a chance of living. Then Evan thought, "I am in pretty good shape for a man of forty," while moving as fast as he could, but then he thought even the fastest sprinter could not outrun a bullet.

As soon as he was passed the edge of his house, he immediately angled himself toward his neighbor's side garden area. The ground was flat, but heavy with vegetation that he possibly could use to cover him. There was a large stand of red-tip bushes that rose some fifteen feet above the ground. A strand of sea grass was in front, so if he stayed low, maybe he could escape. Half expecting to be hit at any moment, Evan concentrated on getting low to the ground, but moving deeper into the dense part of his neighbor's backyard. His neighbor's wife had planted the red-tips and various other shrubs, giving the side yard a wild jungle look. But once the bushes were fully grown, the look became one of an English garden. It was the envy of the neighborhood and was saving Evan at this point.

He crawled behind some holly bushes, getting pricked by their pointed edges. However, he wasn't feeling the pain from the leaves. There was an opening in the shrubs. Evan concentrated on finding a completely dense spot of vegetation. He saw a small area that was totally dark. Not thinking about what could be hiding in the bushes, he pushed himself off the ground by putting his legs on the stone wall behind him and holding onto the holly bushes. It was at this point that he finally began to feel the pain of the holly's leaves digging into his skin. A minor inconvenience, he thought, compared to getting shot.

After a few moments, he started to catch his breath and wonder who was trying to kill him and where was he now. It was pretty late, with very little light, but he thought he saw feet off to the side of the house, coming at him, and then moving off in another direction.

It could have been a cat or even his imagination. All he knew was that he wasn't moving and he was praying that whoever shot Oscar got scared and moved off.

After about ten more minutes of hanging onto a thorn bush, Evan had had enough. He lowered himself to the ground and crawled back along the holly stand to see the back of his house. Not a good idea, he knew. There he was more exposed, and if the killer were patient, he would see Evan before the killer would ever need to expose himself. Silently cursing his stupidity, Evan backed out and moved down to the corner of his house.

Feeling lucky that he was still breathing, the questions came in waves in his mind. Who hated him enough to want him dead? And why? It had to be a robbery. Was the robber just spooked into shooting the first person at the door. Evan didn't want to expose his neighbors, so he decided to play a deadly game of cat and mouse. If it were a robbery, the killer was probably gone.

Evan had taken off his jacket in the car and his cellular phone was in his jacket. Without a phone, Evan made the decision to circle around to the front. The killer wouldn't expect it and he couldn't get to any house except his own without being totally exposed. Evan crawled behind the hedges, ran through the open space between the yards and slid behind the shrubs in the front of the house. Thinking that whoever wanted to kill him was probably still searching down the street, he should be safe going back to the house, maybe, he thought. Then he saw the shadow. It looked like a lump on the side of the driveway in the darkness, but once he got closer, it was a body. When he crawled out of the bushes, he went to the man. He could see that the man's eyes were open and that they looked very dead in the dark. It wasn't Oscar and there was a gun lying on the ground beside the body. It had a silencer, just like in the movies, and Evan could smell the distinct odor of gun powder.

Here appeared to be the killer, but who or what had killed the killer? Evan was used to thinking on his feet and taking a course of action that was usually correct, but this hit him like a "ton of bricks." It was almost as if his brain shut down all thinking procedures and expected his body to spring into his next flight or fight sequence. Evan stood up, searched around for any other movement and went to the bags still in the garage by Oscar. He grabbed his phone from his coat pocket and made the 911 call. "This is Evan Cannon at ten zero seven Lake Forest Drive, in McKinney. Two people have been shot dead." He thought his voice was calm and controlled, but the operator asked him twice to repeat the address and if the people doing the shooting were still around?

"Look, I don't know. There are two people dead in my driveway. One is a friend and the other one is who I think shot my friend. Can you quit with the twenty questions and get someone over here?"

"Sir, the police are on their way and should be there within ten minutes. Don't go back into the house. Go to neighbors until the police arrive."

"OK, I'll wait next door," Evan said mechanically. The big question still haunted him, "Why him?"

He went to the body to see if he had ever seen this person before. Nothing about the killer looked at all familiar. Then his mind started thinking again...who, why, where, how — then all of a sudden Evan realized -- Jake could be in trouble.

He called Jake's house. The "Hello" he heard from the phone was a relief.

"Jake, I just wanted to make sure you're okay. I have to go. I'll explain later. Lock your doors. Bye!"

Evan could hear the siren and knew he couldn't be on the phone when the police got there. A few neighbors passed the house and slowed down, but the last thing they wanted to do was get involved, because there was obviously something wrong. But everyone knew Evan, and more than once he had parties where people ended up lying in the driveway for different reasons, so seeing this situation did not warrant them to stop to investigate.

While Evan was waiting for the police to arrive, Evan walked back over to the assume killer's body. He sat down on the ground beside the body and began to shake. He couldn't control his hands. He tried being analytical, saying he was alive, and this man was dead, but his still shaky hands revealed the truth.

Evan started to look at the supposed killer in greater depth, feeling anger and even rage that he killed one of his friends. Then another question arose. How did the killer die? Had he been lucky that this killer had a heart attack and died? He had seen enough cop shows to know you didn't touch the body, but he started looking all around for any blood marks or bullet holes. He turned the dead man over slightly, half expecting the man to rise up, but Evan was ready if he did. If he hadn't been looking carefully, Evan would have missed the half-inch hole that was in the base of his head. There was a little blood around the hole, but nothing else.

Two police cars pulled up to his driveway, their light arrays flashing and sirens blaring. It created a level of comfort; the cavalry had arrived. Thank God for the cops. Two officers got out of the first police car, hands on their holster guns. They looked at Evan and saw the body and immediately drew their guns.

"Get your hands up where we can see them."

Evan realized they were taking a serious look at him as a killer. "I'm Evan Cannon and I called this in."

The two officers walked toward him at an angle with their pistols aimed at his head. The one on the left came within an arm's length to get a good look at the body and then at Cannon. The officer then said to him, "I need to see some identification."

Evan slowly lowered his arms reached into rear pocket and grabbed his driver's license and let the officer closest to him read it. Evan was smart enough to keep quiet while he looked at the picture on the license and back at Evan's face to make sure they were a match.

"Ok, Mr. Cannon, do you want to tell us what happened here?"

"You will find the body of Oscar Ramos in the garage and probably determine that the bullets that killed him came from this gun. How this man came to be dead is a mystery to me, but there is a hole in the back of his head."

One of the officers went into the garage and called to the other policeman. He and Evan went into the garage, the second policeman keeping an eye, apparently, on the dead man and his gun.

Oscar still had that look on his face, but that serenity and peace was distorted by the blood and damage to the rest of his skull.

Evan explained about Oscar carrying in the bags, seeing the flash and Oscar falling. Just re-telling the event made Evan's head spin, almost like a bad dream, from which he would wake up and everything would be back to normal. Evan stepped over to the front of the garage door. "Here is where I almost got hit. You can see the new gouge marks on the wood." He told the policeman.

One of the cops placed his hand on Evans jaw and looked at his face. "It looks like you may have some splinters in your face from those shots." Evan placed his hand on his face and could feel stubble. It was either from his beard or dried blood from wood splinters or even from the holly bushes.

"Don't touch it if you can. We want one of our guys to take a look at it." They went back to look at the man's body on the ground on the sidewalk. Another pair of cops had arrived on the scene and was looking at the body as well. With them was a man in civilian clothes, holding a large suitcase. He wore gloves.

The evidence technician was examining the head wound, while other detectives where arriving on the scene. By this time neighbors had come out of their homes watching and wondering what Evan had got himself into now. The evidence technician remarked that he'd never seen anything like that before. One of the plain clothes cops turned around and looked straight at

Evan. She was tall, around five feet eleven inches, with an athletic build. Evan could tell by the way she walked that she was in great shape and carried herself with considerable dignity. Her skin was the color of rich milk chocolate. Once she spoke, her voice left no questions as to who was in charge.

"Can I ask you what you were doing contaminating the crime scene?"

Evan didn't know what to say and usually that wasn't good, because he would say anything and face the consequences. "Got tired of waiting, so I thought I would check out the perp."

"The perp, sir? You have watched too many 'Law and Order' episodes."

Evan knew her by sight and reputation -- Veronica Green. She was called "Ronnie" in the media. She was an ex-FBI agent and a North Texas celebrity. She had evidently decided that being a big fish in a small pond was more to her liking. Evan had read about her in one of the news magazines. While assigned to the Dallas' FBI office, Ronnie Green had broken up a terrorist ring in Richardson, Texas. There was a tremendous amount of publicity and her cover was blown. There was an opening for a county sheriff that covered the city of McKinney, which is a bedroom community to Dallas. Aside from print and electronic media coverage of her cases, Evan knew her from the charity work that had brought them together from time to time. Evan would have like to have known her better, but their work schedules precluded this from even happening.

"Haven't we met before?" Ronnie said.

"That should be my line...a couple of times. I'm Evan Cannon, and the last time we saw each other was at the crippled children fundraiser at the country club. And I wanted to talk to you more about your FBI experience, but there were so many people there, I didn't get the chance."

Good grief, Evan thought. He sounded like a complete idiot, but he did notice that his shaking had stopped.

"If you wanted to get to know me better, Mr. Cannon, there are easier ways of doing it than arranging a double homicide."

Evan almost laughed out loud, but his emotions were still on edge. He could feel his face turning red. However, the comment had a calming effect; he relaxed a little and said, "I'm a very shy individual and thought that this was the only way I could get you to come to my house." Evan wondered if he had actually said that.

"You could have just called. I'm in the phone book," she said. A smile crept over his face that he thought had just turned a deeper color red. "You corporate executives always have to find a way to make news these days. Let's go inside and talk about this, but first, I want to look at the dead man." She put on purple latex gloves, dropped into a crouch position, and examined the hole.

"Have you ever seen anything like that before?" Evan asked.

Ronnie looked up at Evan and didn't say a thing. She didn't have to. It was a look that said, "We are in charge here, so let us handle this," but without saying a word.

"The hole looks familiar, but there are a few drops of dried blood around it that don't add up to a normal bullet or other object hitting the skull like that," Ronnie said.

An ambulance was pulling in and another police cruiser joined the makeshift car lot. As they entered the garage and were passing Oscar's body, with a team of technicians examining the crime scene for any clues, Evan stopped.

"What's wrong?" Ronnie queried.

"I haven't gone into the house since the killings."

"Don't worry.  My officers have already searched the house and found nothing that indicates more than one guy was in here."

"Maybe...but, I know I didn't put that hole in that guy's head, and if I didn't, somebody else did and they could still be hanging around."

"Mr. Cannon, you have to realize that whoever stopped that man seems to have wanted you alive, and in that case, you should be fairly safe, except for the fact that someone else wants you dead."

They entered the kitchen and sat down, Ronnie surveying the appliances. She might have had a gun on her hip and maybe another on her ankle, but she was still a woman, Evan thought.

"Stainless steel -- I like stainless steel -- goes well with the granite counter tops." Ronnie said looking around in the kitchen.

"My wife picked everything out before our divorce.  It's very practical, so I didn't think I needed to change anything."

They sat at the kitchen table while Evan walked Ronnie through the entire incident. Evan poured both of them a glass of beer that he had bottled about two weeks earlier. When and if he retired someday, he knew he could make a fortune opening his own microbrew restaurant.

Ronnie got ready to sip the beer, but she realized she was still on duty. She stopped him from time to time, to ask questions, but he explained everything as he had shared earlier with the other policemen. After he was finished, he stood up to pour himself more beer. Stopping behind her, he could smell her perfume, Obsession, he thought. It was the same brand that his "ex" used. He wondered why a County Sheriff would be wearing perfume during work hours.

Ronnie turned in her seat, looked up, and asked Evan, "Where did you just fly in from?"

"My business meeting was with NATO, in Brussels and Madrid, with a third party buyer. Do you think that any of this is because of those meetings?"

"I doubt it. It happened so quickly since you've been home, but it's something that I will check with the Feds."

"I'll give you my contacts. Just let me know before anyone starts to talk to them."

"I doubt if it will even get to that point, and if it does, it will be out of my jurisdiction anyway."

Evan walked back to the chair in front of Ronnie and sat down again. "You know? It's weird. Suddenly, I'm exhausted. Do you have any more questions for me?"

"A few, but they can wait until later tomorrow. We'll still be here for another couple of hours, finishing up the crime scene."

"You have the run of the house and I'll be in the family room behind us sacked out on a couch."

Ronnie smiled and said that was good and they would try to let him sleep as much as possible.

Before that, a police doctor examined his face, removed several splinters and applied an antiseptic, which stung and smelled a little.  He was too exhausted to care. Evan laid down on the leather overstuffed couch and started dreaming right away about the long-legged Ronnie Green with the perfect complexion and athletic body looking down at the body of a possible killer with a hole in his head. Sleep would come, but he knew the nightmares would come as well. Evan rolled onto his side and drifted off to sleep.

# Chapter Four

# Underway

EVAN AWAKENED AT ABOUT SIX-THIRTY THE NEXT MORNING on his couch. His first thought was that he had one hell of a nightmare. But reality hit him full force when he saw a policeman in his driveway. Protection was great, but all it seemed to do was remind him of how close he'd come to losing his life, so after Evan got his composure and thoughts together, he went out to talk to the patrolman.

"I'm making some breakfast. You want to come inside and have some?"

The patrolman looked like he had a bullet proof vest on because his shirt was stretched across his chest and back. He seemed very young.

"No, sir. I am supposed to stay by the crime scene."

"Hey! If that's the case, then you need to be in the garage, where Oscar was shot and I almost got it."

"Well, they are more interested in the shooter and my orders are to stay here."

"The shooter is dead. Now, you're after the shooter's killer. I'll tell you what. If I bring out a breakfast burrito, would you eat it?"

"Sounds great, sir. I wouldn't turn it down."

Evan's "ex" was a great cook and taught him how to make a killer burrito. He liked them spicier then Gail, his ex-wife, but the ingredients were still the key. He made them in bunches and froze as many as thirty at a time.

Once inside, he decided to call Jake and fill in the details that, by now, he was sure Jake had heard about. Picking up his cellular phone, he called Jake on his work number. Jake typically got up at five every morning, so Evan knew he would get him. Jake didn't have a cell phone, and very few people had his work number.

Jake answered, "Can't you stay out of trouble? Glad to hear that you are alive at least."

"How did you find out?"

"Sheriff tracked your car down and told me the whole story. Sorry to hear about Oscar."

"Did you see anything unusual while you were driving my car?"

"I told Sheriff Green that I thought somebody may have followed me, but I couldn't tell for sure."

"Are you in the design center?"

"Yeah, putting together some breadboard designs for the new proposals."

"I'm having a little breakfast. I'll come in as soon as I can."

"No sweat, as long as you bring in one of those burritos for me."

"How did you know?"

"I can hear and smell them over the phone."

"Okay. Sure, whatever you say. I'll see you soon, bye."

Evan could only chuckle at Jake's powers of observation. Maybe he could smell food over the phone. Who knew with that guy?

Evan gave two burritos to the patrolman and wrapped up another two for Jake. Then he called a taxi, showered and quickly got dressed. He really didn't want to linger in his house that morning. When the taxi arrived, the officer in front knocked on the door and yelled that the taxi was waiting. When Evan came out of the house and passed by the patrolman, he noticed that the young man had spilled sauce on his shirt.

"You'll want to soak that in cold water to get the stain out," Evan said to him.

The officer looked down and smiled at Evan. "Thanks for the breakfast. The burritos were great."

"You can thank my ex-wife. She showed me how to do it."

"Be careful out there."

"Will do, friend. One attempt is enough." Evan got into the cab and looked back at his house like he never had before. It was no longer a place of a sanctuary, but a vulnerable building where he needed to be on guard. Then he sighed and opened his metal zero briefcase and picked up the pistol that was lying on top of the papers in it. The gun had been a gift to himself. Maybe it was one of the most advanced pistols ever made, a 9 X 19mm Smith & Wesson with Novak sights, based on the no-longer manufactured stainless steel models 5906, but heavily worked on at the factory. It had a fifteen-round magazine, but a sixteenth round could be kept in the chamber. The recoil was mild, and the pistol was all steel. It felt good in the hand and was extremely accurate with an experienced shooter. But Evan had never fired it in anger; however, he wouldn't hesitate to do so under the right circumstances. It had been registered, so it was legal, but Evan wasn't sure if his concealed handgun license was still valid. Evan loved firing his Smith and Wesson and even gave it a name, Spitfire, after the World War II fighter planes. This pistol was light and nimble compared to his modified Glock 37. The Glock was a .45 caliber that held ten rounds. It was heavy, but it hit like a sledge hammer. He had several more pistols, but the Spitfire would do just fine.

\*\*\*\*\*\*\*\*\*\*\*\*\*\*\*\*\*\*\*\*\*\*\*\*\*\*\*\*\*\*\*\*\*\*\*\*\*\*\*\*\*\*\*

Cannon Electronics had been the idea of Evan's ex-wife. Besides burrito making, she had a good head for business. She suggested that he start a business that would take advantage of fiber optics and use it for military applications. Many large companies were doing the same thing, but Evan found the small projects that large companies couldn't or wouldn't invest time or effort into developing. Once he was successful on several small projects, he noticed that the large companies started coming to him to sub-contract their work. Currently, his company was going head to head with the same companies on medium size projects and they were usually successful in landing the business.

One could also point to Jake, a certifiable genius, coming aboard as the tipping point to their profitability. That was the year Evan took a leap of faith and purchased a fifty thousand square foot facility at a foreclosure auction resulting from the telecom meltdown in the early 2000s. From the outside, the stand alone building looked like a big box. Inside Evan made sure that the office portion was first class and spent considerable amount of time getting it right. Oriental rugs were used, indirect lighting to enhance the décor, and various wall colors that were considered bold, but timeless, which was the wording he remembered from the decorator they used.

The fixtures were what people would use in their own homes. The biggest gamble that he implemented was to have a company sponsored in-house daycare for employees. The daycare was a huge hit and always seemed to get an article every year in the newspapers. Evan got to his corner office, which was right by the main entrance. Usually, presidents liked their office as far from the entrance as possible, but not Evan.

Evan wanted to know what was going on, and to see the people coming and going into his company. Besides, his office was the same size as everyone else's and close to the kitchen. When Evan arrived at his office, he sat his briefcase on his desk. As usual, Brenda, his secretary and assistant, had put all the urgent papers in order. He went over to the kitchen to get a cup of coffee and everyone who saw him mumbled their greetings, but didn't want to look him in the eye. He felt like a dead man walking. Everyone was staring at him, no matter where he went. Eventually, he walked over to Brenda's desk. Brenda had been the ideal assistant and had worked for him since they had started the company. It seemed as if she could read his mind, and in most cases...she could.

As Evan bent over, she said, "I've sent flowers to the Ramos family and a large food basket, too."

"Can you also send $10,000 to the McKinney Education Foundation for scholarships in his name?"

"Of course, is Mary still the administrator of the fund?"

"Yes. I met with their core team last month for our yearly contribution, so the management shouldn't have changed since then. Also, can you informally tell everyone that I'm still alive and quit with the sympathy looks? It's driving me nuts."

Brenda smiled, "You say sympathy; I think its regrets."

Evan chuckled as he walked into his office. He was sure that most people thought that Brenda's duties extended beyond working hours, especially after his divorce, but they were more like brother and sister than boss and subordinate.

Evan walked back into his office and noticed there were notes lying on his desk that enumerated the calls that he needed to make as well as appointments that were scheduled for that day. Then Jake rambled in, sat down and grabbed one of the burritos that was wrapped up on top of his briefcase.

Jake was his most trusted friend, and while he did work for Evan, Jake obviously knew that he had Evan's trust and had a free hand in anything he wanted to do. At the moment, that was eating. Jake unwrapped his food and said in a loud stage whisper, "I hear that you have developed a new ray gun."

Evan laughed as he usually did with Jake. Jake was the same height as Evan, but without any excess weight. His face was angular and looked like he had lived his whole life in the West Texas sun. He wore his typical cowboy boots. Also, typically, Jake was very secretive about what he did, whom he talked to, as well as he was proud to be living off the electronic and information grid. Evan knew why Jake did it, but would never tell anybody, since it wasn't anyone's business.

Evan had met many scientists that wouldn't come in "out of the rain" because of the way they were wired, but not Jake. He functioned as a normal human being that had an IQ in excess of 200.

Looking fondly at Jake that morning in his office, Evan said, "Just to keep you up to date, I called Mrs. Ramos and told her we would like to take her two remaining sons on part-time. I figured they could use the distraction and money. I really liked Oscar, but what happened at your house last night?"

Evan went into the details and Jake just listened, while eating his breakfast. He had told the story no fewer than thirty times. Yet, each time he still felt vulnerable. Evan just wanted to get things back to normal.

"Jake? What are the chances of getting that fiber pay-off system working for that contract in Spain? I have a message from Bob Walters of that VC group who invested in the last round of fundraising we did and I think we both know where that conversation is headed."

With that Jake closed the door, slid over and sat in one of the chairs by the desk.

"Are you serious about the finances?"

"Remember that test at Redstone Arsenal in Huntsville? In reality, it was one of the last shots we had at changing the military's mindset from a mobile tank killer to using an accurate, high tech missile system to disable an armored column. They didn't want to use magnetic directional sensors and any thought of fusing that technology with gyros and accelerometers went out the window as well."

Jake was shaking his head. He was still mad about the way the military had jerked them around. Jake was no longer sitting, but pacing inside Evan's office rubbing his chin. He said, "We passed that test with flying colors. I still can't believe that they threw another unauthorized milestone into the mix in order to prove the concept. I would like to take our FOGMs and do a live test with those contract guys driving the tanks. Also, don't we have existing contracts for coils?"

Evan replied, "We do, but the Mountain Project from Spain could save our butts if the specifications are not impossible. The existing contracts will only keep the doors open long enough for us to land a major project in eight months. After that, it will be painful. I hate to say it, but the large companies, like GE, Dynamic Industry, Boeing and GM, can tie up these contracts, so that they never get awarded, and companies like us will just quietly go out of business."

"Well, I'll bring some sunshine into your life. I talked to Larry and he thinks that the new LCP crystal material can be applied over the fiber and steel core then coiled before it's cooled. That should allow us the opportunity to go full speed with the missiles, without fiber breaking. The three camera output shouldn't be an issue as well."

Evan found himself sitting up, listening to Jake's description of the activities. Maybe his luck was changing.

\*\*\*\*\*\*\*\*\*\*\*\*\*\*\*\*\*\*\*\*\*\*\*\*\*\*\*\*\*\*\*\*\*\*

Evan was in full work mode, oblivious to anyone or anything that passed by his desk. At noon, Brenda walked into his office and told him the Sheriff was on the phone and wanted to talk to him. Evan just grunted and never looked up at her. She walked over to the shade and opened it full.

"Hey, what are you doing? That's going to let the heat in," Evan said in a somewhat sharp tone.

"He speaks in sounds other than grunts and groans," Brenda said jokingly. Evan rolled his eyes, wondered why he put up with her.

"Okay, what is it?"

"I said that the Sheriff is on the phone and wants to talk to you."

"Tell her, I'll call her back."

"This is a murder investigation in McKinney, Texas. You don't call them back when you were one of the intended victims. You answer the phone!"

Evan reached over and grabbed his phone, giving Brenda a serious stare. She fixed his blinds and blew him a kiss as she walked out of the office.

"Yes, Sheriff. What can I do for you?"

"Did I catch you at bad time?" Ronnie asked.

"Yes, but anytime would be bad right now. I'm just trying to catch up with my work from the last two weeks. Oh, but I do have a question for you. Why is a county Sheriff doing the murder investigation when I'm in the McKinney city limits?"

"They had a major crack house bust and it took a majority of their officers to response to that situation. Often we take the lead anyway in major crimes because of the formation of a unique combined task force that covers the cities within our county. We have a seamless working relationship with the cities and so far an outstanding success rate." Sheriff Green responded like she had given that response at least a dozen times a day. Then she paused and said, "Listen, we have some more questions for you, and we thought we could do it over the phone."

"Fire away and let me see what I can do."

"We finished gathering evidence from your home and will leave the key with the officer out front. He will leave once you arrive, unless another incident occurs."

"That's kind of ironic...if another incident happens -- I could be dead," Evan said sarcastically.

Evan was quite irritated just thinking that another person could be waiting for him and then the Sheriff would tell the press, "We would have put more security on Mr. Cannon, if the second attempt hadn't worked."

Sheriff Green said, "I use the term 'incident' very liberally, meaning anything from threatening calls to strangers walking around your neighborhood." Evan took that to mean she would have someone around his area, just not at his house. "Anyway, I see you have some guns and a concealed carry permit that has expired. Do you have a firearm with you now?"

"I'm carrying a pistol in my briefcase. I've nick-named her Spitfire. Does that classify as a concealed weapon?"

"I just want to remind you that most people carrying a pistol often wound themselves rather than getting a shot off, in a case of self-defense."

"I'll try not to shoot my briefcase."

"Why did you name your firearm? What is it with men and their weapons?"

"Do you really want me to answer that?"

"No, but I did noticed there was an ace of spade that had a bullet hole in it in your family room. May I ask, what's the story behind that?"

Evan knew she was checking his capability of firing a pistol -- first the permit and now the framed ace of spade.

"Okay. I'll save you some time. If you really look carefully, you'll find that the card has two holes in it, almost in the same place. That is the result of two .22 bullets hitting the card at the same spot from thirty feet away."

Ronnie paused, "Who, may I ask, is the trick shooter?"

"I am, but that was over ten years ago." Evan was enjoying his conversation with the Sheriff, but somehow felt there were some lingering questions that she wanted to ask. At that, Ronnie stopped talking, and blurted out.

"Whoa... I have to talk to you about what we have just found. Can you meet me in a half hour?"

"You just said that we could do this over the phone."

"I was just handed some information that I think we need to cover face-to-face."

Evan was starting to feel a little queasy about this discussion. "Where do you want to meet?"

"It would be best to come to my office, where I have all the information," she stated.

As quickly as he could, Evan was driving his Hummer down to Ronnie's office. It took about twenty five minutes. Her office was in the restored county courthouse. When he arrived at her office, he noticed that her office was nicely furnished, but very business-like, though. Fax machines and monitors were placed around the room. When he entered her office, she rose from her desk to shake his hand, and for the first time, Evan took a look at her more as a woman than a Sheriff. Many of his friends who had met her previously had been impressed with her intellect. Evan was more interested in something else.

Ronnie was still holding out her hand and Evan shook it firmly. "I guess I'm either a suspect and you're going to play the good cop bad cop thing on me or you have something serious to tell me."

Ronnie's skin seemed to glow when she smiled at Evan's comment. "Last night, it was obvious who shot Oscar. But as far as who killed the murderer and how, we weren't sure. Remember that hole in the back of his head?"

"Yeah, it seemed very strange, almost like it had been burned into his head."

Ronnie was shaking her head. "You're very close, but it's more horrible than that. The medical examiner was doing the autopsy last night, and found half-way through it that there was still slight brain activity. I won't go into how he found out, but the killer was still alive, and if you can imagine the torture and pain he felt while being dissected, then it doesn't get much worse."

"My God! How was that possible?" Evan was nauseated, thinking of the pain. "That bastard tried to kill me, but the penalty seems awfully harsh. Do you have any information about this guy?"

Ronnie handed him her investigation report. "I'm surprised that you care how this guy died."

"I haven't always been a gun toting redneck looking for action."

Ronnie smiled at his remark. "Maybe not, but I've done my homework on you and I think you would have shot first and asked questions later."

Evan just looked at her and started reading the report. The first page basically described the death-like condition and told of previous examples and how it had occurred. There were lots of technical medical terms that were substituted for pain, dying and death. Reading further, he found very disturbing information. The killer was found to be a mercenary with lots of experience, trained, of course, by Uncle Sam. Fred Russell was his name and he seemed to have disappeared for the last three years. His name came up as a possible suspect in over a dozen cases, but he was still loose until the incident of the previous night. Evan continued to read, until he found that Russell had been to Austin. The gas receipt was at a location that he knew well.

He looked over to Ronnie. "Why do you think he went to Austin?"

"I was hoping you could tell me."

"My ex lives down there, but I haven't seen her in over two months."

"We did a preliminary look and found that he had dinner about a quarter of a mile from your ex-wife's house."

"I thought guys like this didn't use credit cards and wanted to stay off the grid."

"Like your friend Jake?"

"What do you know about Jake?"

"I know he has an extremely high IQ, takes his salary in cash and wires it to a bank in Panama. Never uses a cell phone and limits his home line to a maximum of three minutes per call.

He was married at one point and loves animals. It also appears that he would do almost anything for you, including focusing a laser into the back of a guy's skull if said guy had tried to kill you."

"I heard you worked for the FBI and can only speculate that they provided some of that profile. Jake and I were classmates at VMI, and he lost his wife in a car accident. It was a bad few years for him, until he started working with me. Jake isn't crazy enough to kill for me, but I would for him. Tell that to your FBI group and if you think Jake or I would kill a guy who tried to shoot and kill me, yes, we would -- in a New York minute. The only difference would be a bullet in his head, not some laser to the back of his skull."

Ronnie was looking at Evan, obviously to see his reaction to her information on Jake. She imagined he'd responded just like she thought he would -- belligerently and mixed with anger.

"Look. I'm not saying Jake was behind the killing, but I have to investigate every angle, including this Austin connection."

"I'll save you some time. My wife and I have been divorced for a few years, but if you call her, I suspect she would be upset and start worrying about my safety. She hated me enough to divorce me, but not enough to kill me." At that his cell phone rang and Evan looked at the caller ID. It was his ex. "You talked to my wife this morning. Didn't you?"

"Yes. We did. It was about an hour ago."

"She's calling me now. Thanks for calling her before I got the chance." Evan walked away from Ronnie and began the conversation with an apology. He did not want Ronnie to hear what he was saying. He wished he had called his ex-wife first.

\*\*\*\*\*\*\*\*\*\*\*\*\*\*\*\*\*\*\*\*\*\*\*\*\*\*\*\*\*\*\*\*\*\*\*\*\*\*\*\*

Evan was over Gail leaving him, since the blame was one hundred percent his after she got tired of playing second fiddle to his company. It was only appropriate that she got a huge chunk of Evan's business in the divorce. Evan still loved his ex-wife. They still did things together as a couple and people continued to speculate they would eventually re-marry. However, Evan knew it would never happen. The last time they went to Lake Austin for a day on the water, it was pretty clear that she was being chased by a guy and was ready to move on with her life.

Evan wasn't involved with anyone, but he knew it would never be the same as it was before the divorce. Evan finished the call with a promise to call Gail back when he was done at the Sheriff's office. Then he thought back to the Sheriff's report. It speculated that the killer could have been stalking his wife. Why Gail? It brought a shiver of fear into him. Evan went back into Ronnie's office.

"I'm glad the bastard's dead. I bet he was staking my family. I know everyone is okay, since I called my son and daughter earlier. And now, I just talked with Gail. What is he after?"

Ronnie came around her desk next to Evan and sat on the edge, looking him in the eye, to make sure the point got across. "I called some of my contacts in the Bureau and there's something you need to know about that hole, that's not in the report. They have eight, maybe ten different incidents of this hole being left in victims. Sometimes, there are sections of the brain that have been removed, while other times it appear that it was done deliberately to disable, and give the appearance of death. Unfortunately, none of the victims recovered. They ended up like your friend, Fred. One noted electronics scientist, named Windom, I think, had it happen to him, after he died. The electronic records were lost, but the autopsy reports made some people sit-up and scratch their heads. The strange part is that even I got stonewalled about the details."

"Did you say Dr. Peter Windom?"

"Yes, I think Peter was his first name. Why?"

"Jake and I were to meet him, the morning after he died. We heard that he died of a stroke. He was going to help us on some new technology. He really was a great guy," Evan summed up.

Ronnie studied Evan. She had met him several times, but didn't know him. In her investigation, she realized that he was pretty much a "what you see is what you get" kind of guy and she liked what she saw. He was a smart guy with a smart mouth, but could back up much of what he said. Evan stood slightly over six feet, at about one hundred ninety pounds. He had a moderate "spare tire" around his waist, but his broad shoulders and movements bespoke strength. She had done her background check, just in case he might have planned the shootings. He played on club lacrosse teams and went to firing ranges for relaxation. Evan even continued to work out at the local YMCA, instead of one of the fancy fitness centers that were popping up everywhere. She also found out that he jogged over ten miles a week. That was entered on the YMCA computer.

He built his company from sweat equity, and since bringing in Jake Bryant, they had grown to be the largest employer in the city. Evan was handsome, but wouldn't turn heads, if he walked into a room. He had dark hair, a square chin and dimples in his cheeks.

Ronnie had met him several times at different charitable functions and always found him to be quite real and sincere unlike some of the men she had dated over the years.

People wanted to talk to him and hear his opinions. Once, they were at a fundraiser for a daycare facility downtown. He walked in the room, left his check on the table and walked out. Ronnie found out later that he had major issues with the people running the charity, but still gave a generous personal check, because he believed in the cause. It was the fastest dinner she had ever attended. Most of the men left before dessert and joined Evan in a downtown bar. He seemed to lead by example and didn't care who followed.

It was always better to do the homework upfront, Ronnie reflected, and know the person under investigation, rather than get surprised later on. She had developed a sixth sense when it came to judging people. Her impression of Evan was that he could be depended upon to be truthful and was driven to succeed. She had earned everything that had come to her, and knew what it was to make something out of nothing. Maybe that was the mutual spark that she felt.

"You also have to know that the FBI really has no clue as to how these wounds are made. You start putting these data points together and you will notice that someone very powerful helped you out. The other side of the coin is somebody still wants you dead." Ronnie slid off her desk and moved around to the back. She was wrapping up the critical issues and ready to answer questions.

Evan was thinking, but saying it out loud, so he could better understand what was happening. "In my business, there aren't consequences -- only unplanned results. Do you think that my connections to Peter Windom and Oscar's killer aren't related? Right now, I don't know why, but I'd bet my last dollar, we're stumbling into a hornet's nest."

"You've given me a new puzzle piece, but I have to tell you these laser head wounds are a dead end, as far as information is concerned." She was thinking about the next steps to take. "What does your wife have that is pertinent to your company?"

"She's majority shareholder and on the board of directors."

"Not you?"

"I gave the shares to her in the divorce settlement. She plays a pretty active part with the board, but trusts me to run the business."

"That was extremely generous of you. Most divorced couples won't release an extra nickel to an ex-spouse."

"My company was the wedge that separated Gail and me. She was the one that pushed me to get into the business and has supported me ever since. She just couldn't be second fiddle to work. We didn't divorce because we stopped loving each other; it was because I had a mistress that came between us – the business."

"Your company's future could be what this guy was after. They take you out, apply some pressure to your wife to sell, and they have control."

"Not a bad plan, actually, but we aren't doing great things right now."

"Tell me about this new opportunity from Spain? I haven't heard back from the contacts you gave me, but doubt they have anything to do with the murder attempt."

Evan gave Ronnie a thumbnail sketch of the proposed contract. He told her that they had to overcome three distinct problems, and if they do, it would be very profitable for his company to succeed. There wasn't any other company that could do it, if they didn't succeed. Ronnie was following everything he said and even writing notes, when needed. She noticed how he was looking at her and she liked it.

Ronnie told him, "With this new information, I'll call Gail back and see if anyone has asked her to sell her stock. I may have to go and see her and show her some of the photos we have of Fred."

"Isn't Austin a little outside your jurisdiction?"

"By a mile, but we do take trips to visit potential witnesses, with the support of their local law enforcement groups."

Evan had been looking out the window and he turned to Ronnie with a smile. "If you ever go to Gail's house, make sure you take a doggie snack. She has an Aussie Sheppard named Baxter, and he can be very aggressive. The snack is a pay-off, but well worth it if you need to get down to business."

Ronnie smiled, telling him, "I'm used to aggressive dogs. I'll consider your offer, if I end up going down to Austin. On another subject, I need for you to tell me about Jake Bryant. We don't have a lot about him in any databases that we have access to."

Evan started to laugh. "In other words, the information that Brenda, my Admin, gave you and the brief from the FBI didn't leave you with much to work on. I wouldn't worry. Jake has nothing to do with this."

Ronnie could see that Evan saw the direction she was heading.

"Ronnie, you could have access to most any database and you wouldn't know any more about Jake. I'll tell you some details, just so you understand Jake better. We were classmates and friends at VMI because of similar backgrounds. Jake actually was at school on a provisional basis, because his grades weren't what they should be in high school. It wasn't long before everyone knew he might just be the smartest guy in school, including the professors."

"What was his major?"

"He started out in Civil Engineering, but gradually moved to a double major of physics and electrical engineering. I'm really not sure why we became close friends, but maybe you could say opposites attract," Evan told her.

Ronnie was taking notes and more and more felt as if she were trying to break a code. It wasn't that she was looking at specifics, but rather trying to read between the lines. "What did you guys do together?"

"Same thing everyone did at school. Study like hell during the week, then party on Saturday nights. Jake's parents were ranchers in West Texas and very poor. We were in the same company, so we roomed next door to each other for the four years of school."

Ronnie looked up from her notes. "What about after school?"

"We went in different directions. Jake was working for National Electronics and did some pioneer work on MRI equipment. Then he met a great girl, while he was there, and right after they got married, she died in a car wreck. Afterward, Jake was going to leave National to work with a consulting firm on new technologies. The life went out of him after the accident and he ended up drinking his life away. I found him in a homeless shelter in Dallas and brought him to live with us. Gail was very supportive, and eventually, he got to the point where he could live by himself. Since then, he has lived off the net. Jake works on a cash basis -- no credit or debit cards. He has been somewhat paranoid that he was being watched. He never goes home the same way. To say he is brilliant is an understatement. He has a dog that stays with him most of the time. In fact, he's from the same litter as Gail's dog."

"He must have some friends that he sees or people that he comes in contact with, if nothing else to take care of the dog, when he's not around."

"He has a middle school girl take care of his dog when he's gone. By the way, his house has a ton of security equipment protecting it."

Ronnie was confused. "Why all the security?"

"Jake is sure that he's been followed from time to time and that his wife died because of something that he did. The police couldn't find anything that would support his theory, but that won't change his thinking."

As they wrapped up the interview, Evan handed her a card encased in plastic. "My new license to carry a concealed handgun."

Ronnie looked it over.

"You know that I must tell you that carrying a sidearm is contrary to protecting you, in most cases."

"I'll tell you what. If you have anyone on the force that is a better shot than I am, then I'll put it away."

Ronnie felt herself smiling. "Let's go downstairs, now."

They went down to the basement range and set up behind a booth. Ronnie put on her shooting glasses and earmuffs. She press-checked her .40 S&W Glock 22 and ran the silhouette target out to thirty feet. She fired a tight five-shot group into the head, then another into the chest, where the heart would be.

Evan ran the target back for her as she changed magazines and re-holstered her weapon. Evan put up a fresh target and ran it out to thirty feet.

Ronnie realized immediately that his pistol was possibly a one-of-a-kind. It was based on the old S&W Model 5906, she guessed, but had forward slide serrations, custom grips with "windows" for viewing the obviously custom magazine which had matching "windows," allowing cartridge counting. All metal surfaces were "melted," leaving no sharp edges. The finish was a rich black.

Evan fired off ten shots very rapidly, matching Ronnie's points of impact in the head and chest of the silhouette, but the groups half the size of her own.

"I have only seen one person shoot like that and he was in the Agency."

"I know, Greg Hendrix, and I've beaten him every time we square off. You see, I know everyone who's someone when it comes to shooting. I should have tried for the Olympics, but was too busy building a business."

Ronnie asked to examine his pistol. He cleared it and passed it over to her, and then the slide locked open.

"This isn't like anything I have ever seen."

"It's not something you've seen. Smith and Wesson handmade it for me.  It's got a lot of the features of the old Devel guns, but a lot more, too -- fifteen plus one. I never had to use it for self-defense before, but it should come in handy."

He handed her the magazine. "Six in the magazine." Ronnie sent a target out and fired all six shots. She handed the pistol back to Evan as the target was coming back. She shot better with his pistol than her own, but not as well as Evan.

"I don't want to hear about any shoot-outs in McKinney. I've had my fill of dead bodies for a while," Ronnie told him, returning Evan's pistol.

\*\*\*\*\*\*\*\*\*\*\*\*\*\*\*\*\*\*\*\*\*\*\*\*\*\*\*\*\*\*\*\*\*\*\*\*\*\*\*\*\*\*

After leaving the police station, Evan arrived at his office to a typical stack of messages. As he was prioritizing the list, Jake came in with his laptop and plopped into one of the cushy chairs.

"We have problems." Jake was setting up the laptop, so Evan could see the screen. "Larry has done a great job on the fiber coils. We've gone from four or maybe ten kilometers to fifty and even one hundred kilometers, far surpassing the need for forty-five kilometers. We have the lens system, so by pressing a key, you can look from the missile's nosecone in normal mode (thermal imaging infrared and even night vision)." Evan was watching the screen simulation and was amazed by the vision changes.

"Jake, this looks great! We've surpassed what they were looking for."

As usual, Jake waited to drop the other shoe. "Now, we speed up the image to Mach one point eight, which is what the missile will actually fly." The image was blurry and shaky. It would have been extremely hard to pick out any specific target in the sight. "We worked against ourselves. The additional speed from the coils means the sampling rate for the video stream is too fast for existing chips. I tried to contact all of the leading chip manufacturers and there's nothing faster in the silicone family then a terahertz. We're going to need at least five to ten times that speed."

Evan was looking at the simulated screen. "You say in the silicone family. What about other choices?"

"The only other possibility is bimolecular transistors, which actually use bacteria as a base to provide the speed. I've made some inquires about availability, but have yet to get any reply."

"You mean what Peter Windom was working on."

"Exactly what Peter was working on, before he died?"

"Remember that hole that looked like a laser had burned into the head of the killer?"

"Yeah. I remember you telling me about it," Jake nodded.

"I just found out that Peter had one in the back of his head as well."

Jake took in the information and was obviously calculating what it meant. "So someone wanted Peter's technology and may or may not have gotten it by drilling a hole in his head. The same people have now helped you by killing your killer. Is that what we are talking about?"

"In a nutshell, except they didn't kill my attempted killer, only made him semi-conscious. He died when they did the autopsy on him."

"Wow! Tough crowd when they could have just killed him, but it sounds like they wanted to torture him." Jake closed his laptop and started walking out the room.

"Where are you going?" Evan asked.

"If I'm right," Jake stopped half way out of Evan's office, "Whoever took that chunk out of Peter will be sending us chips that will work with the missiles."

Evan turned around and picked up a slip of paper and asked Jake, "You know an Erin Roberts, President of TI? It seems that she wants to meet with me about on-going business concerns."

"Hey...timing is right. Ask her about their advanced organic thin film transistors and if we can get our hands on some of those chips. Also, see if you can wear a helmet to the meeting, just in case it's TI who's having people killed."

Evan slipped around Jake and handed the slip to Brenda and asked her to arrange a luncheon meeting ASAP. Jake slapped Evan on the back. "We both have our work cut out for us."

As Jake was walking away, Evan said abruptly, "Jake? One last thing...Sheriff Green is going through her list of possible suspects and I had to give her some personal information on you. I wanted to make sure she cleared your name."

Jake lowered his head and stared down at the design on Evan's Persian rug. "You probably did the right thing. Do you think she will keep it quiet?"

"So far, she's been pretty fair about everything. She may be going to Austin to talk to Gail."

"I could save her the trouble. Gail might shoot you, but she would do it herself."

"Ronnie seems to think the killer was hanging around Gail's part of the world a little too long. It may have to do with trying to take over our business."

Jake went back inside Evan's office and sat back down in the same chair. Evan watched him starting to put the pieces together. "Evan, I think the Sheriff is right. I don't know how or why, but business is the key component between Peter, you and Gail. Let me "noodle" on it a little more and see what I can figure out." He stood up and finally left.

Evan finished up his business and finally left for home about 8:00pm. After working out and a very light dinner, Evan contacted Gail to give her the heads up about Ronnie visiting. He decided to tell her that his would-be assassin had been in Austin, very close to where she lived. As usual, Gail was very independent and wasn't too concerned, except for Evan's life.

"Gail, this is about your safety. The guy who tried to kill me filled his car up at the QT station around the block from your house. He also had lunch or dinner. I'm not sure which, but at one of the same restaurants store you go to."

"Evan, it's obvious that he tried to kill you. I still don't see why you think I'm in danger. He's dead and not coming back to life. Even if he was a hired killer, whoever sent him will send someone else once they find out he didn't get the job done. If you say Jake thinks it's about the company and wanting control, then it's you that will be in the "crosshairs" not me."

"Yes, he did." Evan was stretching the truth, but he had to get her out of there. If Jake said something, Gail would believe it. "I just found out today that Peter Windom, the guy we were going to see in San Jose, but he died the night before, of a stroke, he had a hole in the back of his head."

"Was he the guy that was making all that progress on integrating ICs with live cells?"

"He was. Jake wanted to take those ideas and apply them to high speed video clarity. We could use it now with the new proposal."

"If you're able to win that new contract, won't it be too late for anyone to try and take over the company?"

"It would be, but meeting the requirements won't be a piece of cake."

"Jake can do anything. He'll get it right. Changing the subject, I have been seeing someone over the past month and it's getting somewhat serious."

Evan's first thoughts were of strangling his ex-wife.

"The football coach from UT?"

"He's very nice to me and it's time you and I move on. I have to think, between him and Baxter, I should be ok. I have a great security system, thanks to Jake, and I'll make sure the company's stock certificates are in the bank's lock boxes."

There was no more hiding or beating around the bush. Gail was moving on and he should, too.

"Just make sure you have protection."

"Is the protection for the sex or intruders?"

"That's too much information. You know what I'm talking about."

"I'm just teasing you, Evan, like you do me." Not really, but Gail knew it wasn't something she could tease him about. Like he, she realized their lives would never be the same as it had been. They wouldn't be able to get back together again, and even the kids were encouraging her to date again.

"I'm sure you like this guy, but if he starts to get physical in the wrong way, let me know."

"My God, Evan! Do you think I'd go out with guys like that? Besides, he's about six foot five inches tall and weighs around two hundred and forty pounds. He does Iron Man competition when football season is over." Then she paused and said, "I think you need to become friends with him."

She was right, Evan thought. Maybe the next time Evan was there, they could go out and have dinner together, so Evan could get to know him. Then Evan could shoot him.

"I'm glad you're happy, Gail. The last jerk you married wasn't much of a catch."

"We had some great years together and raised two wonderful kids. No, my first husband was a pretty good guy."

"Thanks, baby. You know I still love you."

"That was never the problem, was it?"

"No. It wasn't." They both said good-bye and hung up. If Evan hadn't been feeling badly enough, he now felt worse.

# Chapter Five

# Problem Solving

AFTER TWO WEEKS OF TRYING TO SOLVE THE PROBLEMS OF missile payout systems and no new threats against him, Evan was looking forward to visiting with the President of TI. It was a luncheon meeting in McKinney. Since their corporate jets flew out of McKinney, they could meet and have lunch before she went back to her headquarters outside of Dallas. Jake had made many calls, trying to find a chip maker that could meet their speeds without needing to be cooled.

Two days before, a call placed from TI's president's executive assistant to Evan confirmed that they had a new experimental chip and wondered if the president of Cannon Electronics could meet after they arrived from the airport. Evan wanted Jake to come, but Jake begged off, saying, "Give me the designer's name and number and I'll talk to him."

As Evan was leaving the office, Jake came to him, walking quickly, and Evan said, "Change your mind and decided to get that free lunch after all?"

"Is that meeting today?"

"Yes…I'm leaving now. You got something else for me?"

"Go ahead with your meeting, but I may have a solution now."

"Great! Fill me in when I get back."

Evan was to meet Erin Quincy at a lunch place well known in the area called "Heaven's Kitchen." It was started by three women who made lunch from scratch. Because the courthouse was located close by, and the city square was getting a reputation as a great place to shop, the restaurant had developed a significant reputation. It was located on the square in an old warehouse. It had originally been a saloon, with a hotel on the second story. Over the years, the bar had been removed and the whole downstairs was opened up with large windows in the front and back. Because it had been a bar, the wood supports had initials and sayings carved into them. There were plaques over the James brothers and Bonnie and Clyde name.

Meeting Erin, who was waiting by the hostess stand, was a mild shock. She was a knockout. It was really hard not to look at her figure, since she wore a jacket that had a plunging neckline. Her trousers were form fitting, without being cheap looking. Evan reminded himself to keep his mind on the business at hand and not to start daydreaming about what could happen.

As they were being escorted to their table, Evan saw Ronnie. They locked eyes about the same time. She was dressed very stylishly and looking good. Her date was Dave Thompson, the All-Star point guard for the Dallas Mavericks. Evan had heard rumors about the relationship, but seeing them together made him feel jealous.

Erin asked Evan about his background and explained hers briefly. Evan would not have said it out loud, but somehow she really did look familiar. Once he and Erin were seated next to the window that opened to the town square and making small talk while looking through the menu, water was placed in front of them. Erin dropped her menu and Evan reached down to grab it. When he handed the menu back, Evan looked out the window and saw a reflection off a rooftop. The reflection seemed to move and Evan suddenly felt that everything wasn't right. He moved quickly, sliding out of the booth just as the window beside their booth shattered and the table splintered.

"Get down!" Evan shouted to Erin, half pulling her underneath the table.

The entire restaurant turned toward the sound and started moving away from the windows. Ronnie came up to Evan in a crouch, her pistol in both hands. Evan's pistol was drawn as well. He was looking at the rooftop.

Erin shouted, "I'm leaving!" and started crawling away, to the back of the building.

"I don't see anything out there," Ronnie said a little breathless sounding. "Do you know where the shot came from?"

"I think so, but I have to tell you, whoever did it seemed to vanish."

Ronnie was on her phone, calling for help. "Cars are already on the way. Someone else called it in."

The station was less than a block away, and the police and Evan, as he peered over the table and the window frame, could see officers running into the street and toward the alleys, to cut off the would-be assassin.

"It looks like your date bugged out on you." Evan looked at the empty booth where Ronnie had been seated.

"Just as well, we weren't going anywhere. He's not the smartest tool in the shed, if you know what I mean. I will miss those free game tickets, though."

Evan chuckled and noticed that his hand started to shake. He put his pistol back into the inside waistband holster under his coat and looked at Ronnie. "I'm not sure how much of this I can take."

"Well, your date wasn't very impressed. I noticed she left, too."

"Believe it or not, she's the president of TI and we had a business meeting."

"I don't think so. I've met the president of TI and he doesn't look like that -- doesn't even wear heels."

"He?" Evan was confused and was starting to get angry.

"Did she give you her card?"

"Yeah. Here it is."

Ronnie looked at the card and held it by the edge. "I'll see if we can lift some prints --odd about the shot. If the gunman saw you well enough to take the shot, he was terrible with the follow through." At that Ronnie, looked down to the floor, found where the bullet had entered the table. She was drawing a mental line to the large hole in the window, Evan realized.

As Ronnie continued to secure their surrounding she said, "Where did you say you saw the reflection?"

"Over on the roof across the street."

"I believe that we're going to find that the shot came from the roof of the old drug store. Either way, you should be a dead man. I think we are okay now."

"Thanks for reassuring me," Evan told her. "I feel so comforted that people are trying to kill me and keep missing."

"I'm sorry I was thinking out loud. You weren't supposed to hear that. But all things considered, wouldn't you rather that they keep missing?"

"Well, I'm going back to my office. It seems to be the only place where I feel safe."

"I'll come by later, when I have more information." Evan looked into Ronnie's eyes. He found hope in her glance back to him.

He had to quit this fixation on her. He had to concentrate on issues at hand. He had to think about staying alive. And, making these FOGM systems work.

\*\*\*\*\*\*\*\*\*\*\*\*\*\*\*\*\*\*\*\*\*\*\*\*\*\*\*\*\*\*\*\*\*\*\*\*\*\*

Once Evan walked into their headquarters, there started to be a buzz about what just happened to Evan. Brenda read him the riot act for even being there. Everyone else kept their distance. Work seemed to be the only thing keeping him focused and keeping him from going crazy. After two hours, he got a call from Ronnie. She was coming over and they had to talk. Once Ronnie arrived, she was escorted into Evan's office by Brenda, and for the first time, Evan felt that things were bad.

"I have to know who your important clients are and who would have an axe to grind against you?" Ronnie asked as she sat down opposite him.

"I thought you had the list, but I can have Brenda track it down by sales numbers."

"I'm checking the check. We're overlooking something. You see either you are the luckiest man alive or someone is manipulating you into something. First, let's start with your friend from lunch."

"I told you. She was supposed to be the president of TI. We were meeting because she had a new, fast chip that we needed on the FOGM job."

"Well, she wasn't, not even close. Remember the first assassin's background, undercover CIA, and then he just disappeared? Similar for her, except ex-FBI and CIA, very few field agents worked at both agencies...kind of an unwritten rule. She must have some mad skills to have done that. She has been a hired intel guru for anyone with money, basically a corporate spy. Her real name is Karen Adams. On a hunch, I tested the water glasses. Her water glass had enough knock out drug that anyone would have been incapacitated.

"You mean someone tried to kill her?"

"You are so naïve, Evan! She would have switched glasses with you at the first opportunity."

"Then, who was shooting at whom?"

"At this moment, nobody knows the shooter, but I'm willing to guess that the intent was to create enough distraction that the drug wouldn't be used. Or, another theory is that you moved too fast and the shooter missed. Have to say that the bullet wasn't normal lead, either. Seems like some type of aluminum, which also doesn't make sense, but I haven't got all the ballistics reports back on it yet."

At that Jake came in and looked at both Ronnie and Evan. "I just heard about it. Were you able to snag the shooter?"

Ronnie explained the evidence that she had found and the likely two options. Evan could tell Jake had started to weigh the options in his mind. "Well, I don't bet, but if I did, I would bet the house that it's got something to do with the Spanish FOGM buyer."

Both Ronnie and Evan looked at Jake and said "Huh?" in near perfect unison.

"Now, how can you hear this story and just decide like that? That it's the Spanish buyer?" Evan said.

"Evan, from the beginning, you have had two sets of variables, one good and the other bad. Someone wants him dead and another someone wants him alive. I couldn't have given you a reason, until today. We have had a hardware issue for a Spanish proposal that's been impossible to build. Today, I had a manufacturer's representative in here that literally hands me the world's most advanced chipset. It's a Bio-chip, one-of-a-kind. Reps never get advanced products like these, and if they did, it would be limited on certain production runs, and they would want you to sign your life away just to test and prototype them. This guy just comes in here, hands me these chips and says he can get as many as I need. I asked him for performance specifications and he had a folder that had been sealed, only for me to open, with all the needed documentation. It was given to him by a new company with directions to give me the papers and sample chips."

"What does it mean?" Ronnie was still confused.

"Someone wants us to develop this system, while someone else wants to kill me or for this project to fail. The woman with me at lunch wasn't the president of TI, but some type of industry spy. Ronnie, show Jake the photo of our little darling."

Ronnie pulled a photo out of her shoulder bag and handed it to Jake. Ronnie stood up, closed the office door and looked at both Evan and Jake. "What are you working on that seems such a threat?"

Jake held the photo sideways and proclaimed, "We know her. She was with Peter that night we last saw him. Probably the girl he was – uhh – with, when --," Jake let it hang.

Evan stood up and tried to remember. He didn't get a good look at her face, but he did see her figure, and how she held herself.

"Ronnie, you have that photo from the entrance to the restaurant?" She handed him another photo and that generated a memory that Evan could recall. "You're right Jake. I thought there was something familiar about her and it's the clothes and how they fit. Why couldn't I remember?"

"Well, if you used your eyes instead of your imagination, you would have." Jake was staring at Evan with a big grin on his face. As usual, Jake was right.

"Are you guys talking about Peter Windom, who had the hole in his head?" Ronnie asked.

Evan answered, "The same. And he would have been the guy that we would have used on this project."

"I didn't find anything odd at all about your buyer in Spain."

Jake was running all the data in his super-computer-like brain. "We have one company offering a big pile of cash to provide a system that maybe three companies could provide, if they got these new chips. So we have company 'X,' that is trying to kill Evan -- not necessarily to stop the project, but I'm not certain on this point. Lastly, we have another group, killing the people who are trying to kill Evan. I really don't think they are all related, but this is happening all at the same time."

Ronnie asked, "Again what's so special about the system that you guys are trying to build? It's not like you're inventing something that will make today's light bulbs obsolete."

Evan answered, telling her, "We aren't inventing something like a computer, but building a missile delivery system faster than a generation beyond what's on the market. They were offering guarantee payments to us for reaching specific milestones. At first, we didn't want to even bother trying, but they made the conditions acceptable to take the risk."

"How state of the art is this system?" Ronnie asked.

Jake interjected, "Normal FOGM systems operate at four to ten kilometers. They wanted us to get to forty and we actually got to seventy-five on a normal production run. They wanted it to operate at night, and through dust, fog and sandstorms. Yet, the biggest issue was the payout speed. This is related to the strength of the coil. We have been a leader in building strong coils. The absolute best speed obtained has been Mach zero point two, but we were able to get to Mach one and actually made it to one point eight. Until now, the best speed we could reach was Mach zero point two. With the improvements, we reached Mach one immediately and then Mach one point eight. The latest speed is Mach three."

"Now," Evan picked up the conversation, "we are as fast as any existing air to air missile system. It's as fast as the Blackbird spy plane, the SR71." Evan then added, "Existing research is underway that could meet most of their requirements."

"You see, we have received about four million dollars, once we delivered the coils that could meet the speed and distance requirements," Evan told her. "If we are successful in bringing everything in on time, it's a total of one hundred million."

"Who are your competitors?"

"Only two different companies can make coils, but since wars aren't cropping up like they used to, there's not a lot of demand." Evan looked at Jake. "By the way, did the chips work?"

Jake pulled out his laptop. Evan and Ronnie looked over his shoulder as he ran the simulation program. The video was clear and specific potential targets were visible.

"Remarkable," was all that Evan could say. "This will change how we fight future wars forever."

"Really? It looks like a computer game." Ronnie added, leaning against Evan's desk.

"This is a simulation. What we are talking about is to take a supercomputer and shrink it into a semiconductor chip and make it work at elevated military specifications. Some that work at half that speed are available, but you have to keep them in a super-cooled environment." Jake shared.

Ronnie suggested that Evan and Jake start taking extra precaution when driving to work. She also told them that extra cops would be assigned to protect them, whether they liked the idea or not.

\*\*\*\*\*\*\*\*\*\*\*\*\*\*\*\*\*\*\*\*\*\*\*\*\*\*\*\*\*

Meanwhile, a mere seven miles awhile, another meeting of individuals was taking place, who were frustrated over the developments that happened at the restaurant. Eliot Huggins who had assigned Karen Adams to kill Evan Cannon was furious. His face was red and the veins in his neck stuck out. "I don't care that you were shot at. You had the opportunity and should have taken Cannon out!"

"The sheriff was two tables over. Do you think she was going to let me do anything and get out of there? She used to be one of the FBI's best field agents. My plan was to drug Cannon and get him into the car. It was set-up perfectly, until the shooter came into play. What do we know about that? Was he shooting at me or Cannon?"

He sat down and continued to look at her. "You're very beautiful, perhaps the prettiest assassin in the world. But you still failed. At this point, we really don't know about the shooter. The bullet seemed to be targeted for Cannon, but was such a poorly made shot one has to wonder why even try? We are going with the alternate plan. McKinney is too small to get anyone involved that won't be noticed. Plus, everyone is on edge. Do you think you can finish this issue?" The sarcasm was dripping and he was making a point.

"Austin is an easier area to work in. We'll get the papers."

"Fine. But, don't come back empty handed. Your life may well depend on it."

She turned around and left the room. "God! To think I actually slept with him!" Karen Adams said under her breath. She had always been a beautiful girl. Her parents entered her into beauty pageants at an early age. Her intelligence was a far greater asset, however. She learned how to manipulate people.

She had never married, and at the age of twenty-four, was working counter-intelligence with the CIA after starting her career with the FBI. There had been only a handful of people that had made that change. At twenty-seven, she was the youngest person supervising actual spy networks in Russia. It wasn't long before she found out that there wasn't any real money in the government spy world, and subsequently, quit in order to enter the private sector. Karen was still respected in most intelligence circles, but her information pipeline was slowly shutting down. If she retired at this moment, she would be a wealthy person all her life. But if they could finish this task, then she would have more money than she could ever spend in several lifetimes.

She drove to her hotel to quickly pack and change her looks. Karen knew the order to stop Cannon Electronics from developing their FOGM system came from the top, but her question was always why they were so desperate. Killing wasn't new to her, but there seemed to be a lot of puzzle pieces that she didn't have or understand. That in itself was enough to drive her to finish this job.

Between the McKinney police force and the county sheriff's officers, the town was wired over the recent activity. There had been a few multiple murders over the years, but nothing like the intriguing developments that were catching the headlines.

The police force, on their own accord, had several roadblocks set up and was burning up the phone lines trying to determine who was trying to kill one of their prominent citizens.

Ronnie didn't really think any of it would make a difference. Whoever was manipulating these killings was held up somewhere, working out the details of his or her next move. Ronnie had an idea that maybe it was time to visit Evan's ex-wife in Austin.

For the first time in her life, Ronnie was totally confused. She was sure that neither group was from the government. Oddly, the key to this was Jake. If someone wanted to stop the Spanish missile project, then stop Jake. With that, she called over to her dispatcher. "Call in Greg and tell him to keep an eye on Jake Bryant's home. I don't want Jake to know. He'll be at the plant, so there's no need to rush."

Ronnie made her flight arrangements. But she was unsure if going to Austin made sense. She called Evan to tell him about her trip. He didn't answer his cell. She tried his office and just got voice mail. On a wild guess, she tried his house and got him.

"Don't you ever turn your cell phone off until we find who's trying to kill you?"

"Hello, Ronnie. I was beginning to think you didn't care anymore. Just so you know, I got tired of being flooded with calls at the office and decided to get work done here. So, what's up?"

Ronnie had to chuckle to herself. Here was a guy who had cheated death twice and was still at ease with himself. He had a certain charm and she had to admit to herself she was jealous when she saw him in the restaurant with a woman. The next thing she knew, she had invited herself over to his house.

"You can come, but can you cook?"

"Of course I can, but why are you asking?"

"Because I still have work to do and if you're coming over, then you could help me with dinner for both of us so I can go to bed before the sun comes up."

"You're pretty cocky, aren't you? I'll be there in about thirty minutes."

A half-hour later, Ronnie parked by the road and relieved the officers watching the grounds and told them that she would be there for awhile, adding that the next shift could take over once she left.

"Red or white?" Evan sang out as Ronnie came through the doorway.

"Actually, I'm bi-racial, but I can call my father and see if I have any Indian blood."

Evan looked at Ronnie and noticed her eyes were blue and made a mental note to ask if they were natural. Her face had fine features, with lips almost in a permanent pout. Actually, she looked like a young Vanessa Williams. No wonder she attracted so much attention. It wasn't that she wasn't pretty to begin with, but he had never seen her dressed up. She looked like she had stepped out of Cosmopolitan Magazine.

"Wow! What an outfit. You should be a model, dressed like that. Is it all for me?" She wore a black dress, the skirt ending just above her knees, the top of the dress held up with what women called "spaghetti straps." Her hair was up, which accentuated the graceful lines of her throat. Diamond earrings and the stone in each was about the size of a typical engagement ring was the only jewelry she wore.

"You might wish I dressed this way for you, but you are wrong. I had a planned dinner date, but after my conversation with a certain basketball player, he says it's over. Funny, but it seems that so many of these hardcore athletes have such fragile egos. By the way, I like red, but keep the amount small. I sent my crew out for a break and want to stay alert."

"Would that jock be Dave Thompson?"

"It would be the same. He's a good kid, but just trying too hard to be perfect."

Evan smiled asking, "Where do you hide your big gun in that dress"

"Smaller gun. And I don't have any immediate plans for sharing that information." As Ronnie took the glass of wine, she saw that Evan already had dinner in place for both of them. "I thought you wanted me to cook."

"I thought about it and I have a ton of food already prepared. I just needed to defrost it and heat up."

Ronnie went over to the stove and tasted the creamy sauce. "Alfredo sauce with something else added to make it spicy, very tasty!" She turned to Evan as he pulled the bread out. "I'm very impressed. This looks great. I didn't know you cooked."

"I don't. I just re-heat. Since you're still single, my thoughts were maybe cooking isn't your cup of tea."

"I'm single because I want to be. I can cook, but choose not to do so. The FBI wasn't an agency where you had a lot of free time. Once I became the Sheriff, I started dating some of the Dallas area athletes and never got into a nesting routine. Once a publication wanted me to do a centerfold, I was a little overwhelmed that people thought I could be a centerfold, until I found out the story title was something like girls who follow sports guys. In reality, they followed me. I was their trophy girlfriend that they wanted the public to see, but had other girls when it was time for a 'booty' run."

Evan was pleased to hear that. "No disrespect, but you really are centerfold material, Sheriff. And you do look great in that dress."

"I think it makes my legs look good. What do you think?" Ronnie was smiling, baiting him, he knew.

"Really hadn't noticed, but yeah, your legs look good." Evan knew that two could play that game. "Now tell me again. Why are you going to visit my ex-wife?"

"Twice people have tried to kill you. There's evidence that at least one of the persons associated with these attempts spent time in Austin. So, I'm just checking all the loose ends. I also hear she's seeing someone steadily."

"Gail is pretty serious with one of the Texas football coaches. Can't say I'm surprised. She loves football, after growing up in Ohio. Anyway, I hope she marries that guy. We need an ending."

Ronnie stood fully facing Evan. "Does that also include you?"

"I guess so, but --." Before Evan could finish, the lights went out. Ronnie was in front of him, backing him into a corner, her gun drawn. Evan smelled her perfume. Her body was pressed close to him. Albeit a bit idiotic under the circumstances. The lights came back on. He was almost sorry. Evan told Ronnie, "This is a pretty frequent occurrence. They're building a ballpark inside the development."

She still had her pistol in both hands.

"Where exactly did you have that pistol hidden?"

She turned around and whispered, "It's top secret! We learned it at the FBI Academy."

He turned Ronnie around so they faced each other. "I have to tell you that this waiting around for you to catch the bad guy or girl is driving me crazy. Tell me that's a normal reaction."

"My only experience with this was with the Bureau, and it usually made people a basket case, so I would say you're doing pretty well."

"Jake seems to think it's a total power play for Cannon and another 'X' factor wanting us to finish this latest project. Since the two don't have a common interest, we have these conflicts with me in the middle. I just don't see why they don't just go after our board, easiest way to take out a company."

"Do you think Jake is right?"

"He usually is. He's one of those rare guys that can look through a ball of yarn and tell you where the two ends are located."

"What are your ideas, since someone is trying to kill you?"

"I'm afraid that Jake is right, but for the life of me, I can't tell you why. We're in the worst financial situation we have ever been in and now we have one of the biggest single opportunities to get ourselves solvent for many years to come. Between that and the fact that Peter Windom had a hole in his head similar to the one in the head of my would-be killer, it makes me think we aren't looking in the right areas. I looked up laser capabilities and there are medical ones with ultra-fast high power pulsed lasers that will penetrate bone and make a hole like we've seen.

But, its main use is to destroy individual cells -- like cancers -- without hurting surrounding ones."

"That wasn't in any report I got from the FBI. I wonder if they put that together. Do you use a laser like that in your project?"

"No.  Most of the lasers used in communications are made in Japan. For other applications, especially military, Northrop Grumman is the leader in the United States. Hell, they have ones that fit on jets and can knock out pilot's eyes from other jets. All of that was abandoned after a treaty signed by all of NATO. It wasn't lasers that Peter was working on. It was an advanced chip design.  The odd thing is that we're trying to use those same advanced chips, to work our system."

"Did your friend Peter leave you any ideas of how to build one or who to talk to about advanced designs?" Ronnie asked.

"No, but I need to talk to Jake about how we got those chips. Now, are you ready?"

"Ready for what?" Ronnie asked.

"Dinner, of course," Evan told her.

Maybe Evan didn't consider himself a cook, but if taste was the benchmark, he was one.  Ronnie was a little taken back about their conversation. She always prided herself on thoroughness and felt she had missed the boat somewhere, and that Evan and Jake were ahead of her and on the right track.

"I have a personal question for you," Evan said.

Ronnie made a mental note to ask Evan more about his suspicions. "Go ahead. Part of my job is to make you feel comfortable about me and my team guarding you. By the way, I love this pasta."

"Thank you. It's not low calorie, but I doubt it matters to you." Evan paused slightly, "When all of this crap is over, how would you feel about us going out socially?"

Ronnie thought to herself...wow, she wasn't ready for this conversation. "You're probably just feeling that way because I'm protecting you and you feel a strong bond between us. Not unusual.  And, I've seen it many times in witness protection reports."

"I'm a shy guy and it takes a lot for me to ask this. I wanted to ask you out many other times, but felt you were out of my league, dating all of those jocks. You don't have to answer now, but know this: I am very persistent."

"I have to be honest with you," Ronnie said in return. "I like you, but it could get very complicated. At the FBI, we learned that protection details almost always get too close to the people they protect, which is why there's such an effort to keep everything at arm's length -- keep everything un-emotional."

"That's okay. You see, you haven't been protecting me; it's been your officers.  And besides, I fell for you when we met at the Holy Family fundraiser."

"You left a check and walked out. I remembered that. It seemed every man did the same thing, and the rest of us were there making small talk, wondering why. I thought, at the time, that you were trying to create a scene.  But when so many of the guys followed, I realized there was something else going on."

"The organizers were essentially stealing from the fund and I didn't like it. No disrespect, but the law couldn't stop them, so I wrote my check directly to the building fund, so it couldn't be used anywhere else. I think many of the others did the same thing."

"I was impressed and I did investigate afterward, but as you say, nothing I could do to stop them. Now, there is a new board and the former organizers are gone. You started it all by walking out."

Everything in Ronnie's training was telling her to call for the relief guard and leave Evan's house, but she was also wondering if her feelings for Evan were real. Neither of them talked much after that, they merely finished their meal.

Evan didn't really take her response as no. As he was standing, gathering the dishes, he pulled her close and took the leap of faith. He leaned down so that he could either kiss her or be slapped. Ronnie's mouth angled to Evan's and they kissed. Her perfume and soft lips only sparked Evans' desire for more. Ronnie broke the kiss off and pulled back.

"Before we go any further, I want some ground rules," she spoke as she wove her fingers with his. "I get total cooperation from you on this case. If I say we have a person protecting you and Jake twenty-four seven, then we do it. I don't want you to be second guessing me on this." Evan nodded his agreement. "Also, if you are under my protection, you're not to be carrying a gun."

"Wait a minute, you know I'm --." At that, Ronnie touched her fingertips to Evan's lips and looked him in the eyes, almost like a parent looking at a child. She whispered very softly in his ear, "It will be worth your while to follow these rules." Evan took her hand, kissed it and nodded his head in agreement.

"It's been some time since I've felt like this."

"Let me guess. Brenda was your last."

"No! We had one date after Gail left and both of us decided it was like dating your brother or sister. Since then, we've grown closer, but not in a sexual way. She knows as much about what goes on in the plant as Jake and I put together. My last time was with Gail, about four months ago. I went down to Austin, to attend a charity function she sponsored. And one thing led to another. The odd thing is, while we both enjoyed it, we also knew it would be our last time. A final emotional tug that had bound us together for so long had been broken, and we both realized it. Gail started dating Jim Swanson, who's the offensive coordinator at UT, so she found her new life."

"How do you feel about her new love?"

"If she's happy, then that's all I can ask for. I put her through hell, starting the business, and she deserves another chance. Actually, we both do. Let's get back to business."

"Look. Thank you for the meal and the information, but I'm leaving for my house, since I have to get up when the rooster crows."

Evan stepped away and returned a few seconds later with an envelope. "Here. When you see Gail, make sure she gets this. It's a list of new projects we are pursuing, if we have enough funding." Ronnie looked quizzically at Evan.

"She heads up the board and I never want her to attend a board meeting without knowing what we want to accomplish. It also gives her some credibility with the other board members." They walked to the front door and Evan wrapped his arms around Ronnie. "I want to finish this conversation when you get back."

Ronnie initiated the kiss this time and walked down the steps to her car. She looked back and said, "When I get back, I'll show you how I cook."

"Looking forward to it," Evan yelled back.

# Chapter Six

# Two Women

RONNIE WASN'T SURE OF WHAT SHE EXPECTED GAIL TO BE LIKE, but now that she and Evan's relationship had taken a more personal turn, she needed to bear down on the job at hand and not look at Gail as Evan's ex-wife and lover. Ronnie was picked up at the airport by Austin police, and as she surveyed the city on her way to Gail's house, she definite wanted to be back in McKinney before nightfall. She thought about calling Evan and inviting him over to her house tonight, but she knew she needed to get him "out of her head." She knew she needed to stay focused. Just because of what happened with Evan last night, she found herself calling her best friend, who worked in Colorado for the Department of Defense and was also an ex-FBI agent. It was like she was back in college, talking to her roommates about potential boyfriends.

Ronnie spotted the detective immediately outside the security gate and after the introductions; he escorted her outside where his car was parked.

"Thanks for picking me up at the airport," she told the Austin detective. His name was Greg and he looked as though he was around 50 years old and reminded her of the detective character "Lenny" from the TV show, "Law and Order."

Greg wasn't much for small talk, so he got right to the point. "Do you really think that someone may be after Gail Cannon?"

"We know that one of the assassins that was killed spent time around her house," Ronnie told him.

"You say he died, but another attempt was made on Cannon's life?"

"Yeah, Greg, it looks like Evan Cannon may still be in danger. We have reasons to believe they are after control of Evan Cannon's company. Gail Cannon is majority shareholder and maybe knows something that we haven't thought of yet."

"You said over the phone that the assassin was dead on the scene, how did he die?" Greg asked, clearing his throat.

"Well, that in itself is strange, since it looks like a laser shot to the head."

"They say Sixth Street is dangerous, but I have to tell you, I'm not sure if we ever had anyone die from a laser shot."

Ronnie laughed, "Well in McKinney, we have the high tech outlaws." She didn't want to get into how he really died because that would be too complicated. Truth was she hardly understood the medical circumstances herself.

"By the way, are you the one dating that basketball player for the Mavs?"

Ronnie was tired of always answering those types of questions. "Yeah, but we've decided to go our separate ways."

"Too bad...I mean, I was gonna ask if I could get some tickets when the Spurs play there."

That was why Ronnie hated dating celebrities. "I'll see what I can do, Greg."

They traveled the rest of the way in silence and Ronnie was flipping back to her notes, trying to remember if she missed anything. Also, Ronnie was interested to see if Gail still held an attraction for Evan that she didn't even realize she had. Romantic speculation aside, Ronnie needed to know if Gail had or could recall any information about the assassins. For this interview to pay any dividends at all, Ronnie knew she had to be at her sharpest, so total concentration was vital.

Gail answered the doorbell dressed in jeans and a cotton chamois shirt. A dog was barking from the back of the house, probably the Aussie that Evan had warned her of. The aroma of freshly brewed coffee was emanating from the kitchen. As Gail and Greg were lead in and introduced to Jim Swanson, the football coach, Baxter was brought in to check her out. With that, Ronnie put her hand out with a treat and became a friend.

"You must know Evan pretty well to have a treat ready for Baxter." Ronnie could see that Gail was taking her measure.

"Your ex-husband warned me to be prepared for Baxter. He's a pretty dog. He even has gold eyes."

"He's all that and more. Once, we had Jehovah's Witnesses stop by the house. Baxter got out the front door between my legs and jumped into the car. All four immediately jumped onto the hood and trunk with the dog sitting in the driver's seat, very pleased with himself." Ronnie found herself laughing as she envisioned it. "He is one of the smartest dogs I've ever been around -- and maybe the meanest. Jim had a hard time getting accepted by Baxter.  He used to be called 'Evan's curse' to keep us away from each other. Now there are three men and I, who can tell that dog to do something, and he will obey."

"Who's the third man?" Ronnie asked.

"Jake Bryant. Baxter never once barked at him in anger. He has always thought of Jake as one of the family as far as I can tell. Of course, Jake has one of his litter mates, which might make a difference as well."

Ronnie made a mental note to herself about Jake and his relationship to Gail. Ronnie got down to business and started asking Gail questions about people she might have seen and if she could tell her any information that would make some sense of the attempts on Evan's life. After thirty minutes of questions, Jim excused himself and left for the stadium. Greg had a call and took it outside. Once they were alone, a new sense of intimacy seemed to pervade the room's atmosphere. Ronnie looked Gail in the eye and said, "Gail, the men who are trying to kill Evan have spent a lot of time in this part of Austin. I'm just afraid that they may make an attempt on your life."

Gail looked down at her hands and gave Baxter, who had lain down beside her, a rub on the head. "I'm feeling better than I have in a long time. Jim and I are getting married in a couple of months and my kids seem to be successful in their lives. Evan and I have finally come to the point where we understand each other and maybe he will even find someone that can give him some sparks that he needs." Ronnie decided to just nod her head up and down and keep quiet. "I'm not a brave person, but between Baxter and Jim, I feel pretty safe. Besides, I don't want to think about it. Maybe I'm burying my head in the sand, but I don't want to think about someone trying to hurt me. Besides, why would anyone want to?"

"You are the primary stockholder for Cannon Electronics. Have you been pressured to do anything that you thought was out of the ordinary?"

"No. I always tell people that I'm not a decision maker and they need to talk to Evan. Can I ask you a very pertinent question?"

"Sure. I've asked you enough, so I guess it's your turn."

Gail had a lopsided smile. "Who is behind this?"

"We believe that there are two different factions working against each other. It seems as if, every time an attempt is made on Evan's life, it's been interdicted by another party. Frankly, we have no idea who either group is, but the attempts are definitely real." Ronnie decided to avoid some of the gruesome details.

"How is Evan holding up? When I talk to him, he does the stiff upper lip routine, but I know that it has to start wearing on him."

"He is very hardheaded about the whole protection detail. I think he actually believes that he can defend himself. I'm amazed by how accurately he can fire a handgun, but shooting someone is entirely different."

For the first time, Gail was really frowning. "He knows the difference between target practice and killing someone."

"Is there something I should know?"

"I have never told anybody about this but Jake, and that was only when he saw Evan lose his temper and wanted to know how far Evan would go when angry. It was quite a few years ago, when we were just married, and on our honeymoon. This drunken guy started harassing me at a beach in Costa Rica. Evan hit him square in the nose and it exploded in blood. The drunk staggered off and we went back to the room. Later that night, three men, including the guy with the broken nose, jumped us on the beach on our way to a bar, roughing up Evan pretty badly. They took us back to the room, dragging Evan and probably getting ready to rape me. Evan always kept a loaded pistol with us. He carried a permit and used the pistol for target practice. Once we were back inside the bungalow, I could see that Evan seemed almost dead. They threw me on the bed and tore my dress off. Out of nowhere, Evan must have found some hidden energy and he pushed the three guys together and found the gun. One of the men also pulled out a gun, but it was over in seconds. Evan fired three times, all three holes in the middle of their foreheads. We found out later that all three men had guns and probably were responsible for multiple robberies in the area."

Ronnie couldn't believe what she had just heard. "I never saw anything in his file about this."

"You won't, either. The men were Nicaraguans. In Costa Rica, they're used as migrant workers, and once the police saw how badly Evan had been beaten, they just erased the whole episode. Evan had to give his pistol to the local police officer and give them some money for cleaning up the room. It took a long time for me to get over the attack, but Evan took it in stride. He doesn't show it often, thank God, but there are very strong emotions lying under the surface in Evan."

Ronnie was taken back. She had seen people that seemed to be able to turn violence on and off with equal ease. But Evan didn't fit the pattern. "Was that one of the reasons your marriage failed?"

Gail chuckled softly. "Not in the least. I think that his intensity is the reason that we stayed together for so long. He loves as intensely as he fights, either for life or his business." This made Ronnie feel better, that maybe the man she had feelings for wasn't someone with seething emotions ready to boil over at a moment's notice.

"Are you sleeping with Evan?"

Ronnie was now squarely on the defensive. She looked Gail in the face and smiled. "Why would you ask this?"

"You are exactly the type of lady that Evan would desire. Also, I can tell by your facial expressions that you have feelings for him. Honey, it's okay if you are. His and my time has long since been over."

"I have to say that, since we've been thrown together, our emotions...Well, last night, I went over to see him about the latest attempt, and -- well, I left before anything actually happened."

Gail reached her hand over to Ronnie's and gave it a squeeze. "I don't know you very well, but please cut it off with Evan unless you're serious. He's very vulnerable when it comes to love."

"At this point, I can't say that I love him, but I also don't want him with anyone else until I know for sure."

"That's exactly how I felt when we first met. I can say I'm over him, but he will always be a good friend."

Greg joined them, his phone call ended, and Gail brought him a glass of ice tea. For the next thirty minutes, they talked about any details and even old associations that would explain an attack on Evan. At the end, Ronnie and Gail hugged each other and Greg shook Gail's hand.

Ronnie and Greg headed back to the airport, while Ronnie finished her notes. Greg kept to himself, and finally, Ronnie asked him if his call back at Gail's house was pertinent to either Evan or Gail.

"No. It seems that a local biker gang bought up some pretty efficient semi-automatic weapons, and we were speculating what they were planning."

"How much of a problem are gangs in Austin?"

"Not too much, but you never want idiot gang-bangers armed with sophisticated weapons that could be used to kill good, law abiding citizens."

"We have some gang issues in McKinney, but nothing like Austin or Dallas."

Greg added, "Yeah. I was in a task force in Dallas and saw firsthand the problems they have with gangs – scary...bad in places."

Two miles from the airport, Ronnie realized that she needed to know who would get Gail's shares of Evan's company if something happened to her. "Greg, do you know how company shares work if a person dies?" It was a long shot, since Greg didn't look like the type who would know anything about finances.

"Usually, people think the shares are passed down, like money or antique jewelry or whatever, but in most cases, especially in the case of someone who's the majority shareholder, it goes back to the board and they distribute it as they see fit. It happens in cases of highly leveraged companies."

Ronnie looked at Greg with new respect. "Well done, Greg. I'll call Gail and see how they handle it. By the way, how did you know?"

"It's Austin. A new company got started every day for three years in the early 2000s. Lots of greed and many people were killed to obtain majority control of a company."

The question of disposition of the shares was of minor importance, but still a loose end. Ronnie pulled out her cell phone and called Gail. The phone was picked up on the first half ring. She heard the dog attacking something in the background and Gail's plea for help and then the phone went dead.

"Turn the car around -- now! I think Gail is being attacked." Greg turned the car in a hard left, over and across the shallow median on Highway 71. Greg pressed the accelerator to the floor and had his lights flashing, while calling dispatch on the car radio. Also, Greg trying to steady the car while changing lanes at high speed was no easy task, but he was able to maneuver it without crashing. But no matter how fast they drove, they knew they were too far away; perhaps, to save Gail if an assassin was in her home. They could only pray that the Austin police would arrive at Gail's before them and save her.

"Greg? Do you have a shotgun?"

"870 with rifle sights in the trunk, chamber empty, seven-round extension magazine loaded with 12-gauge two and three-quarter Double-O-Buck."

"Are you sure she was being attacked?"

"I heard the dog going after someone and Gail was yelling for help."

"Christ! We were just there. Did they wait for us to leave?"

"Hell, if I know. Let's just get there and see what we can do."

Her next issue was whether to call Evan or wait until she got to the house. Since she really didn't know if Gail was hurt or not, she decided to wait. Gail's house, where she had been mere minutes ago, laughing and talking, could possibly be a crime scene now. A police car was in the same spot where they had parked earlier. The front door to the house was opened. As Greg pulled up, he hit the trunk release. Ronnie was out of the front passenger seat while the car still rocked on its brakes, grabbed the zippered case and slid the shotgun free. She took Greg's word on condition of readiness and racked the pump.

Greg had his weapon out and they announced themselves as they entered, Greg first, followed by Ronnie.

"This is Ronnie Green, Sheriff from McKinney, and she called this in," Greg told the uniformed officers inside.

"How did it come around to you calling this in?"

"I was meeting Ms. Cannon about another investigation we had in McKinney. The Detective and I were on the way back to the airport when I realized that I forgot a question I needed her to answer. When I called, I heard the dog fighting something in the background and Gail asking for help and then the line went dead. We couldn't have been gone for more than twenty to twenty-five minutes."

As Ronnie explained, her eyes scanned what she could see of the house, trying to determine what had happened.

"I'm sorry to say this, Sheriff, but the lady in question, at least I assume it's her, has been killed."

Ronnie knew in her heart that it must be, but wanted to make sure. She only knew Gail for a very short time, but what had transpired was hitting her hard, nonetheless.

"Where?"

"She's in the kitchen. Homicide and forensics are on their way. I would guess that you heard the last words she ever said, since the phone (a land line) was pulled out of the wall and she was shot. Can I ask you about the crime you're investigating in McKinney?"

They were all going into the kitchen together, when Ronnie took in the smell of blood and gunpowder and saw Gail in front of the dishwasher. Blood had already pooled under her body. That sickening feeling of death was enveloping Ronnie, and she always wondered how killers could embrace such a feeling. Maybe it was because murderers were really crazy and had no feelings, she sometimes thought.

"We are investigating a murder and two attempted murders on her husband. I'm starting to believe that they all are related."

Ronnie and Greg crouched down, looking at the details, but not wanting to disturb anything until the crime scene investigators and detectives arrived. One of the officers went over to Baxter and noted, "The dog's been shot three times...looks like he really put up a fight, poor guy. I'd guess he was still alive when what might have been the third bullet went into his stomach.  Killer probably wanted to pay him back for some bites or scratches. Bastard! Whoever shot this dog had to be very close, and it looks like this old fella dog took a piece of his killer before he died."

Ronnie and the others looked at Baxter and another wave of sorrow mixed with revulsion hit Ronnie. It was displaced in the next instant by anger that was intensifying every second.

"You need to notify Jim Swanson. He's one of the football coaches at UT that she was dating. I'll call her ex-husband and then I'll work with your detectives to get all the information together." Ronnie wasn't looking forward to this next call, but Evan needed to hear it from her.

She called Brenda and wanted to make sure Evan was there. "Brenda, this is Ronnie Green and I need to talk to Evan." Ronnie sense that Brenda could tell something was wrong.

"Evan's on the plant floor looking at some new equipment they just installed. Is this about yesterday's events?"

"No, Brenda. Just please get Evan; it's an emergency."

Ronnie questioned her effectiveness. If they had stayed, could they have stopped the killing? Or, would they also have been killed? It was ingrained in her to review everything and determine if the outcome could have been different.

"Ronnie? It's Evan. What's up?" The matter of fact question told her that Evan knew there was a problem.

"Evan, Gail has been murdered. It happened while I was on my way to the airport." She left a pause to determine what Evan was going to do. The loud clang that Ronnie heard was obviously the receiver hitting a wall. She also heard some loud inaudible cursing, but Evan was still not responding and a click happened that told her their connection had been broken.

Her phone rang and it was Evan. "Sorry, that phone didn't work." Ronnie's thought was how many phones did work when someone slammed them against the wall.

"Do you think it's the same group that is after me?"

"Evan, I am so sorry to tell you this. Right now, we can't say one way or the other, but it seems just too convenient not to consider."

"I'm coming down. Can you wait for me?" This was exactly what Ronnie was trying to avoid.

"Evan, there's nothing you can do here. The police have their investigation team here and will be looking for you soon enough to see if there is anything you can add. If you're here, emotion takes over and you will only get in the way."

There was silence on the phone. Perhaps, the silence was a good sign that maybe he was listening. "No. I, uhh -- need to get Baxter and bring him home."

"You can't, Evan. I am so sorry, they killed Baxter as well. He was trying to defend Gail and maybe he got a chunk out of one of them."

"Bastards! That's it! I'm coming down! Who do they think they are? Coming after me is one thing, but my family is something else, dammit."

"Evan, if you come down here and interfere with the investigation, they will jail you without thinking twice. This is Austin, not McKinney. The police don't have time to deal with people carrying a vendetta."

"I'm not that stupid. Besides, I have to help close up some of Gail's bookwork."

Ronnie knew he was coming no matter what. So she told Evan to call her when he got to the airport and she would pick him up. Ronnie knew working with the detectives and going over everything that was pertinent to the investigation had already been tiring and stressful, especially when she thought about all the events that had transpired over the past few days. And then there were the other detectives that were very hesitant about speculating too much until they had Ronnie's report faxed to them. To add to the confusion, Jim Swanson arrived in black shorts and orange polo shirt. It was obvious he'd come from practice and was giving the detectives hell. He wanted answers. Once he saw the bodies, he crumpled up and started weeping. Ronnie had seen it before, but the emotion of grief always left her feeling, she had failed. In this case, she wondered how it could have ended differently.

Time seemed to stand still. Swanson was being interviewed by two detectives, a four person team was going over the crime scene for the umpteenth time and Ronnie was left thinking about why this had happened and wishing Evan would call to say he had arrived.

Two men in dark business suits and sunglasses came into the kitchen. Had Ronnie not noticed the FBI cufflinks, she would have pegged them as Feds, having been one herself. She'd never gone for the cufflinks, though. "We're here from the FBI and need to ask Veronica Green a few questions." All the Austin police turned their heads in unison and looked at Ronnie.

Ronnie wondered how Gail's death would rate FBI involvement. "I'm Sheriff Green, how can I help you?"

After the introductions of both FBI agents and the Austin detectives, the lead FBI agent, a good looking man of about forty, named Matt Kingsley, got right to the point. "We believe that the men who did this killing are part of the same group that has been responsible for a massive computer fraud over the past two years. We don't know for sure, but would like to see what your CSI team comes up with."

"It's a far cry from computer theft to murder. Also I'm the Sheriff of Collin County. These men are in charge of this investigation. She pointed to Greg not wanting to complicate the investigation any more than necessary. Plus, if you look around, you'll see that they didn't leave behind too much to go on."

Ronnie noticed the Austin cops and forensics team watching the FBI agents, probably thinking it was nice to have someone else state the obvious to the Bureau. "I'm out of my jurisdiction. I live in McKinney and these are the guys that you need to talk to, not me. I can make some introductions," she offered.

"Actually, we also believe that this murder is tied to the attempts on Evan Cannon, which is why we want to access what information you might have gathered concerning the attempts."

Ronnie's warning antennae went up, telling her to tread very carefully. She figured that the FBI expected her to be cooperative since she used to be an agent. Another issue was how computer fraud fit into the whole mess. Before she said anything else, there was a commotion at the front door. All of them looked, only to see Evan explaining to one of the police officers why he needed to be there. Just seeing Evan generated an emotion in her. God, she couldn't be falling in love with him, she thought. She looked at her watch. It had only been two hours since she had spoken to Evan over the phone. How had he gotten to Austin in two hours?

Evan pointed her out to the detective stationed at the door. He was walking toward her in a manner she hadn't seen before. It was his body language that spoke of being in charge. If there was such a thing as an irresistible force, then he seemed to have it. She went to him and he put his arms around her. At that point, nothing seemed to matter, except the comfort they gave each other.

"I'm so sorry, Evan. If I had any idea that she was in danger, I would have put guards around the house."

"Gail would have just said 'no.' She wasn't one for any special treatment."

Ronnie was well aware that everyone was watching this scene unfold, wondering about her relationship with Evan. Cops would guess it right off the bat, but she guessed the Feds would be a little slow.

Greg, who had been designated as the lead detective by default, came up, and extended his hand and said, "Evan, I'm Detective Greg Olsen. Can you look around and see if anything is missing or out of place? It doesn't make too much sense to us why this happened."

Evan asked what they had found as he introduced himself to everyone in his wife's home. Evan physically shook from time to time, as he moved about the house. Death was always a hard thing to overcome and he was getting too much practice.

Gail had been there for every event in his life. They loved one another at one time and her loss created a void that might never be filled. The fact that she was going to be married soon really didn't change that. Her spark of life was gone. Evan heard something coming from the back bedroom.

Evan entered the room and saw an enormous man -- Jim.

"Hi, I'm Jim Swanson and you must be Evan." Swanson had his hand out. Evan grabbed it and hugged the big man. No matter that Jim and Gail had found happiness over Evan's silent objections, Evan still felt sorry for this mountain of a man.

They both went outside the back door to talk. They really had nothing at all to say to each other, but neither man wanted to not talk. After many stories shared between them, Jim left followed by the Austin PD CSI unit. A few uniforms were stationed outside to protect the crime scene. Only the two FBI agents, Detective Greg Olsen, Ronnie and Evan remained inside the house.

Evan went out to the side porch followed by the younger agent. Agent Lowe struck up a conversation. "Sorry that it's been a tough couple of weeks for you." Evan shoved his hands deep into his pockets, wishing he could change things, if only he knew why they were happening.

"I will tell you this; I'm going to spend my personal funds to find who's behind this and make them pay."

Agent Lowe looked at Evan with an expression suggesting he thought Evan might be crazy. "You need to let us take care of this situation, Mr. Cannon. Trust me when I say you're way out of your league on this."

Evan was thinking about how he could throw a right hook to Agent Lowe's nose. "I've heard that before in my life and haven't been found lacking yet."

Agent Lowe was staring at Evan and probably couldn't see the white sedan slow down in front of the house, Evan surmised. Evan saw the car, realized it was going to stop in front of the house and was about to say something to Agent Lowe when there was a bright flash from the car.

They were standing some fifteen yards from the car, and with no noise coming from the flash, Evan thought maybe it was some type of electrical short. Lowe's reaction was nothing short of amazing. He must have at last seen the car from the corner of his eye and was actually moving his hand to his holstered pistol, when his body began jerking and blood was splattering in all directions. Evan saw three people come out of the car, two firing into the house and another concentrating his fire into Lowe.

The shooter must have thought that Evan was hit as well, since Evan went down behind the now very dead FBI agent. Before Evan even hit the floor, he grabbed the agent's SIG 229 and rolled behind a line of eighteen-inch flower pots. The assassin was now directing his fire to the house and the only noise Evan could hear was breaking glass and a few shots being fired from inside. The uniformed officers posted outside were likely dead. Maybe Ronnie – but Evan pushed the thought from his mind, even though his stomach was churning, his bile was rising in his throat, and his anger was increasing by the seconds. Evan press checked the pistol. The chamber was loaded, just as it should have been.

He positioned himself so he had a clear field of fire and aimed at Lowe's killer, going for the crotch. It looked as if the killers might be wearing body armor, but most conventional everyday body armor didn't have a groin protector.

Evan fired a double tap, the shots hit their mark and the man screamed in agony as the weapon, some sort of submachine gun, fell and his hands suddenly went limp and the killer crumpled to the ground. Evan fired twice more, this time at the nearer of the two remaining shooters, just as the man started into a crouch. Both rounds missed the groin and struck the middle shooter in the chest, where the armor protected him. The shooter, he just moved behind a tree to protect himself from the crossfire that had developed.

A burst of gunfire hit around the flower pots on the porch, throwing pottery shards and dirt into and around Evan. He paused for a moment to make sure he was still in one piece. He had one target of opportunity, a shot at the right foot of the man behind the tree. Evan fired three shots and the shooter drew up his foot and screamed in pain. The third man had nothing to do, but get out of the gunfire and run for the car. Evan couldn't get a shot, but fired into the car tires and waited for the killer to get behind the steering wheel.

The wounded man, as he crawled to the car, was hit twice from the house, the sound of a twelve gauge shotgun unmistakable. The lone remaining assassin fired a burst toward the house from behind the wheel. In a flight or fight adrenalin rush, Evan ran to the car at an angle, to get a shot and stop the killings. A burst of fire from the broken car window hit Evan in the side. The feeling of something tearing away from his side, followed by numbness, allowed him to fire a couple of shots into the back of the front seat. Numbness was quickly replaced by an intense burning sensation, a pain that brought him to his knees. The car drove off with two flat tires and some miscellaneous bullet holes in the right rear quarter panel.

Blood oozed through Evan's fingers. He made no effort to view his wound, afraid to see the damage. He was starting to shake and felt a cold chill through his shoulders, working down his body. He knew enough that shock was setting in and he was losing consciousness. Hope was the one thought that he hung on to as he fought to remain alert. Evan noticed that, other than the intense pain, he really wasn't bleeding that much. Ronnie came running out of the house, a pump shotgun in her hands. She checked on the two gunmen, and then ran over to Evan.

Changing magazines as he ran, Greg Olsen was there, too, checking bodies. Ronnie told him, "Follow the tire tracks and you'll find the shooter that's left. We have some men down, so radio for an ambulance."

"On my way, Sheriff!"

Evan blanked out, then opening his eyes in the next instant.

Ronnie had dropped to her knees beside Evan. She looked at the wound. Not much blood, but enough.

"You stupid SOB! If you ever do something like that again, I'll shoot you myself." At the same time, she was checking for an exit wound and any other bullet holes Evan might have sustained.

"I'm out here dying, trying to stop some wild–gun toting bastards from killing you because I care about you. And now, I have to listen to a lecture? Agh! That hurts. What the hell were you doing?"

Ronnie was looking all over Evan's body finding the bullet holes and wounded areas.

"Thank God the bullets went right through your side. I don't think they hit anything, but we have to get you to the hospital. It looks like you'll be sore, but you'll live to love again." She gently wiped the dirt and blood away from his face and rolled Evan over to his good side.

"Hey! This hurts like hell. Let me get back on my back."

"This position will slow down the bleeding until the ambulance gets here." She packed her jacket against the wound on his side. "You realize how hard it is to get blood stains out of silk?"

"Ronnie, all I could think of was to kill those guys for what they did. Who knows if they were the ones that killed Gail or not, but spraying those automatic weapons like that, I had no choice, but to come out shooting. By the way, they killed Lowe."

She bent down so they were face to face, took hold of his chin and kissed him on his lips. She dabbed at his face with her thumb.

"I was afraid that you were dead, Evan. The first shooter had you in the perfect kill position. And yet, if you did not put him down, I'd be lying on the kitchen floor. I'm not sure why you are still alive, but I intend to keep it that way. But the FBI guy in the house may not make it, either."

She leaned away from Evan, hunches on her heels, the shotgun back in her hands, double checking that the area was secure again.  Sirens were growing louder in the distance. Surveying the bodies and the destruction, along with the gunpowder and primer smells emanating from the spent cartridge casings were overwhelming to her. She could only shake her head. This was, by far, the worst firefight she had ever been involved with and suspected it would be the same for the Austin cops as well. She'd never used a shotgun on a human being before.

"Ronnie, Lowe was quick to react to the car, but the silencers kept him from pulling his gun right away. Lowe was almost cut in half. He was in front of me and took the full burst."

Another police car came up. Ronnie stood up and started walking toward it, with the shotgun in her hands. "None of this drop the gun stuff. I'm Sheriff Ronnie Green from McKinney, and I'm working with your Detective Sergeant Greg Olsen. And right now, I don't trust anyone I don't know, uniform or not. Deal with it."

She pointed to the fallen killers. "These two guys are alive, but barely." They glanced at Evan and walked over to the fallen killers. The ambulance came soon after the second squad car and one man went over to Evan and Ronnie showed the other guy where the agent was in the house. The paramedic looked at Evan. A second ambulance arrived. By this time, Ronnie felt secure with all the officers and emergency help that was on the scene that she was able to recoil her weapon.

"I don't think there's any major damage," the paramedic told Ronnie as he examined Evan. "We need to stop this bleeding more effectively and check for any internal bleeding." Another paramedic helped to get Evan onto a stretcher, cocooning him in a blanket. He gave Evan a shot and started wrapping his side. The pain was getting worse, Evan realized.

The detectives moved over to the guy whom Evan had shot in the groin. He was conscious. Evan called out to the wounded killer, "Hurts, doesn't it, dick head?!"

"Shot hit him between the vest layers," one of the detectives remarked. The blood had pooled beneath him and was still pumping. A paramedic dropped beside the killer and applied direct pressure with his hands, another paramedic beginning to staunch the bleeding. The man lost consciousness. Evan guessed the killer wouldn't make it.

The last man had a foot wound and was also shot in his hand and arm. Evan stretched his neck to see what was going on. The man was crying out. Regardless, how much he cried out, the cops continued to question him. His yells only got louder, laced with cursing. Evan had heard enough of the noise and yelling. Evan pushed away the medic who was attending him and got to his knees, then to his feet.

"If you want something out of that scumbag give me two minutes with him." Evan took one step and everything went completely black.

# Chapter Seven

# After The Slaughter

EVAN AWOKE IN A HOSPITAL BED, TUBES STICKING IN HIS ARM. He felt around his nose, which hurt like hell, and his face stung from the raised scratches.

"Must be from the flower pots" he mumbled to himself. There was a very sharp pain in his side, where he found gauze wrappings. Beyond the pain, Evan also had a strange taste in his mouth and was having difficulty knowing if he was dreaming or awake. Evan was actually relieved as he felt himself falling asleep once more; hoping all of this was just a dream.

The sedative and pain medicine finally cleared his system and he awoke with the worst headache of his life. He filled and drank two cups of water and wished it could have been Jack Daniels or something stronger, but the water tasted good. He was getting his bearings when a nurse and Ronnie came in. Ronnie flashed a weary smile at him. The nurse asked how he was doing, and if he needed any help voiding himself.

Evan was annoyed and said in a disgusted way, "I'm not ninety years old. I can go to the bathroom by myself."

The two women looked at each other and smiled at some private joke. As the nurse left, Ronnie came over and sat on the bed. Evan wondered how someone as beautiful as Veronica Green could have attached herself to him.

"Ronnie, I know you think I'm crazy for what I did, but they were shooting at me and had you guys pinned down. Once they started to run, I couldn't stand the thought of losing them, after what they had done to everyone."

Ronnie was softly putting her hand on his forehead, and cheek to see if he was warm. She replied, "I was so afraid that you were dead, but then I saw the one man go down -- excellent shooting, by the way -- and the other man direct his fire at you. It gave me time to use the shotgun and clear a field of fire. By the way, neither of the FBI guys made it and this includes the two uniforms, this was a blood bath like I have never seen before."

Evan closed his eyes for a second and thought about both the agents and wondered what they knew? Ronnie continued, "Then, out of nowhere comes this crazy guy running after a car driven by a man with an automatic weapon – and all he's got is a pistol. I should slap you for being stupid."

"I had no idea what I was doing. I was just trying to keep that guy from getting away."

Ronnie bent over and whispered in his ear. "I don't make love to stupid people. I want you to remember that." The tingling sensation of her being so close to him and whispering in his ear, saying what she had said, stimulated him even more.

"Do we have any idea what the Feds were talking about on the computer fraud issue?"

"No. But, now that you're awake, they may tell you what's going on. They've decided that, right now, they want to find out who ordered Gail's death. The lone survivor isn't talking, and they really don't have many options."

"I bet I could make him talk. Where is he?"

"About three doors down, but don't even think about getting up. You know they had to fix your nose because you broke it when you fell."

Evan felt gingerly around his face, touched at the scratches and the bandage across his nose. It was very sore to the touch.

"If this keeps up, I'm going to look like a jigsaw puzzle."

Ronnie put her hands behind Evan's neck and kissed him gently on the cheek. "You look pretty good to me. I'm going to take a shower in your bathroom and change into some clean clothes that Greg brought me, and then, we can talk about what's next." With that, Ronnie went into the bathroom and Evan decided to take a stroll. It wasn't pretty getting out of bed, but it was easy enough to find the killer's room. There were three suits hanging around, talking to each other. Evan was feeling pretty good other than being in a hospital gown, walking barefoot, rolling an IV drip stand.

"I understand that you have the Gail Cannon killer in there."

"We have the killer of two of our agents in there, if that's what you mean." Evan could tell that he wasn't going to get any commanding respect with a hospital gown opened in the back. He wondered how good a weapon the drip stand might make in a pinch. He figured he looked like somebody's crazy uncle, just admitted to the hospital because he thought aliens were after him.

"Can I ask who's in charge?" In one motion, they all looked to the older agent, about Evan's height.

"Mr. Cannon, how can I help you?"

"I can probably get the information we're looking for, if you give me the chance."

"Sure. We do that all the time. We always let the survivors take the first crack at interrogating a perp. Get your ass back in your room and let us do our job."

"For the record, I want you to know that agent Lowe saved me. He took the full burst while pushing me down and away from the gunfire."

"Thanks for sharing that. I may ask you later to write it up."

"No problem. He died saving my lousy butt." Evan figured that he had established some relationship with the Special Agent in charge, so now he wanted to see if he could convince him to let him talk to the killer. "You know, this guy could be headed for the most horrible torture you can imagine." That got the SAC's attention.

"Everyone who has shot at me over the past few weeks has died very brutally." He was stretching it a bit, but still truthful.

"Whoever is protecting me," Evan went on, "and I know you have something on that, actually takes a piece of the brain out through a hole in the back of the head. The guy with the hole in his head shows all the symptoms of death, but is actually very much alive. The autopsy is what kills the guy."

"I have that write up, but is it true?"

"Yeah, it is, and according to the Doc, it is the worst kind of torture, because you can't scream or pass out." After a couple more minutes of discussion, the SAC pulled his agents over to the nurses' station.

Shortly after that, Evan walked into the bad guy's room. He looked at the IV drip and then looked into the man's eye.

"Who in the hell are you."

"I'm probably the guy that put you in that bed."

"How the hell did you get in here? I'm going to call security and have security throw you out."

"Good luck on that, Dieter. I don't see anyone out there." The FBI had run his fingerprints past Interpol, Evan had been told, and were able to determine his name. He strained his neck, to see if anyone was out in the corridor.

"Hey, Bubba, I'm telling you. There's nobody in the hall and there won't be."

"Oh. So I get it now. You're going to be the tough guy and threaten me to tell you information or you'll beat me up."

"Dieter you know the first three letters of your name spell 'die'—talk about coincidence! You know who I am? You killed my ex-wife and my dog." Dieter was going to enjoy this discussion.

"I didn't kill the woman, but I would have liked to. She went for a knife and was killed in the struggle. She was feisty. I would have loved to take her with us and drain some of that out of her."

Evan knew Dieter would try and push to get him angry, but it wasn't going to happen. He was keeping his emotions in check. "Dieter, you're an idiot. I could care less who you are and what hole you live in. Obviously, you didn't hear me when I said 'ex.' Now, I did care about that dog and I can see a great big bite mark there on your shoulder. If you killed him, I'm glad you had to give a little flesh in the process. Do you know that someone else tried to kill me this past week? They found him with a hole in the back of his head. They thought he was dead, even conducted an autopsy on him, only to find out that he was alive. He was sort of in a coma state, but seeing as they didn't conduct a brain scan, they never knew. The Feds aren't interested in you, but they do want the group that puts holes into people's heads.

"You see, Dieter, you're bait, pure and simple. This drip has a 'T' marked on it. You know what that is?" There was no response from Dieter. Evan knew that at the least, Dieter was listening. "The 'T' stands for titanium. They want to monitor your brain scan activity and having titanium in your blood will give them some excellent responses. They hope to catch the person or group responsible, after they drill a hole in the back of your head. That was smart – I tell ya. Then, they'll watch the activity as the hospital staff starts cutting and basically torturing you until you die. Its information they will never have the opportunity to get otherwise. A conscious person will pass out as a self-defense mechanism, but imagine being fully alive while people start cutting open your head. Pain is terrible, but you can't become unconscious and you endure the entire torture routine until the doctors realize you still have a very active brain function. Death will come to you, but not until you endure the greatest torture ever given to somebody, and it will all be legal and accidental. At least that will be the official response."

Dieter's eyes were wide and alert. His expression was no longer smug.

"Hey, Dieter. Go ahead. Don't believe me. Ask the Feds why I was able to walk in here and tell you about the last guy that tried to kill me." Almost on cue, an elderly person came into the room, asking if Mr. Lumera was in that room. Evan said no and the man walked out. Evan looked around the corner and back at Dieter with a smile and said, "Not sure where all that security is. I feel sorry for you. The Feds don't want information from you, but they will keep up the façade." Evan started laughing and walking back to his room. Evan hadn't taken three steps away when he heard Dieter calling for the Feds. The group had followed Evan's suggestions and waited until Evan joined them before responding.

"Just tell him you stepped out for some coffee, and don't know why the guards left the room. He'll talk now." The agent in charge, John Lynn, gave Evan a look of skepticism, but ambled into Dieter's room. Evan was feeling a little woozy and went back to his room to lie down. His timing was perfect. Ronnie came out of the bathroom with wet hair and a loose fitting shirt and jeans. Evan was sure she wouldn't have approved of him walking around in his condition. The nurse came in, asked Evan a few questions and took the drip off. As the nurse left, agent Lynn came in and closed the door.

"You were right, Mr. Cannon. Dieter started talking and hasn't stopped. I'm waiting for him to confess to shooting JFK, at this rate." Ronnie turned her head to Evan, wondering what trouble he had started this time.

"What we have is a very complicated story and you two are in the middle of the longest unsolved case in FBI history." Ronnie looked at agent Lynn with a skeptical eye after hearing this.

"The only case I remember that the agency couldn't make progress on was the international bank theft ring. If I remember rightly, nobody could even prove if there was a theft. Most of us thought it was an urban legend." Ronnie said.

"Your memory is correct and it's just part of what we call the 'New Eden Group.' In 1991 flight three hundred, heading for Paris, experienced engine problems. We had three agents on board and there was a member of New Eden among the passengers. That jet crashed in the Atlantic."

"I remember that crash. It was supposed to be engine problems, but an eyewitness aboard a fishing boat, said he saw streaks of light, like a missile fired into the plane. It was always assumed the crash was a government cover-up." Ronnie sat down on the edge of Evan's bed. "I was brand new with the Bureau when it happened and was doing some of the analysis of the fuselage. There was no way a missile took down that jet."

Agent Lynn pulled over a chair and sat down. He whispered, "You're right. We think that New Eden brought flight three hundred down to save their agent. They didn't do it with a missile, but with a high intensity laser beam."

"I'm a fairly bright guy, except when I get around some gunfire." Evan gave a quick glance at Ronnie, who gave Evan a frown in return. "Nobody could survive that crash. It wouldn't make sense to kill your guy, even if the Feds were after him. Another thing is that I'm somewhat familiar with laser technology and that capability wasn't around at that time, unless it was from one of two major labs in the Northeast."

"All of that was in the summary that was passed around internally at the Agency. The case was closed, as far as we were concerned, until 1993. The NSA had a satellite that was actually going over the area at the time of the crash. It didn't see the actual explosion, which dropped into the sea, but it did capture a small boat picking up a person in the water. It would have been missed by anyone investigating the crash, but analysts are curious people, and when they saw activity even close to the crash site, they investigated. It looked as though the person in the water had a small parachute. They tried to determine who was in the water, but never did get a look at the face. The parachute – there might have been more than one -- was real enough and a boat definitely fished the guy out of the water. And this same person that was on the aircraft showed up again at another location in 1993."

Evan was thinking about the possibilities when Ronnie spoke up. "Why didn't someone take the guy into custody?"

"What you both don't realize is that New Eden goes so much deeper. It has become the Lost Continent of Atlantis to all of the intelligence organizations. It's something we know exists, and yet, it can never be found. There have been no fewer than fifty industry technology leaders that have either come up missing or have died mysteriously, with a hole drilled in the back of their heads.  That's over a span of the past 40 years. Some even think, it goes back to the 50s, but we can't prove it.

"The scientists that have been taken or mangled have been very carefully selected," Lynn went on. "Not the best known, but those who know the applications and specific working details."

Evan was now very interested. "If they took those guys, they wouldn't create the stir compared to kidnapping an Einstein. What fields of technology are they focusing on?"

"From what the FBI and NSA can tell every major technology that has been developed!"

Evan was trying to determine if he could remember anyone in the fiber optics field disappearing or dying suddenly and couldn't think of any. Ronnie spoke up, saying, "I don't believe that New Eden is out to kill Evan. Rather, that's some other entity. If anything, New Eden has been there to help us."

"You are exactly right, Sheriff. And, for the first time, we feel that Cannon Electronics has something New Eden needs and we can do something to either uncover the group or at least capture a few of the group's agents."

Lynn's last statement raised a red flag for Evan. Nobody from the government was there to help his company, only to obstruct. Evan told Lynn, "We came to that same conclusion, but didn't have a name for the group. What doesn't make sense is that we are building a field deployable system for a Spanish company and it doesn't seem to fit your profile of this New Eden group."

"I hate to say much more, but with every major incident over the past fifteen years, New Eden has left their calling card. Also, I will say that their intentions appear to be good."

"Other than blowing up passenger jets?" Ronnie remarked.

"That seems to be one of their rare exceptions."

"Agent Lynn, just how big is New Eden?" Ronnie asked.

"We can only guess, but figure its numbers to be over a thousand, but less than five thousand people."

"Agent Lynn, why would a group of people familiar with various technologies and capable of astounding capabilities, according to you, want to protect me?"

"You are not stating it exactly correctly, Mr. Cannon. They aren't just familiar with various technologies, but they are experts in all high tech areas."

"I don't see how it could be possible. GE, HP, Microsoft, AT&T -- all of these companies have tried to be industry leaders in more than one area and haven't been able to do it. You can throw in the Japanese and European companies as well and nobody has ever been able to sustain a leadership position in all technologies. Now, you're saying some underground group has done it without leaving any traces as to their existence? Not possible!"

"Everything that is known about this group would fit into a single file folder and every bit of it is classified. The only reason I know about it is that I head up the U.S. task force covering their actions," Agent Lynn informed them. "Let me say this. It's easier to prove the existence of UFOs than to have any information about the New Eden Group."

Evan guessed that Ronnie was already thinking ahead, to what would be next. "If we can't do anything about the New Eden Group, then what can we do about the people who are trying to kill Evan, or stop the FOGM project?"

Ronnie clearly said what she had been speculating in order to bring Lynn back to task. Did the Feds care that Cannon Electronics was the new bait, or were they going to pursue those responsible for the bloodbath in Austin? Lynn wasn't stupid, Evan knew, but Lynn's facial expression gave him away.

"We aren't sure why Cannon Electronics has been targeted by New Eden, but we're looking into the FOGM portion of the business."

Evan was trying to look oblivious to their conversation while checking all the bandages that adorned his slightly mangled body. But, he was observing the exchange between Ronnie and Lynn and decided to throw his two cents in. "So, this is where you are in the investigation. You don't know anything about this New Eden Group and you are hoping I will lead you to them, so you can shut them down. You have one of the killers, who isn't part of New Eden, but you haven't figured out who is trying to kill me. Now, my question to you is simple, Agent Lynn. Where do your resources go? Because, the enemy of my enemy is my friend and you don't see it that way."

Lynn apparently decided to play his trump card, saying, "We have an idea who is after you, but can't do anything to stop them until we have more proof. As far as your cooperation, we will review your activities, and if there are any misunderstandings, then we will use the Patriot Act and take over your business activities."

All the cards were on the table, and if Lynn was hoping Evan would submit, Evan decided Agent Lynn wasn't all that good at reading background files.

"I'll tell you what, Lynn. You'll have total access to our activities, and may I suggest that we meet in three days at my facility, so I can show you what we make and maybe why we're being targeted. I would say earlier, but I won't get out of here before tomorrow and I need to get everything together after today's shooting. I also have a burial to help attend to so I may need a few days to get squared away."

Lynn nodded his head and said, "Works for me. Get well." Then Lynn walked out of the room.

"You aren't giving up that easily, what are you planning?" Ronnie asked Evan.

"Ronnie as much as I would like to have you here, I'm going to need some rest. I feel very tired right now. By the way, what were you and the nurse giggling about when I came to?"

"The drugs that they gave you would have the same effect as Viagra. The nurses are watchful to make sure that their patients don't get too frisky."

"I see what you mean. I can hardly believe I'm saying this, but right now, I need to sleep for a week. But, I don't have a week."

"How did you get down to Austin so quickly?"

"My son has a friend who's a pilot. I use his plane from time to time. The airstrip is the old airport in Austin and is only twenty minutes from Gail's."

"Is there anything that we need to talk about?" Ronnie asked.

"Any legal trouble waiting for me after killing that one guy?"

"There'll be an inquest, just a formality….nothing to worry about.  Dumb play that it was, you're a hero. Anything else?"

"Let's talk tomorrow."

With that, Ronnie bent over and kissed Evan on the forehead. She whispered her goodbyes and left Evan to go back home. Evan knew that he didn't have any time left, so once he knew she was gone, he started making phone calls.

Ronnie's drive from Love Field to McKinney was stressful. She had the distinct feeling that either Evan was getting cold feet about their relationship or had finally hit that wall of helplessness. Either way, she didn't get a lot of sleep that night knowing that the next day's paperwork and reports were going to be nightmares in themselves.

# Chapter Eight

# Details

**WHEN WILL GOT THE MESSAGE FROM HIS DAD ABOUT HIS**
mother's death, he was stunned to the point of being in shock.
His sister, Abbey, took the news a little better, but it devastated
her as well. Neither were married, but both had significant
others. Will was involved in making commercials and music
videos in Austin and Abbey was in San Diego, working with sea
lions and dolphins. Evan was proud of them, because they chose
their own path and were very independent.

Neither wanted to hear what their daddy had to say to
them, but followed his instructions to the letter. Their family had
long ago established two different failsafe procedures. It might
have been silly when they were kids, nonetheless, after 9-11
(where terrorists had boomed the Word Trade Center in New
York); they talked about the plan at every family gathering.

Their mother being murdered was not figured into the
plan, but both Will and Abbey agreed to go along with their

daddy's short term solution. The funeral was a sad affair; however, their mother's gruesome death along with the many high profile contacts that she had made and the selected charities she promoted in the Austin area, made her funeral a very somber affair. While the Governor didn't make it, most everyone else in the State government was present. What was surprising to the family was the number of UT football players that were present. Jim and Gail had made a significant impression on these players and it became evident to everyone that Gail and Jim were much closer than was publicly known.

Evan was angry at himself, knowing somehow that he had caused Gail's death. Will and Abbey were raised to be independent. Losing their mom seemed to break down that wall of self-dependence and suddenly they both realized that mom was never to be in their lives again. They needed an arm around their shoulders and someone to tell them that the sun would come up again. Evan wrapped his arms around his kids at the burial and led both of them to the waiting limo.

Later that night, after the guests and distant relatives had said their goodbyes, with only their closest friends, family and armed protection; they managed to discuss the fun and silly memories of the life that they had shared with their Mother. Jim Swanson stayed to hear the stories and imagine what life would have been like if he and Gail had been married. He even shared some stories that none of them had heard.

It was after midnight when Evan gave Abbey and Will their next step in the agreed upon instructions. Both flew out the next morning. They had talked about their hate for their father and the sorrow for their mom. They had blood shot eyes from the tears. Now, their father had convinced them that it wasn't safe for them and they needed to go missing for a while. It took Will an hour to come around to Evan's plan, but he needed to join his father's argument in order to convince Abbey to follow through. Evan called their employers and gave them an appropriate reason for their absences.

They were to fly to Ashville, NC. A man named Dickey Moore would meet them there and they were to follow his instructions to the letter.

They were tired when the plane touched down in Ashville. After getting the bags through security and walking out to the airport curb, a man approached to pick them up. Abbey was a little suspicious, but they followed him to his car. He put the bags into the trunk while Abbey sat in front and Will slid behind the driver. The driver, who looked like a drill instructor from the Marines, turned and said in a voice that was firm, but also compassionate,

"You don't know me, guys, but your Dad and I have an arrangement. If any danger is posed to either family, the other person will make a safe refuge for the endangered family. People won't connect me and Evan, therefore can't trace you to me without a lot of effort. I know what happened to your mother and I'm very sorry. I met her once about twenty years ago and I could tell right away that she was too good for your father, but she loved him to death. When Evan called me for help, he filled me in on the details.

"My name is Dickey Moore," and he went on to say, "and I taught your dad how to fire a pistol and gave him some discipline while he was at VMI. I was a master sergeant in the Army at the time. We met again a few years after that, in Roanoke, Virginia. That was where I met your mother. Your father and I have a company we own jointly, but you'll never find it on any company books. It's a handshake agreement and written in both of our wills. We're going to go over some basic safety rules that I expect you to follow."

Will looked at his sister. He realized she was just as taken back by what was being told to them as he was. Their Dad had never told them the whole arrangement, so they were getting it from a very no nonsense, ex-Army guy and weren't sure of the next steps.

"I picked you two up, but neither of you ever asked to see my credentials or ID. That has to be the last time that goes like that way while you're with me. I could be an assassin that was sent to kill you two. What were you thinking? You can't trust anyone." He turned to look at Abbey with a fire in his eye that would melt steel. "Never get into the front seat with someone you don't know."

He turned to Will and said, "Always sit behind the driver, like you just did. That way, you can grab him from behind and take away an advantage he may have. Sorry to have to give you 'James Bond 101' on the fly, but it's the best way to make sure you two will stay alive, even in my company."

Abbey Cannon was always one that questioned authority and this little episode brought all of her senses into play. "I don't know you, but I don't take this junk from anyone. You may know my Dad, but I'm not a teenager that's at boot camp because she missed curfew." If she had something to throw, it would have found its way to Moore.

Will seemed visibly shaken by all of what had just taken place, but he was the peacemaker, and always had been when it came to his little sister. Abbey knew he'd dive in.

"You have to excuse, Abbey. She --" Will didn't get a chance to finish when she turned on him.

"Don't make any excuses for me, big brother! I'll kick the piss out of both of you!"

Moore started to laugh. "You remind me of your father, young lady -- your spirit. I usually try to intimidate people I have to train or work with. It's the military way. I'm glad to see that neither one of you kids are backing down." Dickey Moore started the SUV, turned into the light traffic and slowly accelerated.

Will started firing questions at Moore. "Why did the two of you – you and Dad -- make this arrangement? It doesn't seem that you two are that close."

"Evan was always thinking ahead and figured that I could be a Dutch uncle if an emergency happened where I need to protect you two and his wife, if the occasion demanded it. As far as being close, he's the closest thing I have to a brother. When Evan was a student at VMI, I was a sergeant teaching marksmanship in the ROTC program. Your father was the best I had ever seen. We spent a lot of extra time at the firing range and he never came off with that superior attitude that most of the 'Keydets' did when working with the "non-comms". For him to get to the Olympics; he really needed to quit playing lacrosse, but he didn't want to. He loved that almost as much as firearms. After he graduated, I lost track of him until I visited a plant in Roanoke, Virginia, to look at some new night vision scopes. I had been re-assigned, by that time, and was getting sent into areas that were considered hazardous to your health. I saw Evan, he gave me a big hug, and after that, we talked a bit. It was right then I started to get warm and my left arm went numb. Long story short, he saved me with mouth to mouth resuscitation, while another guy was pumping my chest until an ambulance arrived. It seems I had a weak heart muscle that chose to quit working at that particular time. I had desk duty for a few more years and then decided to find another career, one that wasn't so stressful.

"By then," Dickey Moore continued, "your Dad was fairly successful and helped me get my business started. He gets some of my profits, but what he really wanted, was for me to take you kids in, in case there was an emergency, and vice versa, of course. But, I never had any family. I am to protect you for as long as possible. So he called, you're here, and nothing else was needed as far as an explanation."

Abbey watched her brother's eyes. Will was thinking this through. He asked, "What do you do now that could protect us?"

"As I said, my heart isn't what it should be, but I still know how to get people in shape and make them perform better. I started a camp in the middle of nowhere and train people in their particular field. It was my idea, but your father was the one who gave me the money and the initial push to get it started. I established a reputation within the pro sports group and I train under-performing players into being better athletes. I have limited communications at my camp and keep a tight lid on who's there and how I train. It's probably the isolation aspect that Evan likes, as well as the fact that I would kill anyone that made an attempt on either of your lives."

Abbey was already running this whole scenario through her mind. It sounded so much like Dad, planning ahead for every disaster that could occur. She also thought that he probably had an ark built somewhere, just in case the Good Lord decided to make it rain for another forty days and nights again.

Will asked, "How much danger are we in? Did dad tell you that they tried to kill him?"

"Yes. He said that they tried to kill him three times and he was in the hospital with gunshot wounds."

Abbey and Will hadn't been told that there had been that many attempts on their father's life. Abbey thought that was so typical of their Dad, not mentioning details that would worry them.

"He called me from the hospital and that's when he told me we had to get proactive on your safety. The wounds weren't serious, but they were enough to keep him there for a while."

"Trust me. Any wound is serious. Infection will kill ten to fifteen per cent of all people hit by a bullet," Abbey informed her brother and their protector.

"Yeah. They die from lead poisoning." Said Dickey. All three of them laughed at that and broke the solemnity.

"Actually, I can use your help, Abbey, Will. I have four people I'm training now and it's really pushing my limits to get everything done."

"What are the sports and who are some of the guys you've trained?" Will asked.

"Do you remember last year's Packers? I trained the two defensive tackles."

"You mean the two guys that they named the Generals, Lee and Jackson? They came from nowhere to make all pro. The Packers should have won the Super Bowl, but the three lost fumbles gave the Browns enough field position to kick three field goals and win the game. So, that's impressive," Will was enthused as Abbey yawned. "What you did with those two guys, can it apply to anyone? Also, you probably have had a boost in PR, of course, if you wanted it."

"It hasn't hurt my reputation. I had to turn down considerable business, because I promised the Packers first choice." Dickey made a lane change, passed a pickup truck and made another lane change.

Abbey found herself wondering how Dickey could make a living with the few clients he accepted. "Just curious, but how much money can you make a year? How many people can you take and train in a year?"

"I only have about five clients a year, but you should know that I charge a good chunk of dinero for each one. If I have two people a year I'm training, then I can make money. It was your father's idea to keep it simple, so the breakeven point was low. Having four in camp at one time is really taxing."

"How many people do you have helping?" asked Will.

"I have one nutritionist and myself. I lay out the PT and start the physical training and then target certain muscle groups. I cut out the baby fat and focus on the mechanics they need -- if it's more speed or power. At the same time, I measure range of motion. You can't restrict a certain muscle, just to get strength."

"Do you use any high speed camera equipment? While shooting a movie in Canada about range of motion, I found that a lot of trainers use the equipment and compare results from different workouts," Will explained.

"I do have some fast speed cameras, but I hadn't thought of looking at results that way. You kids may come in handy after all!"

"I feel a little left out, since most of my work is with mammals that live in the ocean, but incorporating feedback into training is always helpful," Abbey said.

"Yeah, you kids are going to work out fine. But I have to tell you, my camp is in a very isolated location. I have one computer that only the staff works with. And, otherwise, these athletes are focused only on getting better. I keep them going hard for twelve hours a day. They can leave anytime they want, but they have to walk, since I have no phones."

"Has anyone left before their training was done?" Will asked.

"Only one. He plays point guard for an NBA team. I would never tell you who he is. He made the all-star team the next year, but hasn't done anything since. He had the talent, but not enough discipline."

The three continued to talk about training methods versus personality differences on their way to Dickey's camp. Dickey seemed to feel good about the meeting and to enjoy their company. "I'll email your Dad tonight, guys. Let's get back to keeping you guys alive, huh. Here are some more ground rules," he began.

\*\*\*\*\*\*\*\*\*\*\*\*\*\*\*\*\*\*\*\*\*\*\*\*\*\*\*\*\*\*\*\*\*\*

Evan couldn't tell anyone his plans until they were thoroughly fleshed out. No matter how he tried, he kept thinking of Ronnie and how she would react. He knew his actions could permanently damage their relationship, so he was trying to determine a way to keep her in the loop, but not let her know his next steps. And keeping her safe was of paramount importance to him. He had lost Gail, and was afraid for himself, his kids and even the company.

Evan couldn't help but wonder, if he had been less driven, if they would still be one happy family living in a nice neighborhood? The idea that he was responsible for Gail's death brought back enough memories that it was crushing his soul. As he drove back home from Austin, he pulled off the road and wept like he never had before. After composing himself finally, he remembered what Gail had told him the last time they were together. "Our problem wasn't that we never loved each other, but that you loved the company more than me. You can't change and I need to go on with my life. Evan, if I die tomorrow, I would have no regrets about my life." Somehow, that was very reassuring at this moment in his life. Her words allowed Evan to compose himself and get back to the challenge at hand. He had to work out the variables. The mystery was still this New Eden group. If he had time, it would be something that he could look into, but for the present, he would have to be invisible and be everywhere at the same time.

Confusion worked as a good cover for a limited time. He just had to find a way to shake off the FBI and get to Spain. He had sent Jake ahead, to coordinate getting the coils, missiles and controls into one location. Brenda has seen to it that all of the End User Certificates had been properly filled out along with the State Department approvals. These were bound to throw up several more flags, but it couldn't be helped. He had to keep everyone looking at him if they were going to deliver the five hundred systems and master control units. The FBI was going to do anything it could to find out if the systems were connected to

New Eden, even if that meant shutting down Cannon Electronics.

Evan thought about the time line that had been established for payments. This project should have been several months in the making, even a year wouldn't have been out of the ordinary. Everything came together and had compressed into four months. Missiles were a stock item; the coils were a modified version of what Cannon had made for five years. They had a cooling core to keep the cable from melting during the fast payout speeds. The chips and electronics were what made the difference. Jake had made the circuits work, but no way were those chips available on the open market. Tracking who made those chips would take time that Evan didn't have, but it was obvious from that alone that New Eden was involved. The question always came back to why.

Evan needed to disappear for a week, and then meet up with Jake. He could buy one, maybe two days max, by just disappearing on his own, but he needed a plan to stretch those two days out to a week. The FBI was going to be coming back to him again and again. Not for protection, but because New Eden was now in their sights, so he had a choice. He could have Ronnie cover for him or protect her from their interrogation. Maybe it was time to tell her how much he cared for her, maybe it would help.  Or, it could just make things messier. Evan's drive to McKinney took about three and a half hours. There was cell coverage the entire way, and if he was lucky, he might just make his plan work.

Driving into his garage for what might be the last time, Evan felt very lonely. He wanted to call Ronnie, but realized he had to wait. Looking at his home, after everything that had happened, it seemed so barren, no real life in it. If he never came back, the house could be sold as is. It was so impersonal, like a model home.

Evan took his first shower since the funeral and the water stung his wound like angry bees. The pain aside, he felt revived. He re-dressed the wound and was ready to hit the bed when Brenda called. She gave him all the information that he needed, and for the first time, Evan felt like he might get out of this without losing everything he held dear, including his life.

# Chapter Nine

# Dropping Off The Radar

**EVAN'S OFFICE RESEMBLED A TOMB WITH ALL THE FLOWERS AND** cards that were on his desk. Everything seemed to be in place, and by 10 a.m., he was feeling hungry. He thought he should call Ronnie, when his phone rang. Ronnie breathed into the phone, "How are you doing?"

"Not bad, considering I have a hole in my side and I just took my first non-assisted shower in a week."

He could "feel" her smile over the phone somehow and could almost tell what she would say next. "We need to talk. Can we meet for lunch?"

Evan wanted a little more time, but knew he needed to stay on plan. "Sounds good...I'll meet you at the Pastry Market. What's the word on the street?"

"People are saying you're a legend in your own time." At that, Evan started laughing, until the pain in his side reminded him of his latest escapade.

"I want you to understand how much I appreciate what you have done for me and Gail over the last few days. If it was not for you, I would have never made it beyond the driveway."

"Remember, I'm still investigating the initial two murders at your house. So, you're still loosely my responsibility. I met your two children at the funeral and they seemed very poised and intelligent. Are they with you at home?" Funny thing was that Evan didn't remember seeing Ronnie at the funeral. It didn't really matter, though, since there was a big crowd and it made sense that she would be there, other than the fact she hadn't made a point of seeing him. He would store that away as a question to be asked later. It wasn't that important now because he knew she wasn't going to like what he was going to say next.

"I thought it best to keep Will and Abbey away from harm, so I sent them to a safe place. Even Brenda has no idea where they are, but I would like to let you know how to contact them, if anything else happens." Silence wasn't a good thing on a phone call, but Ronnie had to be wondering what stupid idea Evan had for protecting his kids.

"I know you won't listen to me, but you can't protect your kids like we could or even the FBI could."

Evan cut her off short. "I know you don't think it's a good idea, but let's talk about it at lunch."

"Okay, 12:15 p.m. at the Pastry Market in downtown."

There were so many things that Evan wanted to say and tell Ronnie about their relationship, but had decided that such would have to wait until this ordeal was over. The problem was he didn't know when that would occur.

The Pastry Market was in a building over one hundred years old. In Texas, that made it a State historical building. It had been converted into a restaurant to serve homemade food for people who worked at the courthouse. Back then, the population of the town was around sixteen thousand. Since McKinney was the county seat, they had gained a good reputation. McKinney had grown to over one hundred thousand people and many restaurants had come and gone in the intervening years, but the Pastry Market still was the best place to eat lunch. Evan liked the wooden floors that had been restored and re-finished, but most of all, it was the atmosphere and the food that made it a good place to eat. It wasn't fancy, but good basic food.

On Ronnie's way out the door, FBI agent Lynn bumped into her. "Sorry. I wanted to update you on what happened at the hospital. Dieter told us that a blond woman set-up the hit and they were actually looking for Gail Cannon's stocks and bonds. Somehow, it didn't make sense to us, so we went back to Mrs. Cannon's house and discovered where she kept her valuables. We found what we think they were after: stock certificates for Cannon Electronics. The receipt was on her desk, where she had placed them in a lockbox at the bank. Initially, we thought it didn't make sense, because they aren't of great value, even though they are the majority share of the company. But it could make a difference, if someone stole them and kidnapped the owner, and gaining control of the CEO at the next board meeting."

"You just said 'kidnapped.' Gail was murdered; therefore, the certificates would be worthless."

"Dieter admitted, they were only supposed to capture Gail Cannon, but between Mrs. Cannon's dog and her own efforts, they didn't think it would be possible to take her alive. So they ended up killing her. The blonde lady wasn't going to pay for the killing, unless they got the certificates. So they went back to rob the place, when they found you, Evan and our agents. One other thing you should know about. While Evan Cannon was in the recovery room, he told Dieter that the 'T' in the drip was so we could watch his brain activity as he was being tortured by the doctors. Cannon said that to get him to confess and ask for real protection."

Ronnie felt she must have had one of those blank stares. She had "What are you talking about?" on her face, but agent Lynn kept talking.

"It may have happened when you weren't around. Anyway, when Evan told Dieter that the people who tried to kill him were always found dead with a hole in the back of their head, but they weren't dead, but in a coma-like state and people actually..."

"Yeah. I know the rest from personal experience. We had one of those here."

"Well, it made Dieter talk," Agent Lynn said, "but it also foretold what would happen to him. And believe it or not, he died last night or maybe the night before, because we found a perfect hole in the back of his skull and when we sent his body for an autopsy, you know the rest."

"Yeah! And you know what? I have no sympathy for the guy. I would like to know how this happened with your protective guys watching him."

"We don't know yet, but we see Evan Cannon as the key person in this puzzle." Ronnie looked around and could see that two or three of her detectives had been listening and all of this would be common knowledge before long.

"I'm meeting Evan for lunch and you and I can discuss this later, when I get back."

"Well, maybe I can come along and we can determine the best way to capture these New Eden guys."

"Agent Lynn, I would suggest you figure a way to protect Evan, versus making him bait for your bad guys who've got some reason we can't fathom for keeping him alive." Ronnie was wondering if Agent Lynn forgot that she used to be FBI and that she wasn't a stupid country Sheriff that would agree to any suggestion by the FBI. What she didn't know was if this was a way that Lynn thought he could get closer to Evan or her. Either way, she didn't want him around Evan at this point.

"You let a killer get through three people. And now, you think you can capture someone they're protecting for reasons we still don't know? Sounds like you're over-estimating your ability. Let's talk about this later, in my office." She turned and left.

Agent Lynn had anticipated her response. No matter, it gave him the opportunity to plant a bug in Ronnie's office, without her knowing it. He told the cop at the desk nearest Ronnie's office that he needed to use a corner of her desk to write something down. He took a small notebook from one of his inside breast pockets and a pen, then started dialing on his cellular phone. Blocking everyone's view with his body, he was able to plant a bug on the side of her in-box. The color was a perfect match and it would only transmit when the tone of a person's voice would trigger it. If Evan were going to be difficult, then Lynn needed every advantage he could seize.

Agent Lynn finished pretending to write something in his notebook, said good-bye to the time and temperature recording he had called, pocketed the notebook and pen, and as he left, nodded a thanks to the officer at the desk just outside Ronnie's office.

The problem with any plan that Evan thought through was the time he needed to get free in order to make it to Washington, DC. He couldn't fly commercial, because the Feds would get a copy of the passenger list, and if he tried another private plane, he would only get that person into trouble. He knew he had to drive, but needed a good eight-hour head start. The plan could work, but it required great timing and possibly putting Ronnie into a difficult position. However it worked out, he was still at the mercy of whoever was trying to kill him. If he failed, it could mean he would lose the company as well. He had worked too hard to build it up just to lose it through stupidity.

Brenda stuck her head into his office and reminded Evan of his luncheon appointment. She also said that he needed to bring back a Mexican Pizza for her. Evan could only shake his head, thinking if he never came back, he would miss Brenda.

"I guess I'm just a high price delivery boy in this company."

"You can say that again -- and really not even a good one." Brenda called back to him as he went by her desk. Evan grabbed Brenda's hand and placed an envelope into it.

"If you don't hear from me every twenty-four hours, open the envelope. There's no reason to think that anything will happen, but I'm a realist, and from what I've seen of the FBI, I doubt if they could protect their own families. I'll tell you if another attempt happens. Then, I'm going to disappear for a few days, maybe a week. But, I'll call you, either personally or leave a message, just so you know."

While Evan was telling this to Brenda, he could see tears welling up in the corners of her eyes and that hurt just as much as what he needed to do. "There are very few people I trust more than you and this information is intended for one reason: To explain what, when, why and how." Before Brenda could make him even more melancholy, he added, "Don't worry. I'll remember the Mexican Pizza." As he walked away, he heard Brenda sniffing back tears.

Evan met Ronnie in the parking lot behind the restaurant, and together, they went around to the entrance. As they were standing in line, waiting to order, Evan came very close to Ronnie and whispered into her ear, "If something happens to me, Brenda has the particulars as far as my kids. I doubt that the FBI even cares who's taking the next shot at me."

"Listen to me!" Ronnie responded in a whisper. "They do care about the threats against you. They also have an opportunity they want to explore. You can draw out both sides and they won't pass up that potential windfall. That's why I'm going to keep an eye on you personally, so enough of the end-of-the-line talks." Evan was the only one who could hear her. The look on her face would have frozen a lake in the Texas summer. Anyone who might even have dared to try to approach either of them wouldn't, not after seeing their faces, Evan thought. "We will talk about this at five-thirty this afternoon in my office, and if you don't show up, I'll bring you in cuffs, like a common criminal."

"Maybe we can figure out something else to do with those handcuffs that might --"

"I'm not kidding! Don't try my patience, because I'm fresh out." Ronnie interrupted.

"I'll be there. Just understand if I'm skeptical about getting any satisfactory results." Evan almost had to bite his tongue, but Ronnie had to remain in the dark, at least for another day. After ordering their food and washing it down with some new type of fruit tea that Evan thought was too sweet, they reviewed the events which had occurred over the past few days.

Ronnie asked where Jake was and Evan told her the truth, that he was in Spain, in a city by the Mediterranean Sea. What he didn't say was that he wasn't on vacation, but finishing up the missile system. Evan grabbed Brenda's lunch and Evan and Ronnie left together, but the mood between them was more adversarial than when they had arrived.

Evan dropped off the Pizza and went into his office for about fifteen minutes with the door closed. He came out and informed Brenda that he needed to visit the local sporting goods store and would be back shortly.

Evan bought six boxes each of 9X19mm and .45 ammunition. He went into the dressing room to try on some fatigue pants and shirts. He paid for everything, and then went to the bathroom.

Evan's tail was an experienced man. Evan figured someone was following him, but wasn't able to guess who it could be. He thought maybe it was an FBI agent. Whoever the guy was, he was very good, but because of a timely traffic accident that Evan set-up just outside the store, Evan was able to use the few seconds of distraction to shake the tail.

Ronnie had hired him to follow Evan Cannon. She sometimes used a P.I. – mostly him -- when she needed someone more experienced than her own guys. And, experience or not, he had almost lost the man he was following. For a civilian, this Evan Cannon was pretty sharp, but not sharp enough as he thought. Evan left the parking lot, but Lou O'Brien was right behind him. Evan Cannon seemed to be heading back to his office. But as O'Brien slipped behind the wheel; he saw Cannon's Humvee start to sway wildly, and then crashed through the guardrail, still accelerating.

Beyond the guard rail lay the deepest part of Towne Lake. O'Brien left his car and ran toward the break in the guardrail. The Lake wasn't more than one hundred yards from the parking lot. The sounds of automobile brakes screeching, and Cannon's Humvee going airborne, then nose-diving into the water was panicking O'Brien as he watched it as if it were in slow motion. He saw exactly where the car hit the water and also noticed what looked like a bullet hole in the rear window. People pulled off the road to see what was going on and a few even started to pull off their shoes to try and grab whoever was in the vehicle.

Lou O'Brien needed to report to Ronnie about what looked to be a shooting, but also wanted to keep these people from drowning in the water that was moving very swiftly for that time of year. He might possibly be able to save Evan himself.

O'Brien made a 911 call, specifically saying it was Evan's car that had run off the road and that the driver may have been shot. As he talked, he kicked off his shoes. He spotted a woman jogger, who had apparently just gotten out of her car. He unholstered his Glock, pulled the magazine and cleared the chamber, pushing the gun and his phone at the woman, saying, "Please, lady! Hold this!" In the next second, he was over the rail and diving into the water.

He oriented himself, spotting the car, swimming toward it.  There was a window down, but that could have happened before the shot was fired. He didn't see the driver inside or near the vehicle, but it was very obvious that the rear window had two bullet holes through it.

O'Brien surfaced, sucking in air, using the weeds to pull himself out of the water channel. Evan's body wouldn't be too far from his car, but the marks in the rear windshield had O'Brien a little perplexed. He didn't remember seeing two holes as the Humvee went through the guard rail, just one.

Could someone have been down there? Waiting? The only reason would be to make sure Evan didn't get out of that lake alive. O'Brien was an ex-Green Beret and a police officer in a neighboring town, until he found out that a PI made quite a bit more money for doing far less stressful duties. Ronnie wanted him to tail Evan and make sure that he kept an eye out for anyone that wanted to do Evan any harm. O'Brien remembered the accident at the store and started to think that it was totally staged, to keep him from noticing anything suspicious.

He took his gun and phone back from the surprised jogger. "Thanks lady. You might want to try a prayer for the guy who was driving that Humvee," he added.

Once Ronnie came on the scene, people were all over the lake bed. The news vans had shown up and the only thing separating the accident from a circus was the absence of a popcorn vendor. "Ronnie, I'm sorry," O'Brien told her. "I didn't see anyone looking suspicious, when all of a sudden the Humvee was all over the road. He went through the rail and sank right where you see it. I phoned in the 911 and dove in to see if I could extract Evan from the car. His body was already gone. He might have been able to get out of the vehicle, but --"

"But what? You need to tell me everything, Lou."

"I saw what I thought was one bullet hole in the rear windshield, when your guy's Humvee went into the lake. When I went down to pull him out, I noticed two holes." Ronnie's heart sank. It wasn't enough that she hated her mood at lunch and the way she'd spoken to Evan, but now, it looked like one of the murder attempts had finally worked. Evan's body must have been caught on some debris in the channel flow of the Lake, or the killers shot him for good, once they had him underwater.

********************************

Ed Tuggle knew that he and the other people Evan Cannon had recruited to assist him would be very well compensated for their part in the charade. But money wasn't why Ed Tuggle did it. How often, he'd asked himself, would he get the chance to pull such a stunt? If it weren't for the curbside fender-bender distraction, the Humvee driver, upon close inspection, would have been seen as a totally different person from Evan Cannon. Ed was roughly the same size and build, but it might have proven very hard to mimic Evan's walk. Everyone has a very distinctive gait and rhythm that distinguishes him, that is noticeable to even the untrained eye, let alone the guy who'd been following Evan Cannon. The driver of the vehicle pulling out of the parking space was supposedly not even looking if anyone were coming down the lane. The vehicle obstructed the full view of the fake Evan getting into his car.

Knowing who was watching and following Evan Cannon was pretty easy. The man had followed Evan Cannon from the restaurant, and subsequently parked outside the plant briefly, then followed him to the sporting goods store. The hardest part of the plan was finding the right parking space that would do the trick. They got lucky, when the detective or cop or whomever he was parked far enough out that a space was easily found close to his car.

Engineering interns, like Ed Tuggle, needed a lot of structure to keep them busy and productive. Happily, Ed realized, he was just the perfect age for not caring if he bent or even broke a few laws, as long as his boss was asking him to do so.

While Ed Tuggle was learning circuit design from Jake, he was also willing to help the CEO of Cannon Electronics any way that he could. Taking a rough outline of Evan's plan and filling in the details was better than any frat prank his brothers could ever devise. Ed was also a certified diver. The last act was making sure "kids" were playing Ultimate Frisbee next to the Lake. It was their call of seeing two people carrying a body from an outlet pipe that convinced everyone that Evan was either murdered or seriously injured and kidnapped. That would provide time. Ed and his co-conspirators were rewarded for their efforts with roundtrip tickets to Cancun and a week paid vacation on the company. The only catch was that they were never to tell anyone about the "caper." Secrecy made it all that much cooler.

Evan had gone out the back of the store and ridden a motorcycle to his destination. Evan had wanted eight hours head start for whatever his plan was, but it was sixteen hours until Ronnie had started to figure things out. She mentally kicked herself. The final piece of the puzzle had fallen into place when she'd asked Brenda questions about the day's events and Brenda hadn't seemed completely distraught.

"Brenda, you're hiding something and I want to know what it is?" Ronnie had Brenda in Evan's office. She imagined the volume of the exchange could be heard throughout the office area. Alright! Enough of this. I'm arresting you in the murder of Evan Cannon and you can make your call to a lawyer from jail. You have the right to remain --"

"You can't arrest me for murder, since Evan is still alive," Brenda responded very arrogantly. "He called right before you got here, to say he was alive and well."

"How do you know it was Evan?"

"Because he used the code word before he said anything." Brenda got the letter Evan gave her and showed that part to Ronnie. The code word was "Veronica." Brenda told her, "He will call every day or leave a message. If he doesn't, I have the directions for his kids."

It hadn't taken Ronnie long to learn about the motorcycle and the back door. While she dug for information, ordering and obtaining the video records of every surveillance camera in the area in the hopes of getting a license plate on the motorcycle, Agent Lynn used the time to shut down Cannon Electronics on the grounds of national security. Ronnie knew the charge was trumped up, but Evan was now considered a criminal, a fugitive on the run, and they had to find him before he left the country. After that, the chances of apprehending him were slim to none.

While the motorcycle was the best method of transportation, if one were not used to riding, it could bring about fatigue after several hours. Evan took more breaks than he intended. So, it was early evening when he finally pulled into Virginia Military Institute Alumni Hall in Lexington, VA.

The person he needed to see was a new three star general in the Air Force, Jimmy Kern. Evan and Jimmy were classmates, and during those years, they were called "Brother Rats." So when Jimmy's son needed a job, Evan was able to get his son a good position in a venture capital group. Now was the time to call in that debt. It was a football weekend, and since Jimmy was starting safety during his college days, Evan knew he didn't miss many home games. Evan checked into the Hall for two nights. He didn't want his name to appear on any charge slips, until he was able to hit Spain.

Jimmy was on the deck, enjoying drinks with a few other people whom Evan didn't recognize. It could be a problem, but at this point, he had to take that chance.  As Evan approached Jimmy, he shouted out in a joking tone, "You can always tell the kiss a____ in our class; they have stars on their shoulders." Jimmy turned around and gave Evan a bear hug.

"What? You decided to show a little school spirit and support our team?"

Evan smiled, but said in a low voice, "We need to talk." After another half-minute of small talk, Jimmy and Evan excused themselves from the group. "How's Roger doing at Frontier Group? The last I heard from him, he was looking at getting into a Foundation."

"He's still on the fence. He's not in any hurry, since Frontier is really treating him great."

"He's a smart guy and will do well in any venue he goes after."

"Evan? Why are you here?"

"To be blunt, I need a favor. You're in charge of Air Force Research, so you can check this out. But somehow a high-tech terrorist group called New Eden has shown interest in me and my company and I have to get to Spain in a hurry." Evan didn't need to get into all the details, such as the terrorists were the ones protecting him versus the FBI, which wanted him stopped. "They killed Gail in Austin even with federal protection." Another half-truth, but he needed to make sure this moved along.

Jimmy's mouth was distorted from him clenching his teeth. "Why haven't you gone to the FBI or even Homeland Security?"

"They haven't been very effective at stopping these guys. Two agents' died in the shootout in Austin."

"Let me do some research on this new Eden Group and we can look at our options. I'm sorry about your wife. I remember her from our 'Keydet days.' You definitely got the better of that marriage. As ugly as you are, we thought that we would have to get you a mail order bride from Egypt."

"Actually, Jimmy, we had to get you a hooker to make sure you had a date for our big dance when we were second classmen."

"So! Now, you finally admit it, after years of denial. You dog!" Jimmy started rubbing Evans hair with his knuckles. He definitely still had strength in his arms and hands, but Evan ended up picking him up and carrying him around like a sack of potatoes. They laughed and sat down in soft, overstuffed leather chairs. "We have cargo flights going out of Dulles every day for destinations all over Europe. So, if possible, you could be on a flight tomorrow."

"I appreciate anything you can do for me, Jimmy." They shook hands and Evan followed Jimmy back to the deck saying, "Maybe the football team could use you if you had any eligibility left."

"You can't be just smart enough, but you also have to look the part of a general, these days. That's why I try to stay in shape."

The rest of the evening was spent relaxing and catching up with old classmates. Evan had a hard time remembering their names, but that could have been due to stress or too many brain cells destroyed over the years by Jack Daniels.

It wasn't until Evan had been sound asleep for a few minutes or hours, he couldn't tell that Jimmy woke him up. "Get these fatigues on and hustle your way up to Dulles. I'll have orders stating you're to be on a transport to Madrid. You will use our Air Mobility Command or AMC transport. It's the friendly airlines of our armed forces -- sort of our overseas taxi service. There's always a waiting list, so you better be there on time. Follow these instructions and talk to a Captain Murdock, once you get to the airport. I asked for a search on New Eden, and I have to tell you it was the scariest response I've ever received. How did you get involved with them?"

Evan's head was spinning. "First off, what time is it? Second, did you get any sleep? Third, I have no idea -- but I'm trying to find out how."

Jimmy gave a big laugh and said sleep was for wimp and that it was zero four hundred hours. "Look, Brother Rat. I don't know all the circumstances that you find yourself in, but by God, keep your head down. These guys scare the Intelligence group to death. Now, get going and you'll make that zero eight hundred flight, and this is as far as I can go, if you know what I mean."

Evan shook his head. He knew that Jimmy must have gotten some information about him and probably ignored any warnings to call the FBI if he were to surface. "Thank you for everything."

Jimmy was smiling, "You know what they call a Brother Rat in need?"

"A pest!" They both answered at the same time. They shook hands and Evan was on his way north to Dulles airport.

# Chapter Ten

# The Journey

CONSIDERING THE TIME OF DAY, IT WAS GOING TO TAKE EVAN three and a half hours to get to Dulles, so he didn't have too much time to enjoy the scenery. When Evan arrived at the airport, he found the Military Airport without any problems. Then he searched for a place where he could change his clothes and get ready to board his flight. He found a fast food restaurant that was opened 24/7 and changed into the fatigues that General Kern had given him. They fit okay and he was able to tuck the excess shirt width into his pants so they looked more military. He read over the instructions that had been given to him and jumped back on his bike and drove out to find Captain Murdock to get on his assigned aircraft. The operation's office was well marked and easy to find once he got pass the guards stationed at the base's entrance. The office for Captain Murdock was very neat and didn't seem to have a single sheet of paper out of place. Not surprising after seeing this, Murdock was a real stickler for making sure Evan had everything that was required.

There were no insignias on the uniform Evan wore, except a patch that said US Air Force over the front pocket. Evan could see that there were quite a few others that didn't wear rank or unit patches. So he realized this was what the contractors wore when they did work overseas.

Captain Murdock asked if he had any other bags and Evan said "no," but that in his duffle he had two pistols and ammo. Murdock asked to see the weapons and asked where Evan had gotten them. Evan didn't have the energy or the desire to give Captain Murdock the whole story, so Evan just said the weapons were a gift from a friend and had quite a bit of sentimental value for him.

"As long as you put that bag in the baggage compartment, you can take the two firearms. I hope you have a European gun license for them? They have very strict requirements about rifles and handguns."

"Great," Evan thought, "I'll get off the jet and some paper pusher will end up with my pistols." There wasn't anything he could do about it now. "No problem. I have a lot of sleep to catch up on and I like to travel light." Murdock just nodded his head, stamped some documents along with Evan's passport, and then went to help another person. Evan bought a few things he thought he might need, including earplugs and some water. The aircraft was not a military transport, but a Delta Airlines 747. That surprised him, but then again, he had never flown on a military transport before. As his seat was called to board, an airman came up to him and asked if he were Evan

Cannon, and then handed him an IPod and a European Firearm Pass.

"Sir, the pass is good for 5 years and will be needed to go from one country to another. Good luck in your shooting competition."

Evan didn't know what to think about the pass since he wasn't going to any shooting competition and had no clue why he now had an IPod. He figured that Murdock forgot to give it to him on orders from Jimmy. Their take off procedure was the same for the military as it was for normal civilian operations, including flight attendants.

After taking off, Evan decided to try the IPod that Jimmy had given him, except it wasn't what he thought it would be.

"Mr. Cannon, you have been given this so that I may give you instructions on where to go once you reach Madrid. Please listen carefully, since the message will only play once and then be erased. Maybe you should pause this message and take out either a pencil or pen to write down what I'm about to tell you."

Evan stopped the IPod and wondered what the world was going on. Was this a joke from Jimmy or something else? Evan almost expected the "Mission Impossible" theme to start up. So he asked the flight attendant if he could have a pencil or pen, then turned the IPod back on.

"Congratulations on getting out of the US and on your way to Spain. We have been very busy trying to protect you and hope that you realize by now that we do have considerable resources at our command. We are sorry about your wife, but let me reassure you that the people who did this will be taken care of once we have everything in hand. There are people on this flight that are following you. It won't be an issue, unless we fail to make contact in Madrid. If something happens and you don't make contact with our agent, get to the airport in Valencia. There, go to the Avis rental car kiosk at the airport and ask for Ramon. Tell him you are the new 'Bishop.'"

The IPod continued to describe the person in Madrid whom Evan needed to see. Since he checked his pistols, his bag would be pulled and waiting for him to claim it at customs. A "Mr. Watkins" would help him get his bag and provide him a route to his limo, in this case a Toyota mini-van, in which he would make his way to Valencia. Jake and his engineers would meet him at a hotel, and from there, they would travel to the next destination together.

Evan let the player go on to music. He tried to start the player over, but all it played were songs from the seventies and eighties. He needed sleep much more than food, so he quickly found himself going to sleep wondering what he had gotten himself into.

He awoke after a couple of hours, and to him – surprisingly -- sound sleep. Evan started making notes to himself and the mysterious "Mr. X." Trying to remind himself of things to do, once he landed, kept him pretty occupied for the entire flight. His only regret, so far, was the deception he'd played out on Ronnie. There wasn't much chance that he could smooth things over between the two of them; he thought the phrase Hope springs eternal was very appropriate right now. Evan went back to his list and saw the statement he wrote, but had forgotten, 'spy on board' followed by a question mark. Now he wondered if he was supposed to find him or her or let them come to him, so during the flight, he paid close attention to each of the fifty plus people around him. He made a mental photograph of each of them in case he saw one or more of them later. In reality, it was a jet and nobody was going anywhere for a while.

The landing went as expected, and of course, he put up a fuss when his luggage wasn't in the carrousel. Evan took note of the one guy who seemed to be lingering with him -- a tall, older guy, whom Evan ruled out because he was willing to call the head of customs in order for Evan to get his bag back. No spy would call attention to himself like that.

After eternity or maybe forty-five minutes, a very proper Englishman, Mr. Watkins, said that Evan had to fill out proper paperwork in order to receive his bag with the "disgusting guns and ammunition." Watkins puffed himself up and said, "Mr. Cannon, this isn't America, where you can get some fool to sign a piece of paper saying you can carry a firearm and expect it to be acceptable to the rest of the world. There are certain rules to the Euro Firearms Pass that must be followed, so please come with me and we'll see if you qualify for carrying a sidearm."

Evan's first impression was, "Why an Englishman. Shouldn't he be Spanish?" Evan found himself questioning everything, but was actually just too tired to deal with it. He would follow instructions, do what they told him and maybe get some rest on the train since he wasn't going to make the air connection. Almost dozing in a chair that was overstuffed and very comfortable, Evan waited for all the paperwork to be processed. The whole assassination deal, death of Gail, the gunshot wound, and lost sleep had caused him to lose any energy reserves that he had.

He wasn't sure if Watkins awakened him by coming into the room or if he were just on the verge of sleep. Either way, he was listening now and wanted to know what he needed. "Mr. Cannon, this is your permit properly filled out to carry a firearm in Europe. It will have to be concealed and you must carry your ammunition in a separate bag."

"Will I need to show this at every country that I travel through?"

"As soon as the shooting competition is completed, you will need to turn your pass in at customs. Expect to receive a stamp at each event and attach it to the pass. We are guided by Interpol, with no specific country dictating how we operate."

"You must explain why you are English."

Watkins smiled. "I'm fluent in several languages, and because of that, I have been assigned to many different countries over the years. May I say that you look extremely tired? Care for one of those energy drinks that Americans find so popular?" Evan thought about it and said that he would and thanked Watkins for getting his paperwork through the system. Evan shook Watkins' hand. Usually, Evan didn't like something full of sugar and caffeine, but he was willing to try anything to wake up. Watkins opened the drink and handed it to Evan, who took a long draw and found the flavor quite good. It was called "Target" and Evan tried to think if he had seen it before. Watkins said, "Hope you have a successful event."

Evan replied, "Me, too!" He went out and over to the train station, found his berth, put his bag in the overhead and wiggled into his seat and fell fast asleep. They were still in the station when Evan woke up. He wasn't just awake, but felt as if he must have slept over multiple stops.

He was shocked when he realized they were still in the same train station. He looked at his watch. The train was starting up right on time. He had been asleep for about thirty minutes. He wasn't just awake, but alert. He decided that he needed to buy stock in that drink company.

\*\*\*\*\*\*\*\*\*\*\*\*\*\*\*\*\*\*\*\*\*\*\*\*\*\*\*\*\*\*\*\*

Pam King was still reeling from the disaster that happened in Austin. The damn massacre was on evening news in every country that had a newscaster. She had repeated her side of the story to everyone within the organization. Huggins was furious, but they were people he had hired and without anybody supervising, they shot anything that moved completely forgetting about their primary objective. Once they came back empty handed, she insisted they go back to find the stocks. She was actually watching them from three blocks down the street. They used phones to communicate and when they stated there were still a few people at the home, she gave them the order to finish the job no matter what it took.

At first it seemed to go their way, but the one man they didn't kill with the initial onslaught ended up being the man that destroyed her career. From her advantage point, it appeared he had been killed, but he got up and once he took out two of their team members, the mission was done and all the mess left behind. She had been summoned by Dr. Harris to visit him at Valencia, Spain and that probably meant her career, and maybe her life was over. He left messages for which train to take and when. It was admittedly odd, but Harris was a very bright man and no one ever second guessed him. Getting out of the US was pretty easy, but it was just pure luck since the government started putting out APBs on her three hours after she had left the country on a flight out of Dallas. She didn't dare carry a firearm, but she could handle herself and figured if Harris wanted her dead, he could have done that in Austin or any place they had a presence. If this was going to be her last train ride, she might as well enjoy the scenery, so she grabbed a seat so she could see the view.

\*\*\*\*\*\*\*\*\*\*\*\*\*\*\*\*\*\*\*\*\*\*\*\*\*\*\*\*\*\*\*\*\*\*\*\*

Evan got up and walked along the train, hopefully, to the club car. A very friendly conductor, who spoke broken English, showed him the way with exaggerated arm movements. One car down, he saw the silhouette of a pretty blonde woman reaching her seat. Instantly, he recognized the profile as that of the woman who had tried to drug him back at the restaurant and had his ex-wife killed.

He realized his weapons were back in his berth, so he casually backed away and returned to his seat. Evan was thinking a mile a minute. Was she alone? Should he shoot her on sight and ask questions later? Did he want to wait and have her arrested? Did she have any of her friends or confederates aboard the train? He decided that she probably didn't know for sure that he was on the train, therefore, it would make sense that she had armed friends nearby. In order to take any action, he needed help. Evan decided to set a trap. He tracked down the conductor and asked if there were any Interpol people that traveled on the train, like the USA used Sky Marshals. Because the train would be going across country boundaries, Interpol could have a presence when the police of individual nations could not. Evan assured the conductor that he was no expert, but he thought that there were people on board that he had seen at the airport security office. It was a little lie, but he needed some credibility. He asked the conductor where they could meet privately and was told that he could go toward the end of the train and into the baggage car.

"You're kidding me! You actually have baggage cars on trains? I thought that went out in the fifties."

The conductor smiled and said, "Sometimes, they have two that they use for mail and express packages."

"Maybe, then we can meet in the first one in about ten minutes. I will bring the woman terrorist and nobody else would be in harm's way."

The conductor nodded his head as in saying he understood what Evan was planning. "I will get our agent."

The conductor left on his mission and Evan waited for about three minutes to allow time to unlock any doors. Evan was making this up on the fly, but this time, he was armed and ready. He walked by the blonde and looked down when he passed her. He let out a little "Oh!" and started down the aisle in a hurry. Her eyes told him everything he had needed to know. She was very surprised and turned away to pick something up, then she got up from her seat and began to follow him.

Smugly, Evan felt that once he hit that baggage car, he could turn around and hold her for Interpol or even show her to the Interpol personnel if they beat him to the car. He walked steadily and deliberately through each car. But he was getting second thoughts. Would she shoot him from behind or even start running toward him? So far, she hadn't gathered any additional people and wasn't talking on a phone, so maybe this would work. He finally got to the classic baggage car and it was unlocked. Evan went inside, wedged himself beside a locked storage container and pulled his pistol and aimed.

She couldn't believe her luck, after missing this guy in Texas, not getting the documents in Austin and giving up ever getting to Evan Cannon, that she would have him wrapped-up and ready to give to Dr. Harris. Maybe her career wasn't quite done. He had no place to hide, and unless he was armed, impossible in Europe, then he would be little trouble to her. She opened the last door and immediately saw the pistol aimed at her head.

"I have no idea who you work for or why you want me, but I can put a bullet into your left nostril, if I want even on a moving train."

"I know of your marksmanship skills. I'm very surprised you have a firearm on this train."

"Why do you want to kill me? And before you answer, I should warn you that Interpol will be here shortly. So you can remain silent or tell me the truth." Evan walked out of his position, so he could move better if she tried to run.

"We are never given all the details, but let's just say that you have information that we need and we doubt if you are going to give it to us willingly."

"Why did you kill my ex-wife and my dog?"

At that, the door opened and in stepped a guy who should have been a linebacker for the Dallas Cowboys.

"Mister Cannon, I presume. And is this person that may be a terrorist?"

Evan lowered his hand down only a bit, but enough for her to perform a roundhouse kick right into the side of Evan's head. Another kick into the agent's throat shortened his life into minutes.

Evan's field of vision was getting very narrow. He was semi-conscious and really had no idea what was happening to him. Like a TV picture that was collapsing from the edges, his consciousness was rapidly ebbing away. The blonde wasn't taking any chances, so she put her hands around his throat cutting off oxygen until Evan was unconscious. Then she looked over to the pistol that he had, and wondered if he really was that good of a shot. But it didn't matter, even though he was cocky, he still did not have any training on what to watch for when somebody is an expert in killing. The next step was to empty a footlocker, and place him in it and take him right to where they needed. Somehow it just seemed too easy. All the planning of what to do with him either dead or alive and how to bring him over to Europe was not needed after all. She had him and they knew what to do from there.

Evan woke up limp, with a headache that could bring down an elephant. He was lying in the same position where he'd fallen and the conductor was kneeling over him, trying to get his attention, when all the man was doing was increasing the pain in Evan's head. Evan got up on his elbows and saw the agent lying there, still. Evan knew right away that the agent was dead. There was something about a body that had no life. It must be the soul that took with it the spark of life, Evan thought fleetingly. "Is he dead?" Evan asked anyway.

"Si, and I thought you probably were, too. Who did this?"

"A woman, In fact, a very beautiful blonde woman. I'm not sure why she didn't kill me as well. Did you see anyone leave this car?"

"No, but there was a disturbance in one of the forward cars and I wasn't able to get back that quickly. What did you do that caused her to attack you?"

"I asked her why she'd tried to kill me. Also, why did she kill my wife and my dog? Then the agent came in, and as soon as he arrived, she whirled around and hit me on the side of the head. I must have blacked out, because I didn't even hear a shot."

"She didn't shoot him," the conductor informed Evan. It looks like she kicked him in his throat and that was how he died."

"I was stupid to even try and capture her. She killed my ex-wife along with two FBI agents and two policemen in Austin, Texas. For the life of me, I have no idea why, either. But I certainly didn't expect her on this train. She looked surprised when I saw her, but that could have been an act."

The conductor probably understood only forty to sixty per cent of what Evan was saying, but the presence of the dead Interpol agent made it a high priority to try and get as many details as possible.

"Where are you hurt?"

"My head feels like its split open and my throat is sore," Evan responded.

"You need first-aid. We get you off at the next stop, so that the police can review your story."

"No problem," Evan told the conductor. "But where did she go? I really don't want to see her again without my pistol cocked and aimed at her heart." Evan got up, took two steps and proceeded to throw up. The pain in his head was so amplified that he felt he would pass out.

In a car near the dining room was an area that had supplies for just about anything that could happen, along with a bed. The conductor found a doctor on board who examined Evan. The doctor spoke Spanish, French and Russian, but not English. Evan took the doctor for some ex-Communist who'd refused to learn English out of spite.

After the exam, the conductor translated to Evan that he probably had at least a concussion and maybe even a fractured skull. They gave him aspirin laced with codeine and told him to lie down for the next thirty minutes. The train would be at the next stop then and he could have more extensive tests and tell what he knew to the police.

The conductor was a man of about fifty, who looked as if he could take care of himself. Without Evan even asking him, the conductor placed Evan's pistol beside Evan and the overnight bag near the bed. Evan tried to sleep, but had to keep one eye open for her. He made himself a promise that should he ever see her again, he would kill her, making hers a very slow and painful death without even thinking twice.

The train was slowing down, and when it came to a stop, the conductor was at the door. Evan stood up and that was another mistake, and his body immediately told him so by emptying his stomach of anything that might have been left. They actually had a stretcher for him, and while feeling foolish for being the center of attention, he felt relieved that he might make the doctor's visit without any more sickness.

# Chapter Eleven
# Peeling the Onion

**RONNIE WAS MAD AS HELL AND DIDN'T REALLY CARE WHO SHE** took it out on. Her deputies and staff tried to stay out of her way. She was after blood.

After putting together the puzzle of Evan's escape plan, she realized he had left the country. Even after she warned him, he had managed to do it. Then she subsequently discovered the bug that Agent Lynn had planted in her office. She was ready to arrest anyone and everyone associated with the fake death and "slap" any FBI person with obstruction of justice charges. A phone call saved a clerk from being chewed out for not filing the proper paperwork for a case that was to go to trial that week. She answered the call with a very professional "Sheriff Green."

The voice on the other end asked, "Is this Ronnie Green?"

"Yes. It is; how may I help you?"

"Well, my name is General Jimmy Kern and I promised Evan that I would call you to say he has landed in Spain and hopes to have everything tied up and will be back within the next three weeks."

Ronnie was a little stunned to hear from someone about Evan. All it served to do was to upset her again about his deception. "Well, Mr. Cannon has some explaining to do, once he gets back here, and that may include some jail time."

"Sheriff, I've known Evan a long time. He has a heart of gold and will help anyone that he can. I found out that the FBI was after him, but he asked if I could get him to Spain, so I did. Then I did some research and found that one of the companies that seem to have an interest in him is pretty scary. Evan knew that and realized if he stayed around too long, everybody close to him would be killed. I don't know you, but I did know his first wife and she was a gem. I can tell you that he looks like hell, and is exhausted. He will do whatever is necessary to finish what he started. I also got the feeling that you and he are more than just friends."

Ronnie was thinking about what Jimmy had said and wondered why she never looked at it through Evan's eyes. "We are friends, nothing more." Ronnie cringed when she said it.

"Being a friend with Evan is pretty good company. I won't keep you, since I know you are a very busy person."

"General? Was there anyone on the plane aware of who he was?"

"Now, Sheriff, all I can say is the manifest was available to all of the agencies. It's a requirement. But that manifest was given out after the plane took off. It seems that I have some people in my group with sloppy paperwork." With that he laughed and said good-bye.

Ronnie was feeling better than she had for a couple of days. She started to realize that the FBI was only using her and Evan to capture a New Eden person. She was angrier at herself for not realizing it before Evan had.

The General's wasn't the last strange call she had. Brenda called and gave her new information about the client in Spain that Jake and Evan had gone to for delivery of the FOGM system. She found that Brenda really was starting to warm up to her. Brenda even passed on some of the personal information that Jake and Evan sent back, but Ronnie was a little surprised by something that Brenda said next.

"Odd thing about these hotels that my boys are staying at. They have a website, but don't show up on the search engines or travel agents' listing."

"Your boys? Is that what you call Jake and Evan?"

"I have called them my boys since they went on a trip to Arizona. They got into an accident and someone stole their briefcases while they were giving their report to the cops. I had to provide information to the cops, hotel staff (where they were staying), and the rental car company. I knew everything, so the cops asked if I was their mother. I've called them 'my boys' ever since."

Ronnie laughed and wondered if she could hire Brenda for her staff. "I'm sure their client recommended the place and if Evan or Jake couldn't find it, you would have heard from them."

"You're right. I can't tell you how many times they've arrived late and found they had no room. They would get the voicemail of the travel agent and then call me at home. By the way, Evan's last call he wanted me to tell you that he's very sorry about how he left. He wanted to cooperate, but that the FBI was only interested in capturing people who were protecting him, including you. He could see that they were going to be putting a lot of pressure on you and thought it was best to get out of the country without government assistance."

"I got a call from a General Kern and he told me the same thing. It seems everyone understood the obvious, but me," Ronnie added.

"Don't feel bad about that. The biggest mistakes are when people can't see the forest because of the trees. A very smart person told me that."

"Was it Jake?"

"Yeah it was."

"What exactly happened to Jake? Evan told me they were classmates and he put Jake together once after Jake lost his wife. But there's a big hole in that story." Ronnie was afraid that she might have overstepped her comfort zone with Brenda, but it didn't appear to be the case.

"Well, there is quite a bit to the story that you're missing. Evan and Jake are about as opposite as they can be in their personalities and personal lives, but they are both alike in their thought processes and drive for life. Jake is a hermit because he still believes people are out to get him. He stays off the grid as much as possible. He gets his paycheck in cash and never takes the same route to or from work. Evan gave him a puppy from one of Baxter's litters and he has that dog super trained. The dog would die protecting Jake's house or Jake himself. Gail and Jake knew each other before Evan married her. Once Jake came to work with Evan, he would stay with Gail when Evan was gone."

"Now that sounds weird. How did Evan feel about that?"

"Evan knew they – he and Gail -- had issues in the marriage, but Jake wasn't one of them. Jake was company for Gail and vice versa as much as Evan was out of town. When Evan finally realized that he loved the company more than Gail, Jake had a fit. It might have been the only argument those guys ever had."

"Wow! If you didn't know better, you'd say they were brothers."

"They are much closer than brothers," Brenda told her. "And if anything were to happen to either one of them, the other would be lost."

"What happened to Jake's wife?" At this Brenda lowered her voice, as if Jake were going to hear her.

"Gail actually set Jake and Anita up to double date with her and Evan. I gather Anita was from some "high brow" family in Richmond and was serious about her career path. She and Jake hit it off immediately and married as soon as Jake got out of school."

"What branch of the service did Jake go into after graduation?"

"That's another connection Jake and Evan had," Brenda told Ronnie. "Both guys graduated after the huge demand for officers and before the first Gulf War. Each of them had a physical problem. Evan had issues with his knee and Jake with his shoulder. Both were 4-F. Do you remember what that term meant?"

"Yeah. It was a medical deferment that disqualified you for military service."

"That's right. Evan got into fiber optics and Jake went with this high-tech firm that built all sorts of things."

"I'm surprised they didn't work at the same company?"

"They were close at VMI, but got closer after graduation. You see, Jake may have one of the highest IQs in the USA. He just didn't want to become one of those egghead types that become socially backward. Anita also kept him as normal as possible. Anyway, the high-tech firm was in Christiansburg, Virginia. Anita was driving home and ran off one of the narrow mountain roads. It seemed very suspicious at the time. The problem was they didn't discover her until two days later. Jake thought she had left him and when they found her car and tested her, she was drunk."

"God, how I hate to see people do that to themselves," Ronnie sighed.

"That was part of the issue.  One, she almost never drank. If she did, it was beer. Jake always said it was to spite her parents. The second odd circumstance was the road. Nobody remembered seeing her car and she never drove in that area; never had any business in that area. The local cops held Jake for a day, thinking he might have had something to do with the accident. I think their conclusion was that local moonshine rednecks probably thought she had seen something and ran her off the road. To this day, the police think it's an open homicide, but haven't ever been able to figure who was involved."

Ronnie was shocked. She'd wondered why Jake had gotten the way he did and to hear this made her stiffen her back.

"Maybe a fresh set of eyes could help. I could pull some strings and see the file."

"Jake went crazy trying to figure it out and that was when he found that alcohol medicated the senses. Evan came along a few years later, took him in and the rest you know. Hey, I have to go and figure out why our HR group is having issues with some expense reports. Take care and I'll call if I hear anything else

"Okay, bye."

Ronnie's talk with Brenda generated a wave of feeling that Ronnie wasn't quite sure how to handle. She thought about how special Evan and Jake were to each other and actually ached for a relationship that she could point to as special. She had dated lots of people. Her last serious relationship before Evan was with the Dallas Maverick's point guard. After meeting Evan and having to be around him, she began to have feelings that she didn't dare have. The problem was she thought he was a special person. She was irritated with his lack of respect for the law and actually scared of his focus. She had seen him kill a person and appear to have no remorse. When his wife died, he seemed more concerned about that stupid dog than the woman he'd been married to, but knew that was all a brave front that would come crashing down at probably a very inopportune time. Her phone rang again and startled her out of her daydreaming. "You have a call on line one, the man on the line said it was about some test results you requested."

"Hello, Sheriff Green here." The voice on the other end was neither rushed nor controlled, but spoke in a way to disarm her and have her listen at the same time.

"Sheriff Green. We have been in contact with Evan Cannon and believe that he is in harm's way. We believe that you can help him, but you will need to be prepared to leave tomorrow on a flight to Turkey."

"Evan, nice try, but somebody has a job to do and seeing as you and Jake are enjoying the sunny Mediterranean Sea, I think I better keep working." Even if it didn't sound like Evan, she could see right through his prank.

"I'm sorry to say, Sheriff, that this isn't a prank call. We have a serious vested interest in keeping Evan Cannon alive and well; it's proving harder to do every day."

"Who is this?"

"I would give you my name, but it wouldn't matter. Yet, I think you and the FBI call us the New Eden Group." Her blood froze under her skin. She knew that many people for lots of years had been chasing these guys and never gotten close. Now, one was calling her and warning her about Evan.

"Look pal, you can take your little game somewhere else, and if you don't, I'll trace this call and arrest you for being stupid."

"Flight number three hundred. Andrew Cook was the 'Ghost' that the FBI was following when the jet crashed over the Atlantic. Only Andrew escaped with a very light weight parachute and floated to the ground. Blowing up the jet wasn't what we wanted to do, but you had put us in a corner."

Oh my God, Ronnie thought. The only people who knew this much information were the FBI and maybe the NSA, always hard to tell with that group, they were that secretive. She had to throw the voice off somehow, so she tried the insignificance route. "Anybody could have that information. I'm a very busy person, so if you don't mind, I need to get back to some real police work."

"Nice try, but actually, very few people have that information and even the FBI guessed on how he was able to land without a chute. One of your officers will come off sick leave today and will be walking into your office in about ten seconds."

With that there came a knock on the open door. It was a deputy and he said, "Sheriff Green? I feel pretty good. I guess the medicine did the trick. I'll start my late shift at nine tonight, if that's alright with you?"

Ronnie mumbled that she was glad he was feeling better and that would be fine.

"Okay. You made your point. You read tea leaves like my aunt did? Why do I have to help on something that neither Jake nor Evan can handle?"

"We find that people have specific gifts and they will need your talents to get out of the mess they are going to find themselves in shortly."

"Why can't you help?"

"I told you. Your talents are unique and will be needed."

"What do you want me to do?" Ronnie relented.

"Meet me in the private terminal at McKinney airport and we will talk further. I will give you the choice of going or staying."

"I have to get my nails done tomorrow, so I don't know if I can fit it in."

"You will be there tomorrow at 11 a.m., and don't plan on bringing clothes. We have your sizes and will bring appropriate attire."

"What if I don't show up tomorrow and instead have the FBI stage a little welcoming party?"

"Your deputy that just got over being sick will take a turn for the worse and die before the sun sets tomorrow, and more, the infection will run rampant through the town before a cure is found."

"You are a sorry bastard, no good for nothing...how could you kill innocent people like that?" Ronnie demanded.

"I won't. You will, if you don't come." Ronnie slammed the phone down. She shoved her head into her hands and wanted to curl up in her daddy's lap. This was a suicide mission. She would surely die if she went and how many people would die if she didn't. "What a scumbag," she murmured.

What sleep Ronnie could get was in five minute increments. The questions just wouldn't stop coming. How did these people know where the deputy was? How did they know about Evan? What was so important that Jake and Evan would be needed? On and on throughout the night, she rolled one way, then the next. She decided she would take her gun, a change of clothes and underwear.

The next morning Ronnie had written a note that explained what she knew and left it at her house hidden in the bill file, mailed another one to the office in case she didn't make it back and left one at her desk to be opened by the FBI. She decided to talk to Brenda and see what Brenda had found out about her boys. If they were fine, then she had some ammunition to use against New Eden. Brenda's conversation was mixed. It seemed that Evan had an incident on the train and had a cracked skull. The woman who did the damage was the same one who had set-up the killing of his wife and who had tried to kill him in town. Jake was on his way to meet Evan, so they could travel together to where they had shipped their payout coils and could assemble them with the missiles. Jake also told Brenda that as soon as they were done, they would be on the first flight back to the United States.

Brenda also said that, according to Jake, the financial windfall would keep the doors open for some time.

"Ronnie, is everything all right? It's none of my business, but this is the second day in a row that you've called the plant and asked about Evan and Jake. And, you seem to have something on your mind."

"Brenda, I'm a Sheriff trying to protect a prominent citizen from a group whom we don't know who is attempting to kill him. Then we have another group which may be the most dangerous terrorist organization in history, and we don't know what really is going on with them. And the only thing we can conclude is that they are trying to protect Evan. The fact that he's somewhere in Spain getting his head kicked in is adding to my worries. The most maddening issue is that I may have fallen for him, which you already know, so, in answer to your question, Brenda? Yes. I'm just a little pre-occupied."

"You slept with him didn't you. I knew it and bet it was when you two were in Austin. You are a little tramp." Brenda started laughing. Ronnie couldn't help but laugh, too.

"No. I didn't. I probably would have, but Evan made it clear he wanted to be left alone. Besides, why would it be so strange?"

"I don't know. You are ten years younger, could probably be on any glamour magazine cover, you date professional athletes and, by the way, you're black and he's white. Did I leave anything out?"

"You left out that I could probably kick his but in a fight and turned down a photo spread in a girlie magazine."

"Oh! You're liberated, too."

Ronnie laughed again, "Thank you for not being judgmental." Ronnie realized that she had tears in her eyes. "I may be taking a trip related to all this soon, and I want you to know that I will do everything I can to get your boys back," She promised.

Ronnie made her way to the airport. She stopped about two hundred feet from the terminal. If there were anything she could use to her advantage, she would. If she were able to kill one, or better yet, wound one of them badly enough, maybe they wouldn't follow through with releasing the virus. She parked the car right in front of the terminal, so that it was very conspicuous, and walked into the building. The shade and air conditioning inside provided a cool alternative to the glaring sunshine and heat outside.

She wasn't expecting what she saw. There was a group of people probably pilots and airplane buffs surrounding an older gentleman who was explaining the finer details of fuel combustion. He stood over six feet tall and had a head full of white hair. He looked to be in pretty good shape and was dressed in a very expensive suit. He was probably one of the rich guys who kept a private jet at the airport. The next thing that happened was even weirder. "Come on over, Sheriff! I was just pontificating about my aircraft experience. Sort of killing time while waiting on you." What a brilliant move, getting everyone engaged, and then get down to business in front of them, so it minimized the forcible options Ronnie had available, she thought.

"Smart move, Mr. X. If I wanted to shoot you, it would be very difficult under these circumstances," Ronnie whispered to the man as she leaned in toward him to muffle the words from the crowd.

"Sheriff Green, I just want to talk and nothing more." Side-by-side, Ronnie just a bit behind him, they drifted away from the knot of people to whom he'd spoken.

"Our schedule has been pushed back for a few days and I will give you the freedom to decide one way or the other, if you want to join us. No retaliation if you don't come. I just didn't want you to miss this meeting. Also, you can call me by my real name. It's Alfred Johnson, Dr. Alfred Johnson."

"Okay, Dr. Johnson. Can I ask what the hell you do for New Eden?"

"Sure! I created it. I guess you could say I'm the 'CEO.'" Ronnie wasn't expecting to meet with the head of New Eden. She briefly thought about shooting him, but doing so in cold blood just wasn't in her makeup.

"My, what an honor to have the top terrorist in the World come to my town, so I can arrest him!" Ronnie smiled.

"Sheriff, if it would make you feel more comfortable, draw your pistol and keep it on me while we talk."

"You can first explain to me why you killed over four hundred innocent people on flight three hundred, kidnapped several scientists and have stolen who knows how much money from banks around the world. What do you say we begin that little chat first?"

"You know you are prettier than I was expecting, and a bit feistier. Is it because you have a personal interest in our Spain project?"

"A couple of weeks ago I would have shot you on the spot, not caring about the circumstances. You have been protecting a citizen of this town, for which I'm thankful, but in the process, I've seen your group add several more deaths to a total that is probably higher than even I could imagine. Nobody that I know of has had a conversation with you, so now, I want some answers. Yes, I have personal feelings in this case, but why do I think I'm talking to Hitler before WWII? So we sit here, drink coffee, and you can start and I will try to believe you."

"Your opinion of me is based on typical intelligence information that is either half-truths or totally made up, so it becomes convenient. I understand your anger and frustration and my interest in Cannon is extremely warranted, but that will be explained later. Let me tell you why those people had to die on flight three hundred. Do you remember that this was after the attempted bombing of the World Trade Center? That particular group of Islamic terrorist killed a few people, but not near the results they needed to draw new jihadists into their ranks. What you don't know is that an agent from China decided it would be a good time to steal vials of one of the worst and most destructive viruses known to man. He made his way from the Plum Island lab on Long Island, New York, and was on that flight to France. The pass-off would take place in France and would have been used on America or England in approximately three months. The loss of lives would have been well over thirty million and would have spread to Europe and Asia. The scientist didn't even realize how dangerous it was. The finger was to point to Middle East terrorists and then China was going to take over some of the oil fields as retaliation. To bring death to everyone on that flight wasn't an easy decision, but one that would save millions. If there had been a better way, we would have done that, but there wasn't. Some months later, we made sure the NSA received the full documentation of the intent, but that was never shared with any other agency. I made the call to kill those people, but I couldn't take the chance of the viral agent getting out into the population. Here is a name and phone number of the man in the NSA you can call to verify the information. As far as Jake and Evan, they are needed on an important project that will become obvious as time allows the events to unfold. You will need to assist them, if you decide to do so."

"You keep saying that I have a choice."

"You do, Sheriff Green, and you can choose to say no. Just know that we always match the best talents that we can with the projects underway." Ronnie was holding a piece of paper in her hand, looking at the name and number of the NSA contact.

"My answer will be yes, if this story of yours proves to be true. When will I need to be ready?"

"I'm glad to see that you're giving me the benefit of the doubt. I think we have four days, but that can change. I'll be in touch." With that, Dr. Johnson got up, gave Ronnie a salute and walked out to the tarmac. He entered what looked to be a Gulfstream Five, which cost about fifty million dollars. She had doubts that it was only rented.

# Chapter Twelve
# The Reunion

**DICKEY AND WILL WERE WRAPPING UP THE LATEST GROUP** evaluations and everyone was ready to break camp for this session. Dickey was a cruel master, and the camp being without any of the luxuries that pro players were used to, therefore, his clients were very happy about leaving. But before they leave, he would have the position coaches view what they had done and watch the final practice film, with the player present. Will had asked him once if anybody had ever tried to fight him. Dickey replied "My first player was a punk tackle with all the talent in the World. He was cut in pre-season after thirty minutes. The coaches were willing to try anything, so they allowed me to build him up. He came in full of piss and vinegar. He didn't want to work or listen, so I told him he would not be eating, so about four hours passed, then he came at me. It took me about thirty seconds to have him on his knees, crying like a baby. I put the fear of God in him and tell everyone that attends that if they lay a hand on anyone in the complex, they will be sucking through a straw. I make sure all coaches know this up front. Now, players arrive without their egos and chips on their shoulders," Dickey told Will and Abbey.

In the evening, Dickey read all the faxes that had come in and noticed that he and his staff had been invited by the Browns to attend the White House ceremony wherein the Browns would be congratulated on winning the Super Bowl. Dickey faxed back that he would be bringing five people with him. Dickey Moore, you have arrived, he thought. He left to tell the staff, and a paid trip to Washington was scheduled in three weeks.

\* \* \* \* \* \* \* \* \* \* \* \* \* \* \* \* \* \* \* \* \* \* \* \* \* \* \* \* \* \*

Jake was laughing so hard that he started to cry. They had heard about Evan's cracked head and run-in with the assassin on another train, but as he boarded the train to Marbella and saw Evan with this big turban of a bandage wrapped around his head, he just lost it. Evan obviously wasn't in that good of a mood and it didn't help that Jake was laughing at him in front of the techs that they had on site. Everyone knew Jake could do or say anything, but the techs wouldn't dare laugh, at least, not out loud.

"Evan, so I see you got your butt kick before you got here." Jake saw that Evan was serious and stopped for about a second – only to let loose again. "I'm sorry, but your new hat needs a magic carpet to go with it. Did you bring one? That way, we don't have to take the train! We'll just ride the carpet." Jake was laughing again.

Evan lowered his face, shook his head and just gave Jake a big bear hug. "Good to see you, too." His head didn't hurt like it had, but he still had a hard shell to protect his skull and the wrap was to protect the cast. Reality was that the turban made Evan look very distinguished, he thought, a Lawrence of Arabia without the English accent. "I hope my luck is better riding with you guys then it has been on my own."

"We heard how that woman almost made "mince meat" out of you."

Evan couldn't just leave it at that. He decided to see how far he could push this story. "You think a girl did this? There were three of them, and after taking care of the first two, the third came around with some sort of metal pipe. I'm just lucky to be alive." Evan didn't worry about lying, because through experience Jake knew two things: Evan never told a lie unless he was in a good mood and he constructed his lies to be obvious whoppers. Jake would also respect his pride; let Evan play it out until Evan admitted he got clobbered by a woman. Brenda had already filled Jake in on the escaped female assailant.

"Why didn't you shoot her? Forget I said that. I should say that it was one hell of a chance you took. Just how big were these guys anyway?"

"They had to be well over six feet and built like linebackers." Evan saw that he had the techs hooked on the story. "Okay, guys, I just made it up. It was that blonde assassin that tried to poison me back home. I'll tell you this; she is deadly. Her kick put a spike heel into the train detective's throat, crushing his windpipe instantly. He probably died before hitting the ground."

"I knew you are kidding, but why didn't you take care of her?"

"Truthfully, I think it was because she was a woman. It just doesn't seem right, but if I see her again, I won't hesitate to pull the trigger. Another thing is that she is drop-dead gorgeous."

"Like a spider mates, and then eats her mate." The techs had their laugh and walked back to their berths. Evan watched them go, and without looking at Jake, said "You knew all along about the story. Didn't you?"

"Of course, Brenda told me when she found out about it. I will say this; you have managed to get yourself here, which I thought would be impossible."

"I had help."

"Let me guess, from that New Eden group?"

"Yeah! They warned me almost every step of the way. I don't wonder why the FBI and every other alphabet soup agency are scared of them. They're always a step ahead."

Jake took off his sunglasses and turned to look at Evan. "It makes me wonder if they set up the meeting with you and the blonde for a reason. Everything that I have seen so far is that they are playing chess and everyone else is playing checkers. You get hurt, but not captured. She's disappeared and they get you here a little banged up, but in one piece. Do you remember our IT guy who fell at the high school football game?"

"He had a cracked skull and needed rehab for several months?"

"Yeah, that guy. He was in the hospital for several weeks, and still had severe headaches."

"So what are you saying?"

"I'm saying you have been wounded in your side and look how quickly it has healed. Now you have a cracked skull and while not as bad as a fall from the stands, still you are walking around like nothing happened. I'm not sure, but something isn't right and it still has to do with keeping you healthy," Jake declared.

"That's why I pay you the big bucks, so you can think of these things to keep me up at nights worrying."

Everything that Jake and the technicians had been working on was being transferred to Marbella, Spain. They were going to assemble everything there and collect the remaining amount of money and head back home. They had done some simulation training for their customer and more of the same would make it possible that another month or so of training would be enough to get the Spanish Army ready to use the fiber guided missiles. The train trip from Valencia to Marbella was going to consume an entire day, so everyone enjoyed the comfort and used the time to recharge their batteries. At a rather long stop in Granada, Evan decided to take a chance and call Ronnie and if possible the kids, first to see if she would still talk to him and Evan needed to make sure Dickey hadn't killed his son and daughter. Ronnie was a problem and he could understand if she was finished with him and would cross that relationship bridge when he got back. He bought a cell phone at the station and got her on the first ring. "Hey, Ronnie! It's Evan."

"God! It's good to hear from you. You are such an pig! I don't know why I even care for you!" This was a good sign.

Other than the "pig" part, she sounded like they might still have something special going on.

"I didn't mean to leave like I did, but I was only putting you in danger and probably within hours of closing the plant down."

"I finally realized that, but it still hurts that you couldn't trust me."

"I trusted you, but not the FBI. I thought they would use you to get to me."

"You were right on that as well. You knew exactly what was going on, while I trusted the SOBs," Ronnie told him. "Before we go any further, have you hooked up with Jake?"

"Yeah, all of us are riding to Marbella to do the final assembly. We should be home a few days after that."

"I wouldn't count on that. Yesterday, I had the privilege of meeting the head of New Eden and he said that you and Jake would be going through some events where even I was needed," Ronnie told him.

"You're kidding! How do you know he was for real?"

"He gave me a name at NSA and I checked it out to make sure. It verified a few things that made New Eden look a little more positive. They really have a good track record, but it's not shared with any other agency. Evan, I was told things that the Director of the FBI doesn't know. Maybe even the President. I wonder what the guy who runs New Eden has planned for you."

"So far, other than the smack down I got, the project has gone without a hitch. Maybe it's not related to the FOGM project at all, but something else."

"I can't say for certain, just please be careful and watch yourself."

"By the way, what did the head of New Eden look like?"

"He was a guy in his sixties and very vibrant and sharp. His Name was Dr. Alfred Johnson." Almost immediately, the phone started to fade. It hadn't been charged and Evan was using whatever juice was in the battery.

"I look forward to seeing you." Evan yelled over the static. He then said more to himself than to Ronnie, "I love you, girl, be careful yourself." He knew he had to talk this over with Jake and see what he could figure out. One thing was certain. "New Eden" or whatever these guys called themselves had something big going on and Evan and Jake would be in harm's way.

\*\*\*\*\*\*\*\*\*\*\*\*\*\*\*\*\*\*\*\*\*\*\*\*\*\*\*\*\*\*\*\*\*\*\*

Jake had mentioned having had some food before he boarded the train, but Evan was a little hungry, so they went to get something to eat in the restaurant car. As they sat in the restaurant car, they could hear the train wheels clicking rhythmically under them. "Jake, I talked to Ronnie and she said she met with the head of New Eden."

"From what I remember of the stories, I would say that Ronnie has been in the Texas heat too long or your turban is too tight."

"She said they'd contacted her and she would be needed to work with us."

"On what? We're almost finished with this project, and after that, we leave for home."

"I know it's crazy, but she said they would be using her along with us and would see us soon."

"Now my curiosity is way up," Jake nodded, picking at his food. "What the hell are we doing that Ronnie would be needed in Europe?"

"I was hoping you would have some sort of idea."

"None. Who did she said she met with?"

"Some old guy named 'Alfred Johnson,'" Evan told him.

"Alfred Johnson? Not Dr. Alfred Johnson?"

"Yeah, she did say he was a doctor."

Jake stopped eating his fig treat and paused, looking lost in thought for a split second. "Did she say how old he was?"

"She just said he looked to be in his sixties. Why? Do you think you know the head of New Eden?"

"Impossible. When I started working after school at the medical instrumentation group, it was guided by this consultant group. The head guy was a Dr. Alfred Johnson. He let Dr. Hernandez do the operations side and he just looked at everyone's work. He would be in his late 80s or 90s, if he was still around. I must say working with you just creates wave after wave of excitement."

"You will pardon me if I don't share in your enthusiasm."

"I wonder if we're going to be crossed up in Marbella. Everything has been too easy and laid back. They say that this is for the Spanish Army to support NATO, but you and I know that NATO doesn't use FOGMs. I have to say, taking into account all the parameters; we may be looking at an issue on where these FOGMs are deployed."

"Do we have the manpower to operate these missiles with the people we have on this train?" Evan queried.

"No. We need the interface guys to fix the parameters of the fiber spools to the missile software. That would have been done on the follow up."

"How soon can we get those guys over here?"

"We could have the three of them along with the coil engineer here in two days," Jake responded after a beat.

"I just got this phone and it needs to be charged. I'll call and get them to Marbella ASAP."

"That's a lot of expense, if they don't need to be there," Jake reminded Evan.

"I would rather be safe than sorry." Evan went off to charge his phone.

\*\*\*\*\*\*\*\*\*\*\*\*\*\*\*\*\*\*\*\*\*\*\*\*\*\*\*\*\*\*\*

Jake began planning the sequence of what they would need to do if they had to arm the missiles. The idea that Alfred Johnson would be the same guy Jake knew just wasn't possible, but Jake somehow knew it couldn't be mere coincidence.

How could Dr. Johnson look so young? Plastic surgery or whatever people did these days would be the answer. For the original Dr. Johnson to head up such a secretive and powerful organization made sense in one regard. Dr. Johnson was a very capable person, but someone would have had to have known Johnson while he worked there so his consultant group couldn't have been New Eden. If his group was that much in the open, then it was impossible for them to be unknown at this point. Jake decided to keep these thoughts to himself and do some research on his own. His main concern right now was to determine what they would need if they were to see live action. Jake's concern was with their team's safety and their company sustainability.

Although she doubted, Evan realized it, Ronnie heard every word he'd said. She finally knew where he really stood. If she had any issues about going with New Eden, such were dispelled now. The issue she was struggling with was first, did she care enough for Evan to go down this road. Second, if she did undertake this adventure, she needed to plan for and to take a leave of absence from her position as Sheriff. She knew she was trying to kid herself. She either loved that idiot or she didn't. If she did, then she was all in and her life as it was today was going to change forever.

Ronnie was a very organized person, this trait started when she was a child. Her father, who was an officer in the Jag Corps, ran the household with a very steady hand. Ronnie continued that into her professional career. After finding the last bug placed by the FBI, she was sweeping the Sheriff's office twice a day. All of her officers had learned long ago that you couldn't argue with her because usually, she was right. She made her rounds of calls and decided to get a bite to eat at a local sandwich shop. The tables were family style, so she took the one furthest away from the entrance, implying to anyone looking for conversation that she wanted to be left alone. She could also watch the door and part of the street. Her salad was nice and crisp and she was looking at the arrest notices from the night before. Once in a blue moon, you would find that a person arrested for disorderly conduct was also wanted in a murder investigation. Everything was supposed to be cross-checked by a computer, but all the information was entered by people who might have a reason to accidently leave information off a record.

"Do you mind if I sit at your table?"

Other than being irritated with the intrusion, Ronnie could only say, "Sure, be my guest."

"You're the Sheriff of McKinney, aren't you? I saw an article about you in 'Texans Magazine.' Are you still dating that basketball player?"

This was a nightmare, she thought. Maybe Ronnie could arrest the nosey woman for being a drug dealer and then say it was a mistaken identity thing. "Yes, that was me, and no. I'm not dating that basketball player." Ronnie thought it was strange that she didn't say she wasn't dating anybody. Damn that Evan! He was screwing with her and he was ten thousand miles away.

"Well, you are better looking in person than the photos in the magazine."

"Thank you. You just caught me on a good day."

"My name is Claire Huxtopole. It's so good to meet you."

"Same here, you mean like the TV character?"

Claire got up from her seat and went to the chair next to Ronnie. "Ronnie, I'm from New Eden," she said very quietly, making it look as if she were exchanging gossip and throwing off any curious onlookers. "By the way, Doctor Johnson is thinking about changing our name to New Eden. He thinks it's a little more progressive, versus 'AHD,' which stands for Advanced Human Development. We used the name openly for years, to get funding? But once we went underground, the name went with us. He wanted me to relay his thanks for the inspiration."

Well, this was certainly a change in routine, Ronnie thought. "Give the good doctor my regards and remind him that I wasn't the one who came up with the name."

"He knows, but wants you to take credit for it."

"Can I ask why you're here? Please don't try threatening me, because I have had enough and probably would shoot first and answer the required questions later."

"You will never be threatened by New Eden again. The reason for my visit is to prepare you for what's about to happen. Evan and Jake will be in danger soon enough. That is not where you will be needed. Mr. Cannon is an integral part of something bigger and will need another point of view and your expertise to succeed. If he doesn't succeed, then people from many countries will suffer major consequences."

"Where will this danger come from and how can you protect him?"

"Can't give you specifics. Not to keep it from you, but I just don't know all the details. In this stack of papers are law cases on specific issues that you should know inside and out. It doesn't pertain to the present situation, but in the near future. Think of it as a homework assignment. You will be contacted later about meeting up with Jake and Evan." The woman pushed an envelope of paper toward Ronnie. And just like that, she got up and walked out the door, as if nothing had happened. Ronnie looked at the first page. It had a list of laws and what they were about and a corresponding state associated with each.

"What the hell is this?" Ronnie mumbled under her breath. Then, she grinned. She at least had something to prepare for, besides thinking about the dangerous position that Evan and Jake were in. She needed to get to Brenda.

\*\*\*\*\*\*\*\*\*\*\*\*\*\*\*\*\*\*\*\*\*\*\*\*\*\*\*\*\*\*\*\*\*\*

He was an all American kid growing up in Ohio. He became a great athlete in high school and went to Ohio State and started as their tight end for four years. They won the National Championship and he would always be remembered as the guy who caught the fourth down pass to keep their game winning drive alive. A bad knee kept him from the NFL, but Uncle Sam was happy to have him. His ROTC background allowed him to be commissioned as an officer, and before long, his talents became apparent in the intelligence arena. Working hand in hand with the CIA, the next step was a logical progression. The group that targeted him was the most select and secret in the World. There was no official recognition, since the group didn't exist on paper. They called themselves the 'Alpha and Omega Group,' informally sometimes AO for short.  They were either the start of everything or they ended it. Unlike many support organizations, they answered only to the Office of the President of the United States. Once a day, their director had a meeting with the President in order to discuss any directions or projects that needed assistance.  The Group fell under the umbrella of FEMA. There were only thirty-five members in the group and a maximum of one hundred fifty people that knew of the Group's existence. That included the lucky ones that managed to make it to retirement.

The Group had tests that most Navy SEALS could never complete. It took both extreme physical and mental toughness to join. Their final test came after graduation. While believing they were on their first assignment, they were captured and tortured. If they spoke at all, uttering any words, then they no longer belonged to the team. Those that passed wore those scars as a badge of honor. For Owen, the physical training was never the issue. Football had taught him to push his body beyond what he felt was the breaking point. The hardest part was the mental testing and training regimen that they seemed to be under at all times.

Most people could go weeks without really thinking only reacting to their environment. Members of the Group were taught to be thinking about every little detail and how it fit into their mission and the consequences of their actions. Owens's current mission was very routine. He was in charge of finding and shadowing Evan Cannon. The only reason the Group was involved had to have been the presence of AHD; the name itself was a highly guarded secret. This wouldn't be the first mission where the Group had tried to capture someone, anyone associated with AHD. Finding Evan at the last minute before Evan had boarded the military jet to Spain was pure luck. Owen had to give Evan credit; the fellow could be very resourceful and focused. Evan's dossier stated that he was a good marksman. That was a huge understatement. In Owen's discussions with people who knew Evan, a great many said Evan could take a pistol and fire consecutive bullets through the same hole. Owen also found out that Evan was loyal to those in his inner circle. Owen thought Evan would have made a great football coach. Unlike some of his targets, Owen respected Evan Cannon. It would be too bad to have to liquidate Mr. Cannon, but that was the usual outcome for these missions. Now, Owen had to find him again.

Owen, disguised as an old man at customs, helped Evan gain control of his sidearm, but this also allowed Owen to tail Evan to the train. Owen's berth was two away from Cannon and he had two bugs to place in Evan's berth. His assignment was to follow, observe who he talked to, and capture him if he needed to keep him from disappearing.

It never happened. Evan started walking along the cars, and suddenly Evan had three people involved with some type of altercation, where one person died and his prey sustained a pretty wicked concussion. It was a gigantic FUBAR as far as he was concerned. Owen saw the back of Evan's head as he was throwing up, and in general, not making much sense. He never saw any of the people he talked to or how he got clocked. Everything was after the fact. To make matters worse, Evan disappeared again before Owen could tag him with some of his bugs. The last intelligence report said Evan had sustained a cracked skull and was traveling to Marbella, so Owen went there, too.

# Chapter Thirteen
# The Deployment

JAKE AND EVAN HAD DISCUSSED ALL THE ANGLES THAT THEY needed to consider for the project deployment and Evan shared all the details that Jake didn't know, from leaving the US to getting clobbered on the train. Finally, Jake said what had been on his mind. "The person that Ronnie met? Doctor Alfred Johnson? I think I know him."

"Have you been holding out on me?"

"Not really. You remember the company I almost went to work for when Anita died in the car crash?"

"Yeah, a high tech think tank."

"Basically correct," Jake said. "But, they were really interested in the workings of the mind. Doctor Alfred Johnson was the company president at the time and I got to know him pretty well. I doubted that Ronnie's contact could be him, because Johnson was over seventy at that time -- years back. It would make him around 90 if he was still living."

"It does make it improbable, since Ronnie was pretty adamant that the guy was very energetic. Not many ninety year old guys have that kind of capability."

"If you think about what they are developing, then maybe it's not that farfetched to believe he could have slowed his aging process down."

"Do you think that is even possible?" Evan asked.

"Hard to say," Jake responded, shrugging his shoulders. But so many advancements could bring about an anti-aging breakthrough, especially if the New Eden people are as far along as shown so far."

The conductor came through and announced the train was entering Marbella. Evan went to grab his bags.

"I'm not sure if this is the same Alfred Johnson or even if he will help us if it is, but just maybe, it's a bit of intelligence we can use to our benefit," Evan announced.

"I don't know, either. Let's just get this job done and get home," Jake declared.

"You got that right." At that, they fist bumped and left the train together, ready to tackle the World.

After a fairly long taxi ride from the Marbella train station to an industrial center, Jake and Evan rolled up to a warehouse in a taxi, where most of the equipment had been packed for shipment. They met two ordinary looking men inside a room that would be considered Spartan, with enough chairs for eight people and a few tables. A telephone and wall outlets rounded out the furnishings.

Evan came in, looked around and stated, "Nice place you've got here." Sarcasm was never to be avoided, if Evan had his way. In reality, Evan was wondering if this were where the purchasers planned to shoot him and Jake or give excuses for why they couldn't pay what was owed.

One of the men in uniform came through a side door, stepped forward and introduced himself. "I am General Carlos Ruiz. I command the Spanish Foreign Legion."

Evan and Jake looked him over. Ruiz had three stars and seemed very fit and young. Jake spoke up. "I didn't know you guys still existed. You were formed in the early twenties to fight in Morocco, right?" The General beamed. Evan assumed people usually said they'd never heard of the Legion and went right on talking.

"You seem to know quite a bit about the Legion. Si, we were formed in nineteen twenty and still have ten thousand well-trained men, ready to deploy at a moment's notice. Most of my men are in Croatia and Afghanistan, but we always have a contingency left for emergencies. I'm surprised you know of us."

"I always like to read up on the elite fighting forces out in the world." The general was already thinking how this meeting was going better than he had hoped.

"Allow me to introduce you to my friends from the Turkish government. This is Abdullah Sezer. He is the finance minister." He introduced the man closest to him and then introduced the gentleman furthest away. "The gentleman on my far left is Adriano Suarez. He is our lawyer, so you won't be taking advantage of us." Everyone got a chuckle at the lawyer's expense; they shook hands and introduced themselves.

Mr. Sezer started the discussion as they all found a seat around a table. "Gentlemen, thank you for going above and beyond the requirements for the FOGM missile system. There is a problem, however, we need to do the initial deployment ASAP in Turkey. Do you gentlemen think that would be possible?"

Evan knew this was what Jake and he feared. "The problem I see is that, according to the contract, we have two to three weeks after final delivery to do training and the set-up. We do so under non-hostile conditions. And if I'm hearing you right; you want it now, and I'm not sure what conditions we could expect in Turkey."

General Ruiz spoke up, "We did not say anything about setting up in a war zone merely changing the venue to Turkey from Spain."

Evan realized he had jumped the gun a little when he heard them change the location. He was a little paranoid about the safety of his men.

"What are the conditions and where in Turkey are we talking about? We like to keep the training in a classroom environment, so the participants can learn and review their mistakes on a computer, with others watching. Peer pressure works in this case and they can learn from each other's mistakes."

"The area about which we speak is in Eastern Turkey, gentlemen, and would be in the field at final deployment."

"Let me discuss this with my Managing Director," Evan said. With that, Evan and Jake walked away from the other three men and tried to figure out the options. Jake was okay with doing it, but wanted to make sure that they had the right compensation, if anything turned hostile. Evan agreed and they both decided on a number for the training venue change.

"Okay, let's go over what we are agreeing to. One, you pay us now for the entire contract amount, which includes delivery of the missiles and fiber pay-out spools. We also expect payment now on the master control center. Normally, that's done after training, but since we are compressing the schedule, we'll need that upfront as well. We are doubling the training cost to cover the expedited fees, and we will expedite the change of the End User Certificates, which, of course, will be paid by the buyer."

Evan placed both hands on the table and looked the three men in the eye. He said very slowly, "If we run into any combat conditions while personnel from Cannon Electronics are in place, we expect the total price to increase by a multiple of five." Neither man gave a reaction, just agreed to the terms and started making changes to the contract and making instructions to wire money to Cannon's corporate account.

Evan was relieved. So obviously, this wasn't the threat that Ronnie had warned them about. Sezer and Suarez showed Evan and Jake the bank deposit for what had been agreed upon and all shook hands and walked away from the "spectacularly furnished" negotiating room. When they were outside, Jake turned to Evan. "For some reason, I think I should be at the training site."

"Why? Do you think they will double cross us?"

"Not that, there's just so much at stake. Even though, I've tested these chips extensively, but just want to make sure Murphy's Law doesn't spring into action at a critical time."

"Wow, as much as I want to get back home, I guess I'll stay to the bitter end, too. Someone has to watch out for you!"

With that, Jake looked over to Evan and patted his head. "I didn't get clobbered by some whacko like you did."

Evan sneered and said, "She's dead meat." Then he rubbed his own head under the makeshift turban. It itched like crazy.

*******************************

Dr.'s Johnson and Hernandez surveyed the data on the sheets spread in front of them. "So the virus really works like we wanted." Johnson, still studying the sheet, said, "This is as close to playing God that I have ever come. I pray this doesn't get implemented. If we miscalculate any variable, we could change the dynamics of the World. Please make sure we have everything tied up and in sequence."

"Are you concerned that the US will not go along with the proposal?"

Dr. Johnson dropped the sheets on the table and looked at Dr. Hernandez. Johnson was suddenly filled with despair. "I'm very concerned about how they will react. More than any other country, they have been the ones willing to step in and take the body blows that these conflicts generate when left unchecked. Doesn't seem fair, but as we have said before, life isn't fair. Getting back to the Turkey issue, how are the missiles progressing?"

"Everyone is on schedule and we should see it initiate in six days," Hernandez supplied.

"I'm sure that will stir the pot to boiling and soon enough get this resolved," Johnson said nodding.

"Are you sure you personally need to escort Miss Green?"

"Maybe not. But I don't want to take any chances. She will make the right decision when faced with the consequences. Also, she's an attractive woman. That's always a plus. When we get to my age, it's the little things in life that bring us enjoyment. Besides, I need to get out more and see the results of all our work," Johnson added smiling.

\*\*\*\*\*\*\*\*\*\*\*\*\*\*\*\*\*\*\*\*\*\*\*\*\*\*\*\*\*\*\*\*\*\*

Another man was looking at the results of his work. A guard, his limbs at awkward angles, was lying in a pool of blood. When found, it would appear as though he had fallen from the roof of the building, and that was how it was supposed to look. Owen had made murders look like tragic accidents more than a few times and had come to think of his work as an art form. He spotted Jake and Evan going into the building and made pictures of the General and the civilian. The photos had been downloaded to his NOC, located back in Virginia. Soon, he would receive information as to who these men were and what they did. His organization was extremely efficient.

Owen was actually a Captain in the Army, temporarily assigned to FEMA. That covered up any personal questions that might occur. Since personnel from the Group were undercover about ninety-five percent of the time, they collected pay from FEMA and their service pay went to direct deposit. FEMA was the ideal place to put any organization that the government wanted to hide. Their office was located away from Washington and lots of money went in and out due to all the disaster areas in the World. If any member of the group ever retired, he was usually pretty well off financially. The problem was getting to retirement. Average time in the Alpha Omega Group was twelve years; personnel usually die in the line of duty.

The best story Owen had heard originated in the first years of deployment of "AO." President Regan started the program to help him do what was necessary to end the Cold War. One of the AO had been captured in Afghanistan, while showing a local tribe how to set traps for Russian tanks. The Russians captured him because he went unconscious during the firefight. As soon as he came to in prison, the AO man killed the two guards sent to bring him in for questioning. He didn't try to escape; he just sat in his cell. They thought he couldn't talk for the longest time. They would shoot him with animal tranquilizers from outside his cage, bring him out, strap him in a chair, and try to get who he was and where he was from. He must have spoken during his unconsciousness, but every time he woke up, he took out at least one guard. Finally, the rebels overran the compound and he was freed. The Russians, who were still living when he was freed, were treated to a barrage of curses in their native language and shot dead. The AO man came back to HQ and worked in the training group. After 9-11, he was sent back to an area of Afghanistan that was pro-Taliban. Three weeks later, the same tribe was leading the charge against Bin Laden. The AO man's name was Ron and nobody knew much beyond that.

\*\*\*\*\*\*\*\*\*\*\*\*\*\*\*\*\*\*\*\*\*\*\*\*\*\*\*\*\*\*\*\*\*

Owen received a return email on his phone. The Spanish General was Ruiz and the other men with him were from the Turkish government. Owen had heard of Ruiz as had most elite fighting unit personnel in Afghanistan had. Ruiz had a good reputation and his Foreign Legion was an incredible asset that very few people knew about. When everyone came out of the building, Owen checked to make sure Evan was the guy in the turban. He got information that Evan received a cracked skull in the train episode and was wearing a wrap. It made him very easy to pick out and follow.

Owen could read lips and, with the aid of binoculars, eaves dropped on Evan's conversation with Jake. "So he's going to Turkey and not back to the States," Owen said to himself. It helped him to remember if he repeated what was said out loud. Owen left his vantage point, found an exit door leading into another storage area and casually changed his make-up, his look. Information on where and why everyone was traveling was needed and Owen had to keep his identity secret. He assumed the guise of a young environmental activist. He loved acting out different roles. He could deliberately piss people off without any probing into his background. Also, nobody wanted to mess with putting an activist into jail, so the activists got ignored for the most part. He would try his act on the General and his aides, just to see how far he could go.

Jake and Evan sat at a table in the far corner of a local bar studying a map. Evan was drinking Carta Blanca beer and it was a Coke for Jake. The establishment actually had internet available, so Jake had his computer hooked up, looking at maps online to see if they could find this village in Turkey. The area they had to set-up the FOGMs was just outside of a small village named Yuksekova. Not much around it, in fact, they would be trucked in after flying military transport from Mersin. This was a desolate area and maybe that made the most sense. They could practice shooting these off in the middle of nowhere and nobody would either see or hear them. General Ruiz had said his government wanted this weapon to be incorporated into the Legion as a front line strategic deployment system much like the tank that was used today, except a better bang for the buck.

*******************************

Evan was still bitter about the testing they had done a few years ago for the US Army and how the Army had rigged the outcome to favor a new assault tank verses using the FOGM. Granted, it didn't have all the advanced functionality that the FOGM had acquired since, but with very little development, Evan's company could have gotten there pretty quickly.

Jake decided that was water under the bridge and he could move forward. Then Jake made a note on the exact location and turned to Evan, who was drinking his beer and looking at the people entering and leaving the tavern. "Evan, do you see how close we will be to the Iranian border?"

Evan looked at the map and made his own calculations. "We are going to be less than ten kilometers from the Iranian border. If we go with the idea New Eden is involved, that could mean two different strategies. First one is that they plan to hand over the equipment to the Iranian Army, once we're gone. Second scenario is that they have it placed there to guard against a possible threat, if things ever get out of hand. Since we haven't heard any news about a Middle East hot spot happening, I would go with the first strategy."

Jake never liked to jump to conclusions without data, but this time, it sure looked like Evan was right. "I have no evidence one way or the other, but if it looks like we are doing this training and there's even a little chance of them turning it over to the Iranians, I'll put a bug into the software that will crash the entire system."

"Good idea. I hope we don't have to do that, but something is just not right with all of this New Eden involvement and a Spanish company buying military hardware headed to Easternmost, Turkey," Evan said, shaking his head.

"You keep forgetting the part where another group is attacking you and your family, along with the arrest warrants from the FBI, and probably CIA, NSA and the Post Office."

"I think I'm safe from the Post office for now," Evan chuckled. "The rest will probably die down once this is delivered. I just have to be careful getting into the country. As far as the killing part, I haven't forgotten, all I want is some answers," Evan said.

General Ruiz came down to the bar for the obligatory snack, drinks and hospitality with the Americans. He wasn't in a very good mood. One of his soldiers had fallen off a rooftop and died, when he was supposed to be on guard duty. That, in itself, wasn't the issue, but the alcohol Ruiz had smelled on the dead soldier made Ruiz furious. It was a total dereliction of duty and Ruiz would have killed the fellow himself, if he could have. Once he reached the bar, his demeanor changed and he greeted the Americans visitors warmly.

Ruiz admired the technical man considerably. The Spanish government literally had nothing on him, but the performance the man named Jake had built into the FOGM was most impressive. The one called Evan -- Ruiz didn't really like the fellow. He seemed to be like every American that Ruiz had ever met -- cocky, arrogant and brash. Ruiz was informed that several attempts on Evan's life had been tried and that Evan's ex-wife had been murdered. Maybe, because of that, American security groups were also after the man. Ruiz was able to overlook some things, but not much. The thing that really irritated Ruiz most was the turban that Evan wore. Evan looked as if he was trying to flaunt something and Ruiz couldn't understand what or why.

He could see that this night could get ugly if these Americans weren't going to be upfront with everything. "Hello, my rich American associates!"

"Good evening, General," Evan replied.

"Evening" was all that Jake said as they all shook hands again. Evan started rubbing his forehead and scratching underneath the turban.

"You better leave that alone. It will never heal if you keep rubbing it," Jake cautioned.

"May I ask why you are wearing that turban?" Ruiz queried.

"I sometimes forget I have it on until it itches like crazy. I had a little incident getting into Spain and ended up fracturing my skull. The doctor had me wear this, to protect my skull, but for the past two days, it's itched like crazy."

General Ruiz smiled, at last having the rationale behind the ridiculous looking turban. "I suspect that there's a good story behind that and expect for you to tell me before we are done here."

Jake snorted his soda while suppressing a laugh.

Evan seemed to ignore him. "It's a long story, without an ending so far."

"Before we leave tomorrow, come by my office and I'll have my doctor look at it. He may be able to put something less conspicuous on your head.

"I'm for that. By the way, what time is the military transport leaving tomorrow?"

"We'll leave at fourteen hundred hours and the rest of your group will leave at seventeen hundred hours, with the equipment," Ruiz informed them.

"General, this may be something you might not want to hear, but I have to ask. Why is the Spanish Legion going into Turkey so close to the Iranian border?"

Ruiz would have put Evan in his place after that question. They had been paid a lot of money and where they went was of no concern to them. Somehow, though, the tone of the question hadn't been threatening, but curious. Also, after hearing about the fractured skull, Ruiz suspected another attempt had been made on Evan's life. Ruiz didn't press the issue. "No, as you can see from the maps, we are very close to Iran, but think of it as a deterrent. It will be protecting a country against a very unstable government," Ruiz explained.

Evan and Jake both looked at the fire and determination of the General. Evan decided that, for now at least, General Ruiz could be trusted.

In the next instant, a young guy stumbled into the bar, wearing an old Army fatigue blouse with rainbows patches and peace signs above and below the name tape. The man approached the General with a stumbling gait. Evan knew some Spanish, but couldn't understand the man's slurred speech.

It was obvious, however, that General Ruiz knew what was being said and was getting very angry. The drunk pushed the General into Evan and Jake. General Ruiz was a blur of motion, flipping the drunk onto his side and keeping him pinned there on the floor until the bouncer came over to usher the man out.

Owen broke free for a moment, punching very quickly at the General's chest with his middle knuckles extended, impacting right below the General's sternum, and as his fist moved upward, it hit right below the ribcage. Then Owen twirl before anyone could grab him. He lunged for Evan's pistol, hidden from most persons in a shoulder holster under Evan's left arm.

Perhaps ninety-six out of one hundred times Owen could have grabbed the pistol, but when he reached for it, Evan had already pulled it. It was cocked, held close to Evan's body, its muzzle in line with Owen's heart. Owen froze. Evan's actions answered a question. Owen could tell that Evan Cannon would pull the trigger without hesitation.

Owen's drunken act came back as quickly as it had left as two bouncers pinned his arms together and marched him out.

"I see he was a friend of yours General," Evan said, grinning as he holstered his pistol.

"Definitely, no friend of mine. The eho de puta is a peace activist and they think they can do whatever they want to get their point across. Do you have all the proper permits to carry that gun?"

"Yes. And I have to say, carrying a gun legally for a private citizen in Europe is not an easy thing to do."

"Your reflexes are very good. Would you have fired at the man?"

Evan didn't know himself, but if these attacks had taught him anything, it was to act fast. "Probably would have shot his ear off."

"That's not an easy shot especially with a stumbling drunk."

Jake advised, "If Evan had wanted to, he could have parted the prick's hair without touching his head."

"Is that right?"

"Maybe, but when push comes to shove, I'm a pretty fair shot."

"If we get any free time, you and I can see who is better."

"General," Jake began, "I like you, but don't shoot against Evan for money. You might as well just give it to him instead of being embarrassed, and you'll save on wasting ammunition."

"Now, that's a challenge I want to have."

Evan just shook his head and grinned. "We'll just have to make some time," He told Ruiz.

\*\*\*\*\*\*\*\*\*\*\*\*\*\*\*\*\*\*\*\*\*\*\*\*\*\*\*\*\*\*

When Evan woke up, he answered emails for only the second time since he'd left the US. He skipped all of the ones that started, "You are in serious trouble…" or "Under the authority of..." Evan figured he was where he was supposed to be, he had a job to do and he would see it through. Consequences would be dealt with later. He answered all of Ronnie's emails first, then Brenda's and finally, the banks' emails.

Before long, it was time to see the doctor. He made his way over to the General's office. Ruiz's doctor was in the next building. The Spanish Foreign Legion had a lot of bases and most were independent of their main army units. Evan was relieved that the doctor spoke very good English.

The doctor removed the turban and plastic plate and x-rayed Evan's head. After what seemed only a few moments, the doctor came back in and showed Evan the results. "A little unusual, in that you have no fracture now. I can see where the break was, due to the calcium build-up around the break, but it couldn't have happened four to five days ago."

Evan fished a card out of his wallet that had the doctor's name on it, the physician who had treated him when he got the fracture. He had saved it for this very reason. He gave it to the doctor, asking him to call the man.

The doctor left for about twenty minutes, came back and said, "I have never seen anything like that before. It's almost like some miracle potion was rubbed on your head. The other doctor gave me the specifics and even emailed a close up of the fracture. It's gone now, so other than the temporary bald spot you need to cover to keep from sun burning, you have no restrictions."

Evan was becoming used to these miracles occurring around him, but also leery of unintended results. "Thanks, Doctor. I have no idea why, but will accept any improvement I can get." Evan walked back, very pre-occupied. This had to be because of New Eden again, but how were they able to make it happen? He packed and walked with Jake to the transport.

Owen was able to get away fairly easily from the two men that had him pinned him down the previous night. A change of clothes and a ticket to Mersin, Turkey, and he was on his way. Seeing the computer screen with Mersin on it last night was extremely valuable. Now they were in an area where no mistakes could happen. He needed to be on his game, to make certain he could complete his mission.

# Chapter Fourteen
# The Set-up

Jake, Evan, and General Ruiz were arguing over the proper placement of an attack system like the FOGM while flying to their destination. Jake looked out the jet's window, to gather his thoughts, when he saw it. "General? What the heck is that being built down there? It looks like some type of pipeline."

The General peeked out the window quickly. "That is the new pipeline that carries oil from the Baku oil fields in Azerbaijan."

Jake looked over to Evan and almost at the same time they came to the same conclusion.

"General, why are they building this pipeline so close to Iran?" Evan inquired.

"Mr. Cannon, that pipeline has been a thorn in the side of OPEC for several years. They have moved it more times than I care to remember. It's close to Iran, but not anymore so then the existing pipelines."

"General? What do you know of a group called New Eden?"

Ruiz shrugged his shoulders. "I never heard of them." He smiled and added, "I assume they're not some American or British rock group. Correct?"

Evan continued. "To make a long story short, there have been several attempts on my life and most of them have been thwarted by a group that the FBI calls 'New Eden.' Whoever tried to kill me was successful in killing my ex-wife. Now, all of this started once we entered into the agreement to supply these fiber guided missiles. Jake here was given state of the art microchips that allow the video features to work in the controller. Think of them as supercomputers in an environmental hardened chip. We have even been warned that there will be a major conflict using these missiles. So, in light of everything, how did you get involved with something that is being resold from Spain to Turkey, and have you run into any odd circumstances while working on this project?"

Ruiz put his hand on his forehead and shook his head. "This is the most obtuse project that I have ever come across." He went on to explain that his commander had asked him to put together this system and have it bought by a third party. It's very unusual, that we would buy a system using that particular method. Also, a fiber optic guided missile isn't what I would recommend, anyway. I mean no offense. We are an elite fighting unit. Why use us as a way of buying unconventional weapons. In NATO, countries are always buying for others, so the money trail is not unusual. The real reason that I am a little worried is what we needed for camouflage for your system. We were requested to add reactive armor to the cover. Nobody admits to putting that into the specifications. But we actually found something that was too 'state-of-the-art' for me to think it only happened by sure coincident."

Whatever reservations they had between each other dissolved in their discussions, Jake thought. He shared the technology advancements of the FOGM and Ruiz talked about the armaments they were bringing to the site including some weaponized robots that were so advanced that there was thought that they would lose them to the main Legion. Ruiz was especially interested in the New Eden group and their interaction in the whole project from Evan's protection to Ronnie's discovery.

Owen's flight was the same one that Evan Cannon and Jake Bryant were booked on, and when the flight attendants were ready to close the door neither man was aboard. Owen started to consider the changes in his mind. Had they missed the flight or could they have re-booked something a little more expensive, such as first class? He knew they were going to Mersin, but if that weren't the final destination, Owen could lose them in Turkey or wherever they were going.

Owen jumped up from his seat, grabbed his bag and ran to the front of the aircraft, explaining in Spanish that his wife had just gone into labor and he needed to get off. Of course, the flight crew was happy to oblige. Childbirth was one of those few events for which people would usually go out of their way in order to help. Owen had found that to be true every time he needed a quick exit.

Once in the terminal, he called his station and asked for an update on Cannon and Bryant.

"Their reservations were just cancelled, and as far as I can tell, they aren't booked on any commercial flight to Turkey," the voice on the other end of the line informed him. "I'm switching you over to the level three "group" to see if they can find anything out from their end."

Each intelligence area had a separate group number and worked only in its own specialty. Level three dealt with the military and government intelligence gathering operations. Once each group added their own information, a summary of possible scenarios was presented for the operatives. The field guys called the list 'menus.' It was a list of actions an agent could take for his next step. It wasn't always a quick process.

At present, Owen wanted information more than he wanted a list of actions he could take. "We have him traveling to Yuksekova, Turkey, on military transport."

"Let me guess; it's with the Spanish Foreign Legion?"

"You get a cigar."

"Where is Yuksekova, anyway?"

"It's near the Iranian border."

"Alright. Put me through to General Davis." General Davis was the military leader of the AO group handling the thirty odd agents of the Alpha and Omega group on a day to day basis. His rank was sufficient to get favors done in a timely manner and for interfacing with the President. He didn't have any real peers and dressed mostly in civvies.

General Davis picked up almost immediately. "I just chewed out the bunch in level two. How could they let you stay on that aircraft for so long when it became apparent that Cannon and Bryant weren't going to board? I think I need to replace the whole damn bunch."

Owen knew the general had a very bad temper because he himself had crossed Davis many times early in his career. He was glad to be on the soft side of the argument.

"I need a flight to Yuksekova pronto."

"Easy there, Buckeye. The equipment won't be there for three days, so you don't have to get into a panic. Remember, once you are out there, there's no fitting into the background. It's very sparsely populated. You will have to move under the cover of darkness and find our prize and bring him back." "Buckeye" was the nick-name everyone called Owen back at HQ. He thought it was a little ridiculous, until he met the guy from Ball State. He was very glad he went to Ohio State.

"I can get you to Mersin and you can take the train to Yuksekova. If anything breaks, we'll contact you." Every agent had a satellite phone that he could use anywhere. It was coded only to the agent's voice. Losing the phone wasn't an option. It wasn't just foreign "companies" that they didn't want to eavesdrop on them, but also any other US intelligence group. The AO Group worked with no one but themselves. If they had information that was pertinent to a catastrophe, like 9-11, they would pass it along without anyone knowing where the intel had come from. That was how they operated. He needed to get over to a private plane that was going to take him to Mersin.

\*\*\*\*\*\*\*\*\*\*\*\*\*\*\*\*\*\*\*\*\*\*\*\*\*\*\*\*\*\*\*\*\*\*\*\*\*\*\*\*

Evan was finished explaining the murder attempts on his life to Ruiz and told him and Jake what the doctor told him in Marbella. "Somehow, they gave me something that can heal the body very rapidly." General Ruiz was leaning forward with his elbows on his knees.

"I'll tell you this. I wish you had kept the turban."

"Why? Because I would look more like an Arab?"

"No, because it's always good to see how foolish Americans look when they go overseas." Evan enjoyed the joke. A brief shot of comedic relief was what they needed.

Jake spoke up. "Remember how I told you I might know this Dr. Johnson?"

"Yes, but you said it couldn't be him because he would have been too old," Evan answered.

"After what you just told me, I think it's him. You see, he and Doctor Hernandez were both very interested in how the human mind worked. They were consulting to the company I worked for when we built the first Positron Emission Tomography machine." Ruiz asked what that was and Jake explained it was one of the first PET scanning machines that had been developed -- except they didn't use radiation to mark their targets, but an electromagnetic pulse. The project was shut down, but Jake gave examples how the same technology was used today on modern Medical Resonance Imaging machines. "Johnson and Hernandez were after how things worked, not why. The 'why' wasn't their goal."

"I'm not sure I understand," Evan said.

"Nor I," Ruiz added. "But I didn't want to say anything because I thought my English was moldy."

"Rusty," Jake noted, clearing his throat. "You mean 'rusty.' Okay, the goal of the company I worked for was to make a PET scan machine that was three generations beyond what was coming out on the market. Johnson and Hernandez only wanted to know how it worked in the body."

"So you know and worked with the World's most wanted terrorist?" Evan supplied.

"Hard to believe, but adding all the stories together, it has to be them."

Evan turned to Ruiz, "Should we contact someone?" "Impossible, since we can only communicate with satellite phones, Ruiz informed them. "We have a set, but they aren't initialized. We need to get our communications up very quickly, and if I'm not mistaken, we will have to get your FOGM systems up and running very quickly."

"I was serious about putting my company's employees at risk. Any shooting and I'm charging you an arm and a leg."

Ruiz seemed to be pondering his response. "Mr. Cannon, I don't think we are in any danger. I think what we are seeing is a step taken by this New Eden group to guide the world into another direction."

"Ruiz, I hope you are right. Until we land, I'm going to sleep," Evan announced, smiling.

Before long, General Ruiz and Evan were asleep. Jake was too unsettled to sleep. He didn't do much of it anyway, so after getting some coffee, he went back to his seat and saw that Evan's blanket had slid down. He reached over and put it over his friend's shoulders and tucked it in.

Ruiz had nodded off, but was fully awake, wishing he weren't. He'd watched as Jake "tucked in" Evan and wondered how Evan generated such dedication. The technical team of Cannon Electronics seemed to worship Jake and Evan by proxy. Ruiz had noticed Jake and Evan never told anyone what to do, merely what was needed. It might be enough for engineers, but Ruiz was curious what would happen if any real pressure were exerted.

Ruiz knew his men would and had followed him into hell, but these two hombres made a unique team and Ruiz wondered what roles they would all play over the next few days.

Ruiz didn't believe what he told Cannon. He knew they were going in harm's way, but Ruiz had no idea how and that part bothered him.

It wasn't long before the jet began its approach to the airfield. Cannon, Bryant and those few members of their team were wide awake and strapped in tightly, the crosswinds at once strong and erratic, a potentially deadly combination, Ruiz noted to himself. There was no sense frightening the civilians. Yuksekova was located in the mountains, but was nearby a wide valley. They were able to land on the first pass, without more incident than some bumpiness.

Ruiz was surprised how the two Americans just took the landing in stride and joked about how they cheated death one more time.

The next two days were busy with Ruiz's men setting up the base camp, bringing communications online and securing their position. The Cannon team brought in and established the FOGM armament. Evan and Jake were still having a conflict resolving why the Spanish Foreign Legion was in Turkey and with over one hundred fifty men. These weren't garrison and support personnel, but a hardened frontline battle group.

Every time Evan and Jake talked to Ruiz, they got the same story: Ruiz was ordered to bring this company with him while testing the missile system. Jake immediately began to set up their group and control systems in the trailers that had already been installed on site. Dan Wong was Cannon's lead tech and in control of the system operations. Jake was there as the system expert. He didn't want to interfere with Wong's plan. Jake trusted Wong with their multi-million dollar program.

Evan was there for one reason only: if anything went "wonky" with this deployment, he would be the one to order the pull-out. The strangest sight, which had everyone talking, was the camouflaged tents that covered the trailers and the payout tubes. The color seemed to change with the amount of light that hit it.

Evan grabbed a section and held it to the sun.

"Surprised by the weight?" Ruiz asked, smiling.

"It seems to change its color in the light, while being very light. I doubt it will last long during this exercise."

Ruiz laughed and grabbed a loose section and took Evan into a rocky draw. He placed the section over a tree and marked a circle on the side and placed a can behind the mark. He walked back to Evan, who was about thirty yards away. "You say you're the expert. Hit that can behind the circle."

Evan could easily see the outline. "What part of the can do you want me to hit?"

"My friend, just hit the can first."

Evan took aim and fired and the bullet hit the tent material and didn't go anywhere else. "What the hell! There is no way I could have missed that."

"You probably wouldn't have, but that material stops small arms fire and even grenade fragments."

Evan holstered his pistol and went to the tent material. He could see the mark made by the .357 caliber bullet, but the projectile never made it through the material. In fact, the bullet was lying on the ground in almost pristine condition. "This is impossible." Evan declared.

"You don't see half of it. Thermal images won't go through it, nor will radar pick up any signatures. The material seems to take the energy it receives and force it back to the object."

"Impossible. It's against all the laws we know of concerning energy."

"You can imagine my surprise when I found this out for the first time as well. It will make for very protective covering for the entire operation."

"Who manufactures it?" Evan wanted to know, thinking of the possibilities.

"Look like you found your magic chip, a distributor brought the fabric to us."

"What was the company's name?"

"Creative Industries. Not a very big company, but they were given the material to build our coverings."

"I don't see a connection, except for the fact that neither product should exist. By the way, does that terrorist group in Spain have a sister group in Turkey? Is that why you have frontline troops versus garrison support?"

"You mean ETA, the Basque group has been fighting for independence for more than thirty years. No, we captured the leader of that group and all they can do now is set companies up for protection and extortion. Pretty much like your mafia in the US cities. I keep telling you I was ordered to bring my men on this exercise and simulate how we would deploy during an emergency. I know you have a hard time believing that, but those are my orders."

"Okay, General, I won't mention it again."

"Good! Now it's time for, as you Americans like to say, kick some butt time." Evan turned and gave him a strange look.

"I want to challenge you to see who is the better marksman."

Evan gave Ruiz a lopsided smile and said, "Let's get the ground rules down."

"Rules?"

"Yeah. Like, what are the betting stakes and payment terms?"

Ruiz placed his arm around Evan's shoulders. "I admire your confidence," Ruiz told him, smiling.

\*\*\*\*\*\*\*\*\*\*\*\*\*\*\*\*\*\*\*\*\*\*\*\*\*\*\*\*\*\*\*\*

Owen was more than a little upset. He had to hike into this mountainous area under cover of darkness in order to attempt to find where the Cannon missiles were being deployed. All of his assets were left behind and his only lifeline was his satellite phone. He had found out that the Spanish had set up the camp, but the satellite scans which had picked up the images one day could find nothing the next. His worry was that, if there were a hidden railroad spur, they could move their position to another location. The other explanation was they had it moved into caves. Either way, Owen's job was getting more complicated.

It might come to bringing in some additional assets to accomplish the mission while Owen moved on the next assignment. He hated that scenario and wasn't going to let it become reality unless he had no choice.

**\*\*\*\*\*\*\*\*\*\*\*\*\*\*\*\*\*\*\*\*\*\*\*\*\*\*\*\*\*\*\*\*\*\***

Evan entered the cool, air conditioned trailer, followed by an upset Ruiz.

"Jake, Ruiz owes me his first born. What is the price for human slaves?"

"Ten to life, if I'm not mistaken" Jake said without looking up. "I told you not to bet him." Jake turned around in his chair, facing Ruiz.

"I have only lost to two people in my entire life when shooting a pistol. He has ice in his veins – not blood."

"Okay. I'll let you keep your son, but that dinner in Paris is still on." Ruiz walked away, obviously going outside in order to find someone upon whom he could take out his frustration.

"Have you really looked at this material?" Evan asked Jake. Evan went on to tell him what Ruiz had shown him and how it stopped Evan's bullet from penetrating.

"I'll have to look into that later. While you were out gallivanting around, I've helped Wong on the set ups."

"Any issues?"

"No. Went like clockwork. We just needed to test the gimbals for tilt and calibrate the gyros and GPS chips for distances. Now, all we have to do is check our software startup procedure, and then we will be ready to go. Training should be easy and we can head back home in three days."

"I know that's the plan, but there is just too much happening for me to think that everything will go without a hitch," Evan confided.

"And I bet money that New Eden will show up before this is over as well," Jake said.

Evan was turning that over in his head. They both were leaning against a bench inside the mobile control center, essentially a construction trailer with reinforced walls and fancy electronics. Then Jake jerked his thumb that he wanted Evan to follow him out. They walked until they were out of hearing range of all the people around the camp unless sophisticated electronics were in play. They sat on a smooth boulder. Neither man said anything for a time.

Jake picked up a stick and started to make zigzag streaks in the dirt. Evan knew not to fill the quiet time with idol talk. It was Jake's way to gather his thoughts before he spoke. "Here's the way I see this. There's an attack group that will be coming from Iran to take out that new pipeline. We were sent here to stop it without us even knowing it. I doubt even General Ruiz knows that is why they were picked to do this exercise."

Evan nodded his head in agreement. "As usual, I think you pegged it. Ruiz doesn't suspect anything, and if he does, he won't admit it."

"Evan, my first thought is to get all of us out of here as soon as possible. But the problem is I don't think we can. We can't train these guys in fewer than three days, and if we wait until real bullets start flying, we can't get out without probably being shot by the Iranians. I also don't think we have three days before everything hits the fan."

"Well! That's some good news you thought of, friend!" Evan placed his arm around Jake's neck and gave it a gentle squeeze. It was Evan's way of letting Jake know he believed him and would somehow get all of them out of this mess. "Before I go to Ruiz and tell him what you think any last words of wisdom?"

"Yeah. Ask him how the Iranians will attack. They probably have a defense plan for this theater of operations."

"Good point! Let's see how one hundred fifty men can hold off an attacking army of fanatics, like the Greeks did against the Persians, maybe."

"Yeah, but we want to win this time, and not have a movie made about how bravely we died," Jake added. He gave Evan a wink and headed back to the command center.

# Chapter Fifteen
# The Attack

**THE GROUP OF MEN WERE STANDING AROUND A MAP WHILE** General Ruiz, his aide and platoon leaders were explaining the different ways that they could expect an attack to occur. Evan and Jake had done everything they could to convince General Ruiz that an attack was imminent. He checked his intelligence groups and it seemed that a small Iranian force of around five thousand men and equipment had disappeared. This always caused great pain to the intelligence groups, especially since they had been only two hundred kilometers from the Turkey location.

General Ruiz took all the intelligence information along with his own suspicions and released a deep sigh. Then he said, "If the Iranian force does make a move on the pipeline, I am about ninety percent certain we can narrow their route to this pass. The terrain will squeeze them into this narrow valley, which means, the Iranians will probably try to get a brigade through here before the Turkish Army can mount any defense to stop them from hitting the pipeline. With the element of surprise and speed on the Iranian side, the Turkish Army couldn't really stop them before the enemy reached the pipeline in sufficient strength to accomplish their tactical objective."

Jake spoke. "I have two questions. Why would the Iranians destroy this pipeline when it helps one of their allies, and second, isn't this a suicide mission? A group this big will be discovered and eventually destroyed by the Turks?"

"You are correct on both counts, amigo, except our original assumption of which pipeline they plan to destroy. I believe they are after the one that is pumping oil from the Iraqi fields that go directly into Turkey. It makes sense that the force that they have to be there, will be long enough in order to destroy the entire pipeline, by using nuclear isotopes, perhaps. And then they will time the devices, so that they go off at various sections of the pipeline, completely ruining the pipeline forever. A dirty bomb set off every one hundred miles would render the pipeline, the land near it, and perhaps, even the fields at the far end of the valley, a nuclear wasteland for generations. After that, the Iranians would have to fight to get back home, but the mission would be accomplished and they would probably be able to convince themselves this was some sort of Jihad, and dying would actually be an improvement."

Evan asked about the strike force. "For it to happen as soon as our thinking seems to indicate, I would say they must have the missing five thousand somewhere within sixty miles of the route they plan to use, which means they are very close to us right now. That is something that we should be able to find out. They will use some jets as cover, and helicopters will be the way they come in to clean up any opposition. Okay, if we feel pretty good about our capabilities, then, let's make some decisions and get our force into position."

Jake looked up from the map. "Why aren't there any major Turkish troops or units stationed here?"

"There is no reason to do so. This is similar to the US border with Canada. I have contacted the Defense Ministry in Turkey, and there are lots of 'red tape,' as you Americans say, but I am anticipating a return call today."

"If we could keep the jets away, we could defend this area." Both Jake and Ruiz looked at Evan as if he had been out in the sun too long and was saying gibberish. "Hey, we have enough missiles to take out tanks, armored personnel carriers, trucks, command vehicles and even helicopters thirty miles away or more. That puts the Iranians in this pass with nowhere to flank us."

Evan was drawing an arc on the white board, from their position to thirty miles out. "From what I've seen of that material," Evan was using his arm to point to the protective tent material, "they will have a hard time finding us. When the helicopters get close, we can take them out."

Jake nodded his head, saying, "I think you're right. We can set two of the launch pads to go after helicopters. The rest will hit vehicles. It actually could work, as long as there are no jets bombing away or strafing us."

Ruiz sounded unconvinced. "I have not seen a tethered system yet that was at all effective against helicopters."

"You just keep the ground troops off the launch site and I'll show you how to do it," Evan responded. "Just to make this clear, we have to speed up your training because we are not going to be anywhere close to this location, if the bullets start flying." Evan's jaw was set and Ruiz eyes registered that he understood what Evan had said.

"I'm sure we'll have support here and your company can make their exit safely," Ruiz assured Evan.

They continued to work on the plan for another couple of hours before everyone went back to their tents. Evan was mentally exhausted from taking every scenario and deciding how they would react. The plan was solid, and since Jake and Evan understood the system's capability, getting Ruiz to trust that capability was half the battle. The only hole in the plan would be air cover from Iranian jets. There was no reason to believe an attack would take place except the missing five thousand man unit from Iran. Better to be prepared than "caught with their pants down," Evan knew. In that way, military operations were not much different from business.

Evan was soundly sleeping in his tent when Ruiz started shaking him awake.

"Cannon. Wake up! We must get you and your men out of here."

"Good God, man! Can't you wait for me to get my beauty rest?"

"We have a problem. We cannot receive or send any radio signals. Our communications are down."

Evan was sitting on the side of his cot and rubbing his face with his hands, trying to take in the information that was just presented to him.

"We have the Sat phones, General. Will they work?"

"No. We think most of the radio "comms" are being electronically jammed."

"What does this mean?"

"It means we do not have much time remaining before we can expect company."

"Ahh!...I hate when I'm right and didn't do what I should have when we had time."

"There is a chance your men could escape, but if an attack does come, I would be concerned with your group being exposed in the open. At least here, we have some protection."

"Have you told Jake?"

"I did. He continued at his work and told me to wake you and tell you myself."

"Alright. Let me talk to my guys," Evan said, yawning.

Evan and Jake addressed the engineers and technicians. Some had military experience, but the initial reaction to his news was shock, which didn't surprise Evan. But after the shock, he was surprised at how the people seemed to relax. They could be in harm's way very quickly. Evan offered to get all who wanted to leave out and to the village. None wanted to go. They were as crazy as he and Jake. The next thing to do was going to be the hardest. He needed to call Ronnie and the kids and tell them what he thought could occur, but that wasn't going to happen. No communications capabilities.

Evan was glad for the nap, because sleep wasn't going to be easy to come by that night. They went to work putting miracle cloth over every vulnerable area and setting up defensive positions. Those who were free were moving rocks, setting up traps, blocking walking trails and doing anything to make it harder to get to their position. The work was hard, but it seemed that everyone realized it might save their lives. And if they had a week, they could have built some really impressive breastworks, but they only had a few hours, and by the end, they knew they were going to be exhausted. Evan's shirt was soaked with sweat and he was reminded of working on their family farm.

There wasn't any alarm clock, but Evan didn't need one. He had rested, but never slept. He suddenly marveled how soldiers were able to be ready to fight for weeks and months on end. Light was beginning to break through and muffled whispers outside Evan's tent weren't a good sign. Evan rolled out of bed, he had slept in his clothes, and pulled on his boots and went out to see the latest situation. General Ruiz was giving orders to one of his officers. He had made a point to include Evan in all their strategies. They walked up to Evan. "While you had your beauty rest, we have had some unfortunate events unfold."

"How am I going to get better looking if you keep waking me?"

The General smiled and said, "We can agree on that, amigo. Two hours ago, helicopters came in low and dropped troops in the three passes. The closest was ten kilometers away. Another dropped troops to the northwest, about fifteen kilometers and to the southwest at twenty-five kilometers. They don't know we are here, but they total about two hundred men. My men put out sensors that will allow us to know their troop movements along the roads. If they don't use the roads and use the goat trails, it will be useless. As you Americans like to say, 'We could be in a world of harm.' We have to have anyone capable of firing a gun protecting our perimeter."

Evan had butterflies in his stomach. He replied, "By the way, the expression is 'a world of hurt,' not harm. I will need to get my guys on those controls and free up more of your men?"

"Yes. And, any of your people who have combat experience would be helpful."

"I'll go tell Jake. He might have some more ideas."

"I have already told him."

"Okay. Do you have a spare rifle I can use?"

"First, are you sure you want to do this? Second, can you fire a rifle like you can your pistol?"

"Yes. No. And those guys in there are my men. If I can protect them, then that's what I'm going to do."

"Make that two rifles," Jake said coming up from behind the General.

"Can you shoot a rifle?" Ruiz inquired.

"I grew up in Texas. If you couldn't shoot, you moved to somewhere else."

"Whoa, partner! Shouldn't you be in the control center, figuring out how we're getting out of this mess?" Evan suggested.

To Evan, Jake's look was as solemn as Evan had ever seen. "I owe you everything because you have looked after me like a mother hen, but you can't protect me this time. Besides, Wong and I were working on a few things that might help us get out of here in one piece." There was a quiet calm between the two.

Ruiz interrupted the silence. "I will show you your positions, and take some of the protective material with you. Hold your fire until you hear us firing. I expect them in about thirty minutes, and after that, we can expect the other two groups to converge. It's going to be a long day, gentlemen." General Ruiz gave them a salute and walked away.

Jake and Evan watched as they were directed into position and shown their fields of fire. Evan remembered his grandfather's story of holding a bridge during the Battle of the Bulge during WWII. He somehow thought that he would be proud of him today.

\*\*\*\*\*\*\*\*\*\*\*\*\*\*\*\*\*\*\*\*\*\*\*\*\*\*\*\*\*\*\*\*\*

Ronnie was at her desk when she got a call. "You need to meet me at the airport in one hour. You won't be coming back for at least a week." The man hung up after that.

She shook her head. No "hello" or "good morning" -- just jump." More than anything else, that pissed her off. She always felt it was demeaning and didn't mind calling people on it. Now, she had to make the decision to do what the man said. It wouldn't be because of love for Evan, but out of duty to see this through. At least that was what she told herself and it wasn't really too convincing. She had already put her arrangements in motion. She just needed to pull the trigger.

\*\*\*\*\*\*\*\*\*\*\*\*\*\*\*\*\*\*\*\*\*\*\*\*\*\*\*\*\*\*\*\*\*

A man she didn't recognize – older, like Johnson -- was waiting for her once she arrived.

"Who are you?"

"I'm Dr. Hernandez. Alfred couldn't join us. Don't worry. Everything is on schedule and I'm up to speed on the events."

She carried a small bag of legal documents and personal items, as instructed. She walked straight to the aircraft. The door was opened and she could feel the blast of cool, nice smelling air. It reminded her of the forests of Washington and Oregon. Hernandez was waiting at the top of the stairs and before she could say anything, he apologized to her about his abruptness.

"I will tell you where we are going and why. The "how" may not always be understandable. I will say that Evan and Jake have proven their worth, but may need some help that you can give them. However, we will address that as we're in flight." Ronnie wanted to know everything, so she could help, but realized that this was way out of her league.

"I will do everything I can to save Evan and Jake, but don't think for a moment that I won't come after you, if I think it will save them."

"Bravo, young lady! That is exactly what I wanted to hear. Let's get out of here and head to Turkey!"

"Turkey?! What the hell could be happening in Turkey?"

"Nothing, if we have our way."

Ronnie sat in the front couch. It had everything one could imagine. There were no seatbelts, which was more than a little surprising. The cushions themselves seemed to hold her as they accelerated off the runway. After they reached altitude, which wasn't long, one of the passengers came up to her and showed her what was at her disposal and how to operate whatever controls she might require. Any food that she wanted could be made and plenty of fruit and snacks were delivered to her table.

\* \* \* \* \* \* \* \* \* \* \* \* \* \* \* \* \* \* \* \* \* \* \* \* \* \* \* \* \* \* \* \* \* \* \* \* \* \*

Owen was tired, hungry and in a foul disposition. Never had his group missed travel connections and lost communications, as they had on this mission. He couldn't use roads, except at night, and even then, he almost got caught when a crazy Turk thought he was stealing livestock. He had found a pathway from time to time, but generally, such would dump him back on the road. So Owen stayed in the shadows, moving carefully during the day, trying to make up the time during the night. Breaking a leg was a real possibility, so he kept a steady, but safe speed.

Morning was just breaking and Owen couldn't believe it, but there was terrain in front of him that looked very much like a farm valley. If he could just find something that resembled real food, he could get back on track. Owen took advantage of the high grass and made his call to HQ or "The Puzzle Palace" as it was called. Luck was with him; he was able to get through. "Can you tell me why I haven't been able to get through for the past thirty-six hours?" Owen, all but spat into the secure satellite phone after submitting his code number.

"We aren't sure, but it appears that the problem is on your end."

Owen gave out a loud disgusted sigh while holding the mute button. "They must know I'm coming and blocked the signal."

"We don't think that's possible."

"Possible or not, it is happening and we have yet to catch one of these guys."

"Concerning your pursuit, we found the Spanish about ten miles away at heading seventeen degrees north. They seem to be entrenched, but there are no signs of the FOGM missile launchers."

"Could they be in a cave, where they roll the launchers out as needed?"

"That's our thought, so proceed with caution. This is either a well masked exercise or you are going into a hornet's nest."

"If it were easy, you wouldn't need me. Has the mission changed? He was still to observe and look for possible New Eden contacts?"

"Yes. And, if necessary, use Level Five force."

"Roger and out." Owen didn't like this new turn of events. He was just instructed to use necessary force to eliminate support and capture New Eden contact. This could get very messy and he wasn't looking forward to an evacuation plan that went through Iran. He decided to stay in the grass and keep a low profile and run in stretches. He would stop and use his thermal instruments, along with binoculars. Owen wasn't really expecting any threats, just wanted to stay away from any locals. He passed a few goat herds and even had his hand stepped on by a particularly heavy goat. But, Owen was able to avoid any detection or disruption of the herd. The government had spent a great deal of money on him being able to blend into his environment, and he was very good.

During one of his stops, he took a sip of water from his bottle and was about to take off on a run, when he spotted a group of people angling down a hill, toward the road. He waited for a minute and pulled out his binoculars, to get a closer look.

These weren't locals, because they wore uniforms. He checked the insignia and realized that they weren't the Spanish Army also. They could be part of the Turkish Army, in some sort of joint exercise. Then he waited for them to come closer before moving again because He did not want one of them to spot movement or reflection. The army came very close to Owen, but he was not spotted, and judging from how careful they were in reviewing their options, before they entered the road, it appeared that they were serious about their intentions.

"Who in the hell are these guys?" Owen said to himself. He followed them from a half-mile away. They had a two man rear guard that kept vigilance for anyone or thing coming down the road and they were about a quarter mile behind the main unit. Owen counted seventy-five men, and oddly, they were marching in formation. They were making good time. It was odd to see them march so confidently.

Owen dropped back and fired up the telephone again. The response he received wasn't what he wanted to hear: Follow the men until he needs to break off the trail and look for the Cannon group. That was just great news, since Owen had no idea where they had hidden themselves. Then a thought occurred to him. He verbalized it. "These guys in uniform must be trying to link up with the Spanish Legion."

That was the only explanation. There were many consequences when it came to his job, so his decisions had to be right. After following the uniformed men at a safe distance for about an hour, two jets over flew the valley. The uniformed men raised their caps and waved. Owen could see that the jets' markings were Iranian. He also started to hear gunfire in the distance. The wind was bringing the sound toward him; otherwise, he doubted if he would have heard it.

There was a short burst at first, soon followed by the steady sound of machine gun fire and individual rifle fire. Owen noted. Someone was in a firefight and these troops were on their way to join the fray. Without warning, two explosions detonated within the troop column. Owen almost fell backward because of the suddenness. He was afraid of the noise he'd made, but realized he didn't need to be worried.

Owen found his binoculars and swept the area. It looked as if almost every man in the column were dead. Body parts were scattered around the twin holes in the ground. A few bodies were crawling, but they looked like they had been hit by shrapnel and couldn't stand or walk. There were about ten men left standing and gathering around one man. They were talking very frantically, it seemed, and pointing to the area where the sound of fighting was coming from.

They took off at a run away from the road and spread out to avoid another hit like they had received. Unless those were bombs from the jet, they had to be missiles from the Spanish Legion. Since the jets were cheered by the troops, it looked like the Spanish troops knew what they were doing. When it was clear, Owen went down to the fallen soldiers. The sights of slaughtered men still had an effect on him. He had killed numerous people with his bare hands, but to see the life taken away so suddenly and brutally had a very sobering effect on him. He picked up an Iranian copy of a SIG 226 9mm pistol with a few magazines and one of the Iranian copies of a Chinese Type 56 AK-47 rifle. Also, he gathered up some spare thirty-round magazines for the rifle, and as he looked to see if he could find some sort of orders or intel, he discarded the useless materials and kept the shoulder strap-fitted canvas bags for carrying spare magazines. He saw nothing recognizable as a field ration. Owen decided to give up on his search and call in the latest intelligence. Maybe he was witnessing the start of the next Middle East war.

Evan could hear the gunfire and realized that he and his people might not see tomorrow's sunrise. He bowed his head and said a prayer. No time like the present. At one point in his life, he had been a very devout Christian, but through the years, had given up most of his disciplines. He still believed and now more than ever he needed help. When he was done, he saw Ruiz running in a crouch toward Jake. They talked for a minute and Jake waved to Evan that he was going into the bunker. At that, two jets over flew the camp. They were Iranian.

"Of course, we can't seem to catch a break. Why wouldn't they send in their jets?" Evan said out loud to himself.

Ruiz was running zigzag patterns from Jake's position to Evan and jumped into Evan's small foxhole. "Not a nice day for a stroll, General Ruiz"

Jake almost said the same thing. "We have engaged the Iranian pathfinders. They have retreated, but I know two other groups have received orders to come this way."

"So we can expect another one hundred fifty men?"

"Unless Jake can whittle down the odds and find the troops before they get here."

"Jesus, Ruiz! We fire off those missiles and those jets will zoom on back here and make mincemeat out of us here."

"We have to take that chance." At that, four missiles left the launchers. Evan and Ruiz both looked at them take off, Evan still amazed at how quickly and how far the missiles could go, tethered to a fiber cable.

Ruiz was seeing it for the first time. "Are you sure that doesn't break the fiber?"

"Yes, but I don't see how we will be able to find those reinforcements. We made it possible to control the speed, but still need to get the missile in the general area where you want it to go."

"We know where they are within a few meters. We deployed sound and movement sensors that we were going to test later in the week. I guess now is better than later."

"We'll soon see," Evan nodded.

At that, Ruiz left in his low crouching run, zigzagging across the open expanse. Evan heard muffled explosions and wondered if Jake had had any luck. The jets were coming back; ready to release their firepower as soon as they found a target. Two were closing in, while two more were barely visible to the north. Their pilots would know missiles were fired and were looking for the launchers.

Evan wondered if the netting was going to work. Actually, he prayed that it worked. All four jets were circling base, hunting for a target. They must have gotten ground information because the jets started to fire their missiles into the Legion's defensive positions. The ground rocked with the energy of explosions, spraying stone, dirt and debris everywhere.

Evan looked up and saw that the team in front of him was gone. His practical sense said they had moved to another position. He knew in his heart that they were gone. Fear held him back, and wondering up to this point if everything would work out. He had had enough. He remembered his wife and the shoot-out at her home and whatever fear he had was replaced with anger. He had placed innocent civilians at risk in order to build a business. He had lost those close to him, and now would probably lose his life. Hell, he thought. He'd even lost Baxter, and that was the last straw. He picked up his two pistols and the M-14 marksman's rifle and ran to the area brave men had defended only moments before.

Through the dust and smoke, he could see men running up the hill, attacking. They were about two hundred yards away and he was going to make his rounds count. The first two men he hit fell but crawled away to safety. They had to be wearing armor. Evan thought. "Okay," he said under his breath. Then, he would just hit their legs and heads.

The attackers were coming en masse. He didn't hear the machinegun and figured the enemy must have silenced it in the last pass. It didn't matter. Evan would take as many as he could. His aim wasn't as good as before. And he cursed himself. "Slow down, damn it! Take your time." Then he started hitting his targets. They weren't coming as rapidly or as boldly as in their previous charge. The Iranian's return fire wasn't directed to him yet, but he knew it would be soon.

Before long, it was quiet again. Evan knew these moments were the calm before the storm. He wondered how many Legionaries were left. The jets came back. And of course, he knew the enemy's jets were going to shoot the defenders in order to support whatever ground assault the attacking troops were planning. That was in every country's plan of action since World War II. It was a good plan. Don't use men, when a bomb will work just as well. One of the jets started its run, but never made it within striking range. A missile flew from the netting and hit it before it could even swerve to miss it. The fireball was the prettiest thing Evan had ever seen. The other jet banked quickly to the north. Another missile was released, following it. It was a question of speed, maneuverability and distance. If the jet could move faster than the missile, its pilot was safe. In this case, the Iranian jet could not match the FOGM missile's speed, especially when, at launch, the missile and its target were within a quarter of a mile of one another.

So the pilot started to pitch and roll to no avail. The second explosion was further away, but was still a fantastic feeling.

"Jake, you did it!" Evan yelled and didn't care who heard it.

The Iranians didn't like to see their jets go down, but they had to have seen where the missiles had come from. This was definitely true because the Iranians started pouring fire into the net area. However, they had no idea that it was useless, but it did pinpoint their position, therefore, the Legion returned fire.

Evan didn't see the group of men that were circling around him until they were in place. They were going for the launch pad, he realized, and didn't have any intention of being stopped. Evan saw the stones rolling down the embankment. He couldn't hear the cascading rocks with all the noise around him or the five men climbing down. Then, apparently, at about the same time, he spotted them. Evan brought his rifle up to his shoulder. From a crouch position, Evan fired off three short bursts.

The first Iranian fell on his back and the other two fell in the next instant, landing awkwardly after being shot in their legs. None moved to defend themselves, so Evan ignored them for other targets. Evan jumped out of the rock hole he was in to get better protection behind a rock outcropping. If more troops came from above, he would be in a more naturally defensible position. It was a bad position if he needed to defend the entrance to the control center, however. Suddenly his rifle was shot out of his hand and broke into two pieces. He grabbed his two pistols and realized his right hand had been hit. He drew out his 9mm twenty-one-shot custom made handgun and was going to go down swinging.

He stood up quickly, but smoothly, and turned sideways. His hope was that they would miss because they would fire in a hurry. It didn't matter; he fired at the two men that he'd ignored and hit both in the face. He dropped down and checked for wounds. His right hand was bloody and too slick to hold anything. He knew he only had one chance to return fire if there were men in front of him coming down the cliff or behind him that would target him for death. Then another burst hit around his back. This time, Evan leaped to the side and lunge his pistol forward to get off one more shot. The soldier was firing at the rock hiding Evan and had started to walk his fire to where Evan landed. Too late for the Iranian, the bullet hit him in his leg. The man dropped his rifle and Evan's next shot hit him square in the face.

Evan ducked back over the rock and into his foxhole and looked for any enemy on the hill and the cliff in front of him. Maybe a dozen hostiles were crawling into protective slips and Evan thought it was best he take his position down closer to their position. It was actually Jake's old position and Evan placed his remaining magazines and his other pistol on a cloth he spread on the ground, where he could grab what he needed when he needed it. He could see Jake at a position that would be the last point before the control center was breached.

The Iranians were stopped for the moment, but it was hard to tell if they had retreated or were waiting for reinforcements. At once, several missiles left and were sent toward their targets. Evan saw what looked like helicopters. The plumes of smoke and then the sounds of explosions reached Evan, but he didn't need to know what had happened. The FOGM worked beautifully. It was an application that nobody had a defense for, so one helicopter after another fell into burning wreckage. Evan finally knew what General Lee meant when, at the Battle of Fredericksburg, he had said, "It is good that war is so terrible so that we don't become fond of it."

Jake exited the control center and got into position to protect Evan's back; Evan realized that Jake would be the last guy to get past before anyone hit the launchers. Evan was stationed at Jake's left flank, so they were in good position to protect each other. It had been done haphazardly, but still effectively. Evan could see Ruiz running through each position, dodging enemy fire. The Iranians apparently dug in, awaiting new orders. The General, as any commander, was probably checking to see how everyone was on ammo and fine tuning his troopers' fields of fire before the next push. Then Ruiz half-slid, half-jumped into the shallow foxhole beside Jake.

"Did you beat back the Huns -- and now you want me to organize a victory celebration?" Jake inquired.

"Ahh, Jake. It is that short fellow who is rather unkempt and doesn't know how to shave -- the President of Iran, himself -- who wants to surrender."

"General -- not to dispute your report, but it's going to be very hot very quickly."

"Yes, my friend, and that is why I'm here. Can you fire those missiles and hit ground troops if they are within one hundred feet from where we are positioned?"

"I can, but those two jets will see the missiles and come back and give us fits."

"Yes. I am hoping for that."

"Are you crazy, sir? We told you; we can't track a FOGM to a jet very far. We got lucky with the other two. I'm not one to play the odds against us too often."

"If you notice, amigo, those jets slow down when they start painting ground targets. So, if we hit their ground forces around us and deplete their reinforcements, it will bring their jets in for support. We can bring them down in a short sprint."

"Maybe, General. You might have a point. If it doesn't work, we'll be dead anyway," Jake told Ruiz brightly. "They are waiting for reinforcements and those two jets will make sure they drop their armaments into our laps. Let me try. I'll wave to Evan so he knows I'm going inside." At that, Jake caught Evan's attention with a wave and ran inside.

Once inside, the gravity of the situation hit Jake. This wasn't a drill, and if they weren't careful, it would be doubtful they would see another day. It wasn't as if this were a declared war. It was a damn invasion by Iran into a country where the only opposition was a small elite military force that was only there by accident. Prisoners weren't an option. "Well, it's time to earn our pay and see if Wong had any luck on those other toys," Jake said to himself. Jake was able to link his GPS coordinates to the sensors that Ruiz had placed. He would do this himself, since it required some adjustments to his software.

One group of approximately seventy-five men was right on the sensor and Jake released the first two missiles. The platform almost lifted itself off the ground. It was like an "X-box" game. He could see the men and he placed both missiles within the group. The feelings he had after the first explosion were very odd. He knew he had taken human life, but the destruction was also very remote. There was a big screen monitor placed, so every technician had seen the results. There wasn't clapping, but only determination to complete this day and live until tomorrow.

Jake began explaining how to take care of the remaining jets. Whatever radio traffic the invaders were using, the massage got back to their air support. The jets, while cautious about getting hit by the missiles, also had to support this troop advance.

The fighters came in low and fast. Jake and three other operators released over ten missiles. The jets went down much more easily this time and without releasing a single bomb. Soon more Iranian helicopters came onto the encampment's radar and these were dealt with in similar fashion. The targets were now numerous and in position. It appeared that the Iranians were not letting their lack of air support slow them down. The airwaves were alive with chatter that the control center could hear as command vehicle after command vehicle was taken out. The Cannon techs had a priority list of targets and they stuck with those.

Some of Jake's technicians were becoming concerned about the destruction they were reining upon the attack group.

Yet, the battle that still raged just outside their tent flaps brought out their determination. The small arms fire was becoming louder and increasing in frequency. Jake could only get the missiles so close to the camp's defensive perimeter and that meant there were a lot of angry guys at the wrong end of a rifle. What these men didn't know and Jake did, was that, of the one hundred fifty men Legionnaire force that was protecting the technicians, only thirty were still available for combat. Many were wounded and temporarily safe in the compound, protected until the defenders outside were either overrun or, more likely, killed.

Evan was still closest to the FOGM command center and could see Ruiz one hundred yards to his front. Ruiz was tightening their defensive position. Evan's hand was beginning to throb. The bandage that he tried to put on the wound was no help. Jake apparently had his engineers in synch with their duties and plan of action and had decided that his services were needed outside. Rifle in hand, he took up his original position.

"I decided to come out for some fresh air. Could you stand some help?" Jake shouted to Evan.

"Jake, I'm sorry I got you and our guys into this."

"Don't be sorry, we could have left, but Ruiz and his men would be dead and this equipment would be in the hands of those crazy people trying to take that pipeline."

"How are our babies doing?"

"They are performing better than even I anticipated. Some of Ruiz's guys are bringing the new racks in and connecting them up like it was child's play. The only problem is that we may have done too good of a job in taking out the Iranian command centers. The boots on the ground keep coming into these valleys, with nowhere to go, and start piling out of their trucks and carriers before we can take them out."

"That explains why they keep attacking out here. They have a new supply of troops because they don't have anywhere else to go." At that, there began a massive attack almost the width of their line. Without mortars or artillery, the defenders could only lay down suppressing fire from a few machine guns. Those were deadly enough.

Jake brought his rifle to his shoulder and started firing, once the attackers were within one hundred yards. There was no cover, so the attackers were very exposed. It could have been a turkey shoot, except for the machine gun fire. Albeit hard to believe, the Iranians didn't know where the launchers were and didn't direct their attack directly toward Jake and Evan. The attack force split, half toward the launchers and the other half against the Spanish positions. The attackers were close enough to see pass the netting and realize what they needed to do in order to stop the missiles. But all Evan could think of was Ronnie. He was sorry that he wasn't going to be able to keep his promise to her, as he fired his pistol at one target, then another.

## Chapter Sixteen

# Help in Many Forms

**RONNIE WAS DAYDREAMING, LOOKING OUT THE WINDOW.**
Flying afforded some wonderful sights. The first thing she noticed was their altitude. It was almost dark out; and yet, they were still in daylight. She realized they were flying considerably higher than most commercial jets. In fact, she guessed, higher than any aircraft except space exploration and spy planes. A woman with average build and a beautiful face came to Ronnie and asked if she could come to Dr. Hernandez's office. Ronnie was trying to figure why the woman was so pretty. It was her skin -- very smooth, no blemishes and slightly tanned. Just like many on board she saw.

"Can you tell me how high we are flying?"

"We are in middle space, flying at about the same altitude as Blackbirds, except, we can fly here faster and go further than almost anything the USA can put into the air."

"I don't need to know the technology, which I doubt you would give me anyway."

"I'm sure you will have more questions before we are done and I have been instructed to answer all your questions, within reason, but right now you are needed in the Situation Room." Ronnie was a little surprised about the pretty woman's response. But Ronnie followed her to the Situation Room. Then they stopped in front of a white panel door, which opened on its own.

"Ms. Green! How do like our little spaceship? You will notice that the wings have retracted. It's not your run of the mill Gulfstream Five jet."

"How do you keep this whole jet pressurized?"

"Basically, the same as they do on the space shuttle. We just do it better with better technology. I'm afraid we don't have too much time, so if you don't mind if we get down to business? I'm going to show you what is going down between the Turkish and Iranian border."

The satellite map was showing real time information, Ronnie realized. The first impression was multiple forest fires, but once one looked closer, each fire was wreckage from either an armored assault vehicle or transport truck. Equipment was scattered all over the mountain range and it looked like many of the convoys had been destroyed en masse as they tried encroaching on Turkish soil along winding roads not built for much other than a horse cart.

"The big picture is really simple. Iran was going into Turkey to take control of the new pipelines. They planned to destroy the oil pumping facilities throughout Iraq, but not before they took out the pumping stations for the supertankers."

"I don't see how they could do that from the eastern part of Turkey?"

"The Iranians planned to send nuclear warheads down the pipeline, and once they reached their targets, set them off. It would dry up the Middle East oil for years, if not forever."

"Where did they get the nukes that would fit into pipelines?"

"Russia. There's a bigger plan in place and this is the first strike. And after they are finished, Russia, China and Iran would be the only countries left with a healthy economy. Of course, they have no plans to fix the worldwide depression they started. We know where the warheads came from, but that isn't our concern at the present. This is the start of your job. We need to know where those isotopes are located."

"The last time I checked, I didn't have any mystical powers. What am I supposed to do to find these nukes?"

"You can't, but you have a friend, Rachel Thurman, that can."

"Rachel has the highest clearance you can get. We joined the Bureau together and became best friends and stay in touch, but I doubt she would tell me anything. She never has before. We are like sisters and I would do anything for her, but she would die before she told me anything about her job."

"We agree with everything you have said, but you have to try. Are you familiar with ILC or ILS?"

"No. I never heard of either term."

"'IL' stands for 'Intelligence Link,' and 'C' stands for 'Classified,' while 'S' stands for 'Secret.' Think of it as two different internet links, 'Internet C' being easier to access and S being very hard to access."

"I'm putting in the call to her and the commanding general now through ILS."

In about ten seconds, Rachel's computer screen came on line. "Is this Major Rachel Thurman and General Thomas? This is Doctor Hernandez. You know me as part of New Eden. By now, I'm sure you have people tracing this call and I'm fine with that. I have bypassed your security link and have access to your files and folders. As long as you cooperate, we have no reason to access those folders. You can run your seeker program, but it will only be destroyed by our system. Our computers are one hundred times faster and have one thousand times greater storage capacity than anything you work with now. It's a bio-electronic system. If you turn us off, I will only turn it back on, so do I have your attention?"

Hernandez didn't wait for the reply, it was a rhetorical question. "I need both of you to see the satellite real time downloads on your screen. This is a view of Eastern Turkey, where Iran was making a play to destroy a new pipeline and the Gulf ports used to load the tankers. As you can see, they haven't been successful, but we need for you to tell me where the ten isotopes are located in that mess."

In the background, alarms were sounding and people were shouting orders. The most secure intelligence complex in the world had just been hacked into by the most wanted terrorist on earth. General Thomas spoke first, through clenched teeth. "I'm not sure who you are or what I'm looking at, but we'll have agents at your office in six minutes." Ronnie couldn't wait any longer. The longer this went on, the less likely they would meet with success.

"Rachel, this is Ronnie Green. Doctor Hernandez is who he says he is. This has been in operation for some time. You can't touch us; we are in space. I have friends in that mess and they need help."

Rachel's voice was steady and sure, "Who are your friends that are in trouble?"

"Evan and Jake from Cannon Electronics. Evan was being protected by New Eden and Cannon is the entity supplying the equipment that is being used against the Iranians."

There was discussion between the Major and the General. "If you are Ronnie, then you can answer this control question. What was the strange issue with my Aunt Margret?"

Ronnie at first thought it was a trick question, but answered it immediately. "Your crazy Aunt Margret had one blue eye and one brown eye." Maybe three people knew that about Rachel's aunt. General Thomas's plan had to be to keep the conversation going long enough for the supercomputers to get a location on them or even disable their computer.

The General stared at Rachel as if she were someone he didn't know. She looked at the General. "That's Ronnie and, if she says it's New Eden, then I bet it is. What do we do now?"

Before they could get the next thought out, Doctor Hernandez spoke again. "You have an asset in the area following Evan and Jake. He can be the field agent in charge, but you must hurry because the Iranians could overrun the compound and still make it to the pipeline. At the least, the nukes should be neutralized."

Ronnie shivered in fear. She was sure that Jake and Evan were down there in the middle of that battle. Thurman and Thomas must have received corroborating information. "We have the data, pinpointing the bombs," the General announced.

"Excellent! I will be landing close to that area within three hours. I will leave the instructions concerning what to do with your asset. I would advise your asset to follow those instructions." Just like that, they were disconnected.

Ronnie turned to Hernandez, emotion in her voice. "Where are Evan and Jake?"

"They are on site with one hundred and fifty Spanish Foreign Legion troops. I can't tell you exactly what we will find, but we will be there soon."

"I heard three hours. I want to know why you protected Evan, just to have him die in Turkey?"

"I don't know he's dead and neither do you. We will be there in two hours, I fudged it a little and we will see the situation firsthand. We have to get in our seats for the rest of the journey. The pressure of someone in the seats creates a plasma positive pressure force on the passenger. It's like putting your brain on some sort of relaxant, but it feeds extra oxygen into your body. It provides a feeling best described as 'euphoric.'"

"I noticed it, but thought it was just the trip and all the excitement. I just want to say, Evan isn't one to back away from a fight. If he thinks they will be overrun, he's going to fight. You realize that you put him in that situation?"

"This is just the beginning for all of us. I need him alive more than you can realize." Ronnie looked into Hernandez's eyes and realized he was telling the truth.

\*\*\*\*\*\*\*\*\*\*\*\*\*\*\*\*\*\*\*\*\*\*\*\*\*\*\*\*\*

Crouched on a high ledge, Owen was able to get his satellite phone working and was describing the situation. "I can see two columns, about five kilometers apart, stopped and pretty much destroyed. Multiple tanks, APCs, command and control – everything stopped about eight kilometers inside Turkey. There's also a lot of smoke coming further west, so I suspect there's damage there as well." The Group would be making notes and recording Owen's observations.

"Can you tell if the damage goes into Iran?"

"Negative."

"Say again."

"I'll have to climb higher and expose myself to Iranian units that are trying to re-group and mount some sort of attack. Most are heading back to Iran. Can't say I blame them. They've gotten their tails whop today. By the way, where are the Turkish Air Force and ground troops?"

"They were caught looking the wrong way. This was planned so they would have no forces in their eastern area, leaving them very vulnerable. How is this group able to keep Iranian jets and helicopters grounded? Have to think a few attack copters could destroy the center."

"I saw three helicopters destroyed in the air along with at least one jet. Could be more, but that's what I saw. They must be using some kind of fiber guided missile," Owen told the voice on the other end.

"Are you sure they're using fiber guided missiles?"

"I'm almost sure. They took out a couple platoons of troops marching together. We don't have anything close to this capability."

"We just found out that there are nukes in that wreckage about twelve kilometers east of where you are currently."

"Nukes? What in the world were they going to do with the nukes and how many did they bring to the party?"

"Ten and it looks like New Eden will be there in a few hours."

"I have to know how you got that information. By the way, there's a fly in the ointment. The compound is under heavy attack. It's a good bet they will be overrun in about an hour," Owen advised.

"I'll tell you the story about the intelligence source once you get back with New Eden, but that compound can't fall to the Iranians."

"It's not like I can do anything to help. They are being outflanked as we speak. Lay down some cover fire and this party is over."

"How many men are defending the compound and do you think they have any reserve support?"

"The Spanish had over a hundred men to start with, but I only count around forty still returning fire. I doubt there are any troopers in the cave."

"The cave would provide great fire support, allowing a few men to delay and destroy a larger force. They have to have a fallback position."

"I don't think there is a fallback position in the cave, because Cannon and Bryant are in the last position before getting to the cave. They aren't there for giggles," Owen told his contact. "They've made the Iranians pay for every foot the Iranians have taken. The way everyone is firing tells me they are very low on ammunition. Where's the air support? A couple of well placed bombs and these guys are off the hook."

"Long story on that, too, but air support is forty-five minutes out."

"I'll keep you informed, but the Iranians are hammering them at this point. I count seven men ready to lay down fire between the entrance and main body of Ruiz's troops." Owen saw something out of the corner of his eye -- a flash of movement. He switched positions with his binoculars and really couldn't believe what he saw. "What the hell just came out of the opening?" He muttered it more than reported it as fact. "Jesus! The cave walls aren't walls, but great camouflage. Two tanks just burst out of the curtain that I thought was solid rock. They're not really tanks, either, but weaponized robots. They have machine guns -- look like thirty calibers -- on the turrets. The guys driving them must not have a lot of experience, but the fire they're laying down is effective. You should see this! In a matter of moments, there must be ten, maybe fifteen dead soldiers that were going to be storming into the cave or compound. They were caught out in the open. I can start making my way down to the compound. What do you want me to do?"

"Stop the missiles, and see if you can capture the New Eden people arriving there in an hour."

"Roger and out."

"Out and good luck."

Owen still had to be careful. The Iranian soldiers were going to be in a foul mood and he had to figure out another way in. He calculated he could reach the compound in thirty minutes and get into the control system without anyone seeing him. He took one last scan of the scene below. He was anxious to see what toys and technology they had that could stop an entire Iranian Brigade in its tracks. He also wondered why the USA didn't employ the same technology. Maybe it had all come from New Eden.

\*\*\*\*\*\*\*\*\*\*\*\*\*\*\*\*\*\*\*\*\*\*\*\*\*\*\*\*\*\*\*\*\*\*\*

Jake looked at Evan. "How much ammunition do you have left?"

"I'm down to my last magazine for my nine millimeter and out for my 0.45."

"I have maybe half a magazine left." At that, three men kept firing at their position and kept them from returning fire, allowing the maneuver element to their left to take cover behind some pretty large rocks.

"You know what they are doing?"

"Yeah," Jake said. "They're getting ready to clean our clocks. They have moved guys on our left. We can't return fire, and once they get into position and if we aren't perfect..." Jake didn't finish the sentence. He didn't have to. Evan knew what he was saying.

"Why did I bring all of us out here to die?" Evan was despondent. They had no chance to live except to give up and neither man was ever going to do that. Besides, who was to say they would have been taken prisoner. This wasn't a war where they had to keep you as a POW and treat you to any Geneva Convention rules.

"Evan! Don't be a wimp on me now and wuss out. I'll make sure they pay for pissing off a Texan."

Evan managed a smile and chuckled. "Well, if a Texan can kill three, then by God, someone from Virginia can kill at least seven -- maybe more!"

"That's what I'm looking for!" Jake was smiling. He wanted to get Evan into a better frame of mind. Evan realized this. And if they were going to die, they needed to buy as much time as possible.

"Remember the Alamo!" Jake yelled as loudly as he could.

"Just great! You had to choose a battle cry named after a battle that was lost."

"The Spanish didn't think so." Jake gave his lopsided grin and moved to confront the attack that was coming.

The sound wasn't subtle, but not really threatening either. It was behind them, and by the time they turned to see what they were listening to, it took their breath away. Salvation came in strange ways. Coming out of their command center were two large, tracked robots that had twin machine guns mounted on them. They traveled about thirty feet, came to a halt and started firing at the rocks and the men between Evan and Ruiz's command, or what was left of it. It was obvious that the controller wasn't very good, because the robots moved very erratically and the machine guns came very close to Evan and Jake.

The operator may have been a little inexperienced, but twenty-five enemy personnel caught in the open had nowhere to hide. Men fell very quickly. Those who survived ran quickly out of range of the robots, but also out of the crossfire from Ruiz's men. The crossfire and sudden loss of manpower seemed to stir up enough fear that the Iranians were leaving and withdrawing over the embankment where they had started their attack.

The General's troops were laying down fire at the retreating troops, and when both robots got into position, they fired a steady stream into the retreating ranks. Men were dying quickly, and just like that, the men of the encampment held the high ground. Evan and Jake saw the robots up close as they sped by and noticed that they were tethered by one of their spools of fiber cable. A lone man came out from the netting. It was the strangest sight that Evan had seen in a while. One of their techs had the oversized command module on his head. It was cockeyed because he hadn't put a regular helmet under it for support. He looked like a character out of a science fiction movie. He was still working the joystick, controlling the robots when one of Ruiz's men came to take over the controls. He looked at the tech and gave him a huge slap on the back and took off following the robots.

The technician was Wong. Everyone knew him as the brightest man they had in the field.

"Wong? Who gave you permission to tear apart one of our coils and attach it to those robots?" Evan asked in mock anger.

"Mr. Bryant did and showed us how to use the fiber tether versus RF."

Evan chuckled and said, "You just saved a whole bunch of people. I'm not even sure how to repay you for this."

"Sir, there were other guys involved and guys covering other duties, so we could get it running. Mr. Bryant had seen the robots before all of this started and found out they were waiting on the RF control systems that would allow the General's people to control the robots and guard the command center. He suggested we use some of our coils and take an 'X-Box' controller and see if it would work. We got so busy and nobody worked on it until you told us that we might have to fight our way out of here. Jake thought we had better try the robots, before it got too late."

"You're timing was perfect! Thank you for saving us."

General Ruiz approached Evan, Jake and Wong. "I will not ask how you were able to get those working, since there were no controllers. I guess I have seen too many miracles in the past week to be shocked, but I am indebted to your group." Ruiz evidently noticed Evan's hand and the blood drenched improvised bandage. "Does your hand hurt?"

"Not as badly as it looks. I don't think there's any nerve damage, because I can still move my fingers, but it hurts when I move my wrist."

"I suggest you stop doing it and it won't hurt." General Ruiz was obviously happy with himself; he had told a joke at Evan Cannon's expense and enjoyed it. It was likely; he was also happy, however tentatively it might be, because the military situation was improving. But he would still be on guard, knowing that they are probably not out of danger yet.

Ruiz turned to Wong, saying, "I want to shake the hand of a true hero."

Wong was obviously embarrassed by people telling him how great he was. "Thank you, sir.  As I just told Mr. Cannon and Jake, a lot of people worked at getting the robots running."

"Spoken like a true Spaniard! I'll have more for you later." Ruiz turned and left, but stopped after taking a few steps and yelled back, "Let me know the location of the Iranian column. I need an update."

As Jake and Evan waved back to him, Evan said to Wong, "Wong? Were you born in the USA?"

"Yes, sir! I'm an ABC -- American Born Chinese!"

"Just checking. General Ruiz will try to make you into a Spanish hero. And you know something? Let him."

They walked into the control trailer and Evan gave Jake a cockeyed look. "Did you expect those coils could work on those robots and save our butts?"

"Truthfully, I'd forgotten about them, Evan. I didn't even know they had ammo for the machine guns."

Evan knew Jake was probably lying, but it didn't matter. Jake would never take credit for anything, anyway. The temperature controlled trailer was a relief, after being in the field, and Evan wanted to find a shower or even a bunk and lie down, but also knew they had to see if they could find any mass of troops. If they could, he wanted to see the FOGMs working firsthand. The sixty-inch LCD screen was showing the multiple images that the launched missiles were seeing. The array was dizzying to look at the first time, but after a bit, the eyes and brain were able to integrate what was happening. Evan noticed that there were no tanks left to hit and enemy forces were actually retreating, but the missiles were following them and destroying anything that had any significance. They were also doing it on Iranian soil. Evan thought about it for a second and then shrugged it off. "Too late to worry about diplomacy," he thought aloud. Jake was looking at the different stations, searching for more of what didn't work.

The retreat was full bore and very chaotic, however, there were pockets of men in quite a few places surrounding the control center, trying to re-group and form some type of force.

Evan asked, "How is it that we're seeing the battle field this far away? We don't have any drones, do we?"

The tech closest said, "We sent up a missile and slowed the speed back and did a far field view. It wasted a missile, but we don't have that many targets left and it gives us a better idea of where we should concentrate the fire. Is that alright?" They all glanced up at Evan. He had been known to verbally tear into someone when he felt they had done something stupid.

"I can't tell you how proud I am of you guys." Evan looked down; he didn't want them to see him with tears in his eyes. Then everybody went back to their work. Afterward, Evan went behind the consoles, sat down, and starting unwinding his bandage. As he did, Jake came over near him and pulled out a couple of discs that Evan assumed he was going to use to back up the data. They would never have any better chance for real fire information than what had transpired and they could look at the results and make adjustments for future deployments. Also, the same server was sending all of the visual information to the General's harden PC outside. Evan knew Ruiz was making suggestions on priorities. Jake seemed tired and running on adrenalin as he sat next to Evan. "Do you think this system will ever be used again?"

"Jake, after people find out what happened here; the intelligence communities everywhere will want a system."

"Yeah, and there won't be any chips to make the system go. We will have to assign a supercomputer to every launch platform. People will ask soon enough how we were able to get teraflops of data into a format that could be controlled by a simple game console."

"I know, and we also have issues about how we can control speeds, spool strength, camera selection between night vision, thermal and focus length. Hey! There are a thousand and one problems you solved with this prototype. But the beauty of it is that it worked perfectly!"

"Yeah, it did, didn't it." Some of the missiles were hitting close enough to the control center that they could feel the vibrations. Neither of them commented about that. They had seen enough death today and they knew that each explosion meant more lives were ending. Jake was standing up when the door opened, and instead of General Ruiz, whom they expected, in walked someone they didn't know.

Jake leaped at the man. Maybe it was an automatic reflex that hadn't existed until a few hours ago. The stranger's response seemed automatic. Jake and the stranger rolled across the floor. With a twist of the stranger's arm Jake's neck was broken and Jake slumped to the floor.

There wasn't time to think, Evan's good hand was wrapped around his pistol and he fired at the most vulnerable part of the stranger's body. The stranger's kneecap exploded and he fell opposite from Jake. Evan glanced at Jake and he felt sick to his stomach.

He exploded on the stranger. "You die here!" Another figure appeared at the door. Evan was pulling the trigger, but nothing happened. In fact, he realized he wasn't really pulling the trigger. He had been slammed against the cabinet and was paralyzed. He could think and feel, but just couldn't move. The same was happening to the guy that had harmed Jake -- except he was pinned to the floor.

# Chapter Seventeen
## Aftermath

"I AM DOCTOR HERNANDEZ," THE OLDER MAN ANNOUNCED. HE calmly walked over to Evan and took Evan's pistol. He did the same with the stranger. "Everyone keep their seats. We aren't the enemy. We will need for you to evacuate this compound. The Turkish Army and Air Force won't be in a good mood, and it's better for everyone to be gone when they get here. We'll take care of Mr. Bryant and Mr. Cannon." People were already working on Jake and the stranger. Evan didn't know what was happening, but he was going to kill the murdering SOB as soon as he could break free.

Evan slid down from the cabinets and found he had enough feeling back that he could crawl. The stranger apparently wasn't as fortunate. The pain in his knee had to be excruciating. His body wasn't able to pump adrenalin into his blood stream and his pain was amplified. He came out of the stun phase screaming. Then he vomited and screamed some more. Two people grabbed him and put him on a stretcher, as they had done with Jake.

Evan looked up to Hernandez, "Who the f___ are you? That bastard killed my friend."

"I'm the man who kept you alive and who is going to pay you a lot of money for what you did today. I couldn't have you kill Owen Schmidt, nor have him kill you. I hit both of you with a stun gun that will keep you paralyzed for a short period of time." Evan didn't know what to say. He stared at Hernandez with confusion and hatred.

"Your friend Jake has had his neck broken, but we can make him whole. We already have him breathing and we will give him a full recovery." He bent down and whispered so that only Evan could hear him. "Jake has always been one of us. We will take care of him. As far as Owen Schmidt goes, he has a more important job to do, so we can't have you killing him now, can we?"

"Are you New Eden?"

"Yes, we are and we have some important plans for you Evan Cannon."

"God! Can't you leave me alone?"

Ronnie walked in and almost took Evan's breath away. She dropped to her knees beside him and kissed him on his lips. "If this isn't real, don't wake me up." She had his face in her hands.

"I saw them take Jake out on a stretcher. They say he will be alright. Are you going to need one, too?"

"I don't think so. The professor there said I would be immobilized for a bit." Evan got up on his elbows. "I thought I was going to die today. It hasn't been very pleasant these past few days." The men of his company and the few Legionnaires started filing out. They were looking at Evan, and once they saw Ronnie, elbowed one another.

Hernandez reminded everyone, "We must hurry along, now." He looked at Evan. "Mr. Cannon, you should be able to get up completely in about a minute or two. Once that happens, we will be leaving in a hurry."

"What about my crew?"

"They are leaving, too. The only people the Turks will see are what's left of General Ruiz's command." Almost on cue, General Ruiz walked in and started talking to Hernandez. Evan couldn't hear their conversation, but could have cared less. He was concentrating on Ronnie. Ronnie finally helped him up and it was his turn to kiss Ronnie.

"Cannon, you left this outside. Are you OK?" It was Evan's pistol that had been made just for him by Smith and Wesson.

"Ruiz, I think I'm fine. I made a promise to this lady to stay away from situations where I would need that. I'd rather you keep it, because I won't need it anymore." Ronnie held out a hand and introduced herself to General Ruiz.

"I do not think I will ever understand America. When the men get in danger, their women come to bail them out." He kissed Ronnie's hand and said, "You are more beautiful than Evan described."

Ruiz returned his gaze to the custom-built weapon.

"Just do me one favor, General? Learn how to fire it."

"Is there anyone else that can shoot like you?"

"Only one man and I don't even know if he's still living."

Ruiz took one step back and gave Evan a salute and then kissed him on the cheek. Evan shook his hand with his very limp left hand. "Come see me if you get back into the U.S."

"I offer the same for Spain -- this time, without all the excitement."

"I would like that."

"I don't know how the assassin made it to the control center. I'm sorry for the injury to Jake. We all would be dead if not for you and Jake."

Evan's emotions went from melancholy to sorrow. "I don't know what is happening except your team is the only one that can be found on site. Frankly, I have had enough, and right now, I'm not in a very charitable mood for these New Eden guys."

"Evan, tomorrow you will be getting better and you will be regaining your strength. Don't do anything foolish that will compromise you, Jake or this lovely lady."

"Genera, well said. And I will make sure Evan holds his tongue." Evan had a flood of emotions going through him. He was getting back all of his senses and almost had full strength back.

Ronnie held one of his arms as if she didn't want to let go.

Evan looked along the compound. Spanish personnel were still piling up the dead and there were many more around the wreckage of the three columns that had been destroyed. He had seen and caused some of that death. His close friend and ex-wife, whom he still loved, had been killed. And after all he had been through; Hernandez said they were needed for an even greater event.

They loaded into New Eden's jet, and Wong and the engineering crew got into the Spanish aircraft. Hernandez greeted Evan at the door. "Your team has all been accounted for and is on the second jet. We just didn't have room on this aircraft, with the hospital facilities set-up."

"Where are you taking my people?" Evan asked

"They will go to Istanbul, and from there, to Paris for the weekend, and then back to the States. They will, of course, be flying first class."

Evan didn't know what to say, except "Thank you." Evan looked and noticed that there wasn't a runway, just a flat surface of about two hundred feet. "You landed this jet in this small field?"

"Yes, but this isn't what you think it is."

"For the past few weeks, nothing has been what it appeared to be."

There were two seats together in the second row that Ronnie and Evan took. Evan took her hand in his. "I hope they have a bathroom on this jet."

"It's not a jet."

"What the heck is it?"

"More like a shuttle that can get pretty quickly into space."

"Do you know where we are going?"

"Hernandez is taking us to his headquarters. He said that it's the only place they can start working on Jake."

"Is the name 'Hotel California?'" Evan asked, smiling.

"I doubt it. If I had to guess, he'll keep us a few days, tell us what's next and send us on our way. Maybe, we'll even have a room together." She leaned into Evan and gave his hand a squeeze. He yelled over the pain and Ronnie cringed realizing what she had done.

"Sorry about the squeeze." Ronnie said with a pained look on her face.

"Not sure I would ever see you again. The thought of losing everyone at our launch site was secondary to the thought of never telling you that I loved you."

Ronnie teared up. "Remember I told you that I couldn't love someone who wouldn't listen to me?"

"Yeah, but let me tell you what I had to do."

He didn't get to finish his sentence. She placed her fingertip on his lips and whispered "I was wrong. This was bigger than anything I could ever imagine." She kissed him.

It was as if it was their first time; yet, he somehow knew they were a couple, a team.

The take-off was quick and almost vertical. Whatever it was that was holding them in their seats gave Evan a very euphoric feeling, almost as if he were on drugs.

"God! What a rush!"

"Hernandez explained it to me. It's like a rush of oxygen into your system and a force field that's pushing us into our seats."

"What kind of guys are Hernandez and Johnson? Jake knew him and actually worked for him before Jake's wife died. We didn't get into too many specifics, but Jake said Johnson was always asking questions."

"I have never been around people like them before. They have developed so many technologies then many could even dream about, and yet aren't consumed by what they have accomplished. I'll tell you – they have everything planned out before it happens. A chess player that's five to seven moves ahead of you. If the government wants to catch them, they'll have to wait until one or the other dies or goes into a coma, which isn't likely for sixty year old men."

"According to Jake, Ronnie, Johnson's at least eighty, if not ninety."

Ronnie seemed a little taken aback by that. "I'm usually pretty good at telling age, but if he's conquered technological roadblocks, he's probably been able to make the 'fountain of youth.'" Both Evan and Ronnie slipped into sleep.

******************************

They both awoke at about the same time. They were in a huge bed, dressed in their underwear. The room looked like one from an upscale hotel chain. The king-size bed had a large headboard and a console on the left end table. There were shears and heavier curtains covering a window that ran the length of the room. There was a glow of light, not bright enough to wake anyone, but the whole room had the glow. You couldn't tell where the light source had originated. The art work actually looked like real paintings and not reproductions, but it was hard to tell for sure in the low light. There were pillows scattered around the bed and sheets were so soft that Evan thought the thread count had to be greater than 1000. Evan's body and his wounds had been cleaned. Ronnie rolled over on an elbow and asked, "Who put us in here?"

"I'm not sure. I just woke up myself. They also gave me a bath or shower or something. My wound has been re-wrapped.

Do you think we are alone? How did I get cleaned up? I don't remember anything but going to sleep in the jet."

"Same thing with me. Sleeping was my last memory. This looks like a hotel room, but I think it's part of the New Eden compound. The room is probably private, but I bet everywhere else is secured."

"Why do you say the bedroom is private?"

"Something that Doctor Hernandez said on the way to Turkey," Ronnie told Evan. "Everyone needs a private bedroom to talk and be intimate. The exception is for recovery from injuries or surgery, where people need fellowship to help the healing process."

"Doctor Hernandez said that?"

"Yes, he did. So, in this room, we probably have privacy. Once we leave this room, we'll likely be watched at all times."

"I hear people out the windows and it sounds like ocean waves, could they have placed us in a hotel close by?" Evan went to the console, and of course, it was a remote for everything. He pressed the button for the curtains. It opened to a brighter wall but no windows. He got up and walked across the wood floor and touched the window that was nothing more than a bright wall. "Damn, its solid and definitely no window."

Ronnie was sitting up on her elbows looking at Cannon from behind. Here was a guy that had a three inch scar along his side, a bandage with a huge red stain on his right hand standing in his underwear looking at a window that was really a blank wall that was getting brighter by the minute. She couldn't help but start giggling.

"What is so funny?" Evan turned around and asked her.

"Because here we are in our underwear in a hotel room by ourselves and you're looking at a wall and not making love to me."

Evan gave a big grin and crawled back next to Ronnie. "They won't have cameras under the sheets and I have a lot of questions to ask you."

At that there was a knock on the door and a male voice announced that they were being asked to get dressed at their leisure and have coffee with Dr. Johnson and Dr. Hernandez, so that they can explain to the both of them the events of the past few months.

Evan yelled back "Give us about thirty minutes and we'll be ready."

Ronnie lying on her back wrapped her arms around Evan and said, "Thirty minutes, my foot, we'll be done in ten!"

**The Beginning**